BREAKING TO PIECES

A BEFORE I BREAK NOVEL

AWARD WINNING AUTHOR

A. L. HARTWELL

Copyright

Breaking to Pieces is a work of fiction. All names, characters, locations, and incidents are the products of the author's imagination or are used fictitiously. Any resemblance to actual events, locales, or persons, living or dead, is entirely coincidental.

Editing by Pure Grammar Editing
www.puregrammar.com
Cover Design by KP Designs
- www.kpdesignshop.com
Published by Kingston Publishing Company
- www.kingstonpublishing.com

Table of Contents

DEDICATIONS

Callum, thank you for putting up with me when my head was lost in the clouds. Your encouragement and support are second to none. I love you.

Mum, you fill my days with encouragement and let me geek out with you about the characters I've created. I hope you find all the answers you need in this one. And welcome to the dark side.

Richard F, although you never got to see me publish my first book, I know that you would be incredibly proud. If you were here today, you would scold me for all the swearing, but also be the first to tell everyone and their dog to buy it. I miss you dearly.

And to the Bookstagrammers who are second to none in their support: You lovely ladies brighten my day with your kindness- this one is for you.

CHAPTER ONE

Olivia Heart

"LET HIM GO."

I felt the invisible handcuffs slip around my wrists as soon as the words left my lips. With three small words, I solidified myself into Luca Caruso's life, accepting my place by his side once and for all. I had chosen Black's freedom and given Luca everything that he wanted.

I'd given him me.

Given him maximum control when I saw there were no real choices, no options, and not a single way out. A man like Luca, the devil reincarnated, wouldn't just let me walk away. It wasn't in his nature to watch his prey run free, not when he enjoyed the hunt so much.

Luca's dark eyes seared into mine. "That wasn't so difficult now, was it?"

Through bared teeth, I hiss, "Fuck off, you sick bastard."

Bones shoved me hard between the shoulder blades, warning me to shut my mouth. I used my elbow against his ribs in retaliation, but he barely flinched. Fuck, it was like fighting a brick wall.

Unfazed by my snarling hatred, Luca smugly turns to Chen. "Get her out of my sight."

Chen, the diligent asshole, yanks me backwards by my dress and I teeter dangerously in my heels. Bones catches me, keeping me upright with his brutish grip on my elbow. Their touch makes me want to vomit and claw at their eyes.

Chen's voice only stirs my hatred. "Yes, sir."

Luca watches me with ice calmness while I'm dragged back into the house and away from the destruction that was still unfolding by the pool, ruining the once tranquil setting.

My hands lash out, my words burn with acid, and the tears finally dry up. Rage, now my only friend, comforts me and warms my skin, leaving me without the burden of fear as I fight Chen and Bones with every step.

I'm done crying over this man.

Done being dragged backwards and forwards.

I'm done.

Under the layers of searing anger that were twisting and shredding my recent happier memories of Luca, I felt a new feeling bloom under my skin. Overtaking my anger was a satisfaction so great, that I stopped fighting Chen to focus on it. Satisfaction whispered to me, reminding me that I had Luca's secrets and he couldn't hide from me anymore.

The mask that he wore had finally slipped *enough*.

We were evening out faster than he could control.

The look of fear that glinted in his eyes only minutes ago told me all I needed to know. Luca may have control over my life and what I do with it, but I have control over every part of him. I was the center of his universe, the weight around his heart, the reason he barely clung to his sanity when I denied him. I was everything and more.

The pinnacle of his existence.

The gravity that kept him on this godforsaken rock.

He could spend the rest of his life treating me this way, forcing me to submit by his side, demanding that I accept him, but he will never be able to control his feelings towards me.

Only I had that power.

I'd never thought in my life that I would find relief in knowing I could hold so much power over another human being. But I did, and I told myself over and over again that I shouldn't feel an ounce of pity for the man that had taken me in the middle of the night.

Not again.

****

Rum, on strict orders from Chen, tied me to a chair with zip ties in a room that's unfurnished and cold. I was somewhere deep in the underbelly of the house, where the only light comes from small windows from the wall to my right. It's dark and eerie, smelling of dampness with the litterings of forgotten tools. Maybe this room was supposed to be an indoor pool, it's certainly big enough, but holds no remnants of a near future.

Like me.

My laugh echoes across the empty space, bouncing off the empty walls and right back into my ears.

My heels lay haphazardly on the cold, tile floor in front of the door. A reminder that even when they shoved me in here, I had fought. The tear on the right side of my dress is another badge of honor. I had managed to wiggle myself free, enough to slap Chen across the face until Rum caught me, pulling me back by my dress until it tore.

I smirk into the darkness. The look on Chen's face alone was worth being tied to this chair with zip ties eating at my skin.

Smug bastard deserved it.

11

Even with the zip ties dragging their teeth into my flesh, I didn't stop trying to free myself. All I needed was one more shot at them, and I'd be able to make peace with myself. At least, I could tell myself that I had *tried* when I looked back on this day.

Noisy steps creak from above and I know that it is Bones coming to see me. He has a pattern and a particularly heavy step sequence that I recognize from his time as my shadow.

The door swings open, and he blazes over to me. I brace and prepare to be ripped back up, but instead, he snatches off his tie and advances.

"Fuck off," I growl, turning my face from his outstretched hand "Don't touch me!"

"Don't be stupid, Olivia," he hisses, as he shoves the tie into my un-wanting mouth, stretching my lips painfully until the material takes up all the narrow space at the back of my throat.

I gag against the musk and smoke coating the material and try to dislodge it with my tongue.

Rage swirled with panic as the material begins to choke me.

Bones crouches down, his right knee creaking as he grabs my face.

"You're in enough deep shit to last you a lifetime, be quiet and don't fight him on this, okay? You might just come out of this unscathed."

I glower, throwing my body forward to attack him with a feral growl.

Pushing my shoulders back he pins me to the rickety chair, barely moving a muscle.

I growl around the tie, my saliva coating the foreign material.

"You should have left that boutique the moment Black stepped in, Olivia. Black's nothing but a psychotic liar-"

The door behind him bursts open again, slamming against the house and we both flinch.

"Out. Now," Luca barks at Bones, with a tone full of unrelenting violence.

Bones threw me one last glare before backing up and turning on his heel. Nodding sharply to the man I despised more than anything in this rotten world. Bones disappeared through the door and left me with the monster.

So much for protecting me.

I watch with bated breath as Luca strides across the room, holding a folder and enough arrogance to smother me more than the tie in my mouth.

Power vibrates off him as he pulls up a chair, choosing to sit a foot away from me where I am still easily accessible.

"Are you calm enough to have a civil conversation? If you are, I'll take the tie out."

I growl around my gag, ignoring the urge to choke when it tickled my tonsils.

Fuck you.

He chuckles darkly before letting his eyes travel from the tie and down my body, taking great care to stare at my exposed thighs. My dress was bunched high, exposing far too much skin for his viewing pleasure.

Luca licked his lips, contemplating his dark fantasies, and whether he hated me enough to go through with them. I shrink away, trying to shift my hips so that the dress would fall.

Leaning over he tugs the hem of my dress down, his knuckles brushing my thigh, and my heart freezes. He glares up at me before pulling down my dress and removing his touch.

"I'll take that as a no." Opening up the folder, he leans back and begins lazily skimming the hidden document.

I shift in my seat, trying to rid the burn he had left on my skin.

"Want to know what this is?" He waved the folder in front of me, smirking. "They found it in the back of your *friend's* car."

I swallow thickly- worrying about Black and what was coming next.

Luca leaned forward and grabbed my knee with the hand that had my initial tattooed on it. His touch caught me off guard again, but I was smart enough to resist the urge to pull away again this time.

I wouldn't give him my fear.

I'm still in control.

He squeezed- hard and I cringed.

"Your eyes are full of pretty rage for me, Olivia, but yet your body gives you away." He slides his possessive hand from my knee to the top of my thigh in one quick sweep. My teeth ache from clamping down on the tie in my mouth, but I resist the urge to vocalize my fury.

He'd only win.

There was nothing more I wanted on this earth than to feel disgust at his touch, but it never came. Instead, expectation and sizzling apprehension produced goosebumps across my flesh.

Fuck, I'm more damaged than I thought.

Snickering, he pulled back and returned to the folder. One quick lick of his finger, he pulls out a piece of paper and begins to read. I watch his eyes dart across the paper while curiosity gnaws at the edges of my consciousness.

"Traumatic grief and acute trauma. Interesting... I'd agree with the grief, but trauma?"

I've heard those words before, somewhere in a distant part of my life and it triggers a cold response across my skin.

He looks at me from under his dark lashes. "Olivia has severe distrust in men, stemming from the traumatic death of her father, who was the closest to her at the time of his death. When her father is mentioned, she regresses to anger—"

I gag in shock, coughing around the tie that's made a home in my mouth. Painful memories sting my eyes, and all my anger evaporates into the air around us.

"Something the matter?"

A memory demanding that Luca leave this part of my life alone presents itself with cruel clarity. He had looked me in the eye and gave me his word that he wouldn't. Now, he was taking great pleasure in exposing the second most painful time in my life— his promise empty, like the many we had made to each other.

I shrink away.

He drops my gaze and returns to his revenge. "Miss Heart's refusal to take prescribed medication has caused concern with her grandparents after a recent outburst—very interesting."

Raw memories tip upside down and empty back into my head. Flashes of a pill bottle and forcing myself to be sick burn me with embarrassment. Those feelings of desperation feel like fire licking against my skin. I was desperate to feel anything but numbness from the medication doctors pumped me with, and now, I'd give anything to go back there.

My gag suddenly feels heavy in my throat. I'm going to suffocate, and he's barely acknowledged me since he started reading aloud. The monster I had glimpsed sits across from me today on his throne of power.

"Miss Heart has trouble recalling positive memories in regard to her parents."

My mother's face presents itself before I can block my unwelcome grief. She stares at me with a cold disapproval and suddenly, I feel like that child who couldn't do enough to win her mother's approval.

"Miss Heart has a fear reaction to fire... interesting."

A noise slips around the gag and I hate myself for it.

Luca doesn't falter in his desire to punish me. If anything, my anguish spurs him on.

"Miss Heart has struggled to maintain relationships with friends—citing a lack of need for companionship. During our most recent sessions she has made it clear that she isn't interested in expanding her relationships beyond family."

The file in his hand is his weapon of choice and I'm an open target. Each sentence feels like a burning knife entering my skin with slow precision of leaving permanent marks.

I'd done so well all these years to block out that part of my life and to bury it so deep that those feelings were just echoes of pain, almost nonexistent and bearable.

Until now.

Forcing my head back, I try to drag in as much air through my nose as I can, but my lungs are too scared to cooperate, they know more is coming.

"Miss Heart blames her father for abandoning her. Abandonment issues will continue to hinder her future relationships if she doesn't—"

My muffled scream halts his enjoyment abruptly. In one tug he rips away the sodden tie from my mouth and grabs my jaw.

"Had enough?" he demands, glaring darkness into me.

"You said you wouldn't read those files. I-I had your word," the words are barely a whisper between us.

The smirk that turns my stomach is back. "And I had yours, didn't I Olivia? We made plenty of promises to one another."

I close my eyes because behind my lids he doesn't exist. The coping mechanisms I'd learned as a child return like the opening of a parachute, ready to soften my fall.

His fingers trace tears from my cheeks until they dig into my chin, forcing me to open back up to him.

"But you chose to disregard all of them. Ignoring all the hard work we put in for a prick with empty promises."

I twist my chin out of his reach and pull back. Luca had gone far beyond the scope of cruelty by finding that file. If he thought this would be the perfect way to punish me, he was right. I was beyond punished.

Black had tried to protect me from this—I was certain of it. It would have been his job to provide Luca with everything about me, but he purposely kept this one file hidden.

The one person who had my back in all of this was probably dead.

"Where is he?"

I needed to know that I hadn't given up my freedom for nothing.

Luca leaned back, my question tipping him from anger to white-hot fire.

"Chen is deciding his fate as we speak," he bit out through clenched teeth.

A strangled choke splutters from my lips. "But I made a choice. I gave you—"

Luca stopped me mid-sentence by throwing the file and grabbing my chair between my legs. I'm yanked forward and our knees knock together painfully before I can finish my sentence.

"Black gave you information on their families, Olivia." He moved a piece of my hair and gently tucked it behind my ear, contradicting the dark glint in his eye that tells me the last thing he wants to be right now is gentle.

I shiver under him.

"He went against his own code and put them in a dangerous situation. Now it's up to them to decide what's the best way to deal with *their* traitor."

"No, he was just trying to help me! Just let him go." I tug at my confines trying to free my hands from the zip ties, desperate to do something other than be punished.

Black had tried to help me, but he wasn't going to risk anybody else. It was simply an empty threat in case they refused to let me go. He doesn't deserve to suffer because I had been stupid to come back.

Luca watches me carefully, cold eyes scanning mine. "How naive you are about him, the man that knew very well what he was getting himself into. He wasn't trying to protect you, Olivia, he was trying to extort you."

My stomach drops into oblivion at the confidence that vibrates through his words.

"You're lying," I snap, tugging at my wrists.

"Am I?" his fingers trace the edge of my jaw. "How would you know?"

"He played the voice recordings, Luca, he told me your plans and—"

"Did he tell you his pathetic attempts to blackmail me for his silence? Did he tell you he wanted five million dollars, or he was going to take you for himself?"

My hands twitched to cover my ears.

"I didn't lie when I told you that Black had forced my hand and I didn't lie when I told he was seeking out my enemies." His fingers dip into my flesh, painting my skin with bruises. "I took you to keep you safe while I cleared up the mess he made. The *people* he went to, had the good sense to stay away, but he couldn't let it go. The rat that you've tried to protect was quite relentless in getting what he needed out of you."

My face burned with embarrassment, but it was nothing compared to what my heart was feeling. It screamed and thrashed against my ribcage, wanting justice for the pain it felt—already questioning whether Luca was telling the truth.

Luca's touch turns to gentle caresses, with his fingers wiping away the tears that had settled on my cheeks. But it wasn't enough to divert me away from the look of betrayal in his eyes.

"You're lying." I tip my head down, trying to dislodge his gentle touch.

He grips my jaw and tilts me back up. "You're a smart woman, Olivia. You know I'm not lying–I can see it in your eyes."

Smart? Me, smart? A smart woman would have never let you in.

"Why didn't you tell me this from the start?" the barely-there whisper that comes from my lips only infuriates him more.

"Because I didn't want to worry you until I had taken care of it all," he laughed darkly, before removing his touch. "You put your trust into a man that was going to use this file to get what he wanted, instead of giving me the chance to tell you the truth."

My eyes find the folder laying at his feet, its corners crinkled, and there was a coffee stain where it had been carelessly left in Black's car.

My head and heart tangle in a screaming match, blaming each other for the mess we find ourselves in. My head wants scalding hot retribution on Black, but my heart begins to question whether Luca's being completely honest.

Impatient as ever, Luca tilts my chin back up and pins me to my seat with his harsh glare.

"I told you that if you ran your security would be tighter and there would be zero options. Do you remember?"

Of course, I remembered.

My eyes have no choice but to stare right back at the monster. I steadfast realize I'm facing hell now that heaven is fading between us and there's nothing I can do. Once again, I'm completely helpless.

Sealing me behind the gates of hell are his lips as he forces his mouth onto mine. His tongue demands entrance without pause, and he pours his violence into my throat. I'm drowning and kissing him back. Hating him and wanting more.

My heady confusion is abruptly stopped when he pulls away. Possessiveness and unspoken promises greet me, pulling me into him.

He smiles. "Welcome to your life of zero options."

Zero options.

Did Luca really believe that he could keep me locked away forever, with his money and guards? Did he think because I had been tricked by Black that I would give up?

There is no such thing as zero options when you have enough tenacity to fight, and I would fight. I'd done it before when I fought my way out of depression, fought my way out of my grandparents' hold when they tried to control my life, and now I would do it with Luca.

Looking at him, I watch as he scans me with his unforgiving stare, his eyes darkening with every beat of silence.

And I smile back.

I still have one option left.

CHAPTER TWO

Luca Caruso

I've been betrayed many times and always sought retribution. Found satisfaction in hurting those that have come for me—but there is no satisfaction here for me tonight. No real winner.

I can't see beyond the rage, can't seem to find my grip on solid reason as I stand above her, watching her wilt under my power.

I'm seconds away from picking the file back up and carrying on the purge of her final secret.

But my feet don't agree, and I leave with only the file that's offered no real satisfaction. I'd expected to feel strong and in control with the final piece of her in my hands, but it had only softened me.

I need to get control of this situation once and for all without her judgment coating my skin.

As I move throughout the house, I train my thoughts on the secrets still in my hands.

Olivia's psychiatrist hadn't been kind in his assessment, calling out the sufferance, guilt, and hatred for her father who she deems responsible for his own death. Her mother, the woman that focused more on her career as a

22

neurosurgeon, had a fragile relationship with her. It's noted in the file that Olivia felt guilt for making her mother's life more difficult when she didn't show up to her school recitals or birthday dinners.

Olivia had been painted as a bratty, only child, but I saw right through it.

Olivia's parents, Robert and Lilly Heart, died in a house fire while Olivia was at school. From the detailed autopsy, they had succumbed to smoke inhalation before they were found by the authorities. Their smoke alarms had been turned off while her father worked on the kitchen renovation — another factor added towards their death.

Olivia was riddled with grief and anger, and she turned her pain inwards — or so it says in the psychiatrist's report.

I saw the grief the day she gave me her ticket. Saw it lurking behind her eyes and realized days later she'd pick pocketed my heart. But not because hers was damaged and she needed a new one. No, because she had recognized the damage coming my way and stole it to protect me from it.

It had taken me only a few weeks after meeting her to realize what she had done, and by that time, it was too late to stave off the beginnings of my obsession.

The angel with big doe eyes and a warm smile was all I craved.

"Take her to my room, but leave her hands tied," I barked at Chen, as I stormed my office. "I don't want her fucking up my shit."

Dante stood up, slowly gauging my mood while Chen nodded and left.

"Prenditi un minuto Luca. Ricorda la tua testa." *Take a minute, Luca. Remember your head.*

Snatching the glass up from my desk, I shot back the cognac and poured myself another. I could still taste her sweetness on my tongue, and right now, I needed something else.

"Fuck off, Dante. Just fuck off," I hissed after the second drink. The burn in my throat was the perfect distraction from the hammering in my chest, so I poured another. "I don't need to hear a damn word from you."

Dante pinched the bridge of his nose before throwing himself back down into his seat. He didn't have to say a word. I knew exactly what he wanted to say and if he was smart, he would swallow his opinions, or I would make him choke on them.

"Chen's team is holding Black. I'll take care of it once they pass him over."

I looked up from my glass and nodded. I would have killed Black by the pool if it wasn't for my pact with Dante and my respect for Chen. Oh, and the possibility of his blood getting in the freshly cleaned water.

"Good fucking riddance."

Dante raises a thick eyebrow my way, but I ignore his look of disdain and pour another drink. Right now, was not the time to worry about turning into the man that had raised me.

"What are you going to do with her now?"

I scoffed. "Whatever I want, there's nothing hanging over my head anymore."

"What does that mean?" he stood up and took the bottle of cognac from the table and poured himself a drink.

Shooting back my final drink, I slammed the glass back onto my desk and fixed him with a cold glare. He knew exactly what I'll be doing with her from now on.

"Maybe you should let her go. Olivia doesn't want to be here and that's not right for the both of you. Let me speak to her, Luca, and I'll make sure there's a solid plan in place for her silence."

Let her go? Impossible.

She's mine.

I hadn't tortured myself for eight years just to let her go.

"Suggest that again, Dante, and I'll put a bullet in your knee cap. Understand?"

Sucking in a deep breath, he swiped a hand over his face and nodded, but not without his shoulders sinking into exhaustion.

****

Chen was waiting for me outside of my room with his hands in his pockets, leaning against the door. There was a bruise forming on the top of his right cheek where Olivia had slapped him earlier — the real reason for her hands still being bound.

She was a feisty bitch when she was angry.

It had been me that her anger had been aimed at, but he stepped in and took the brunt of her unravelling. Even underneath my rage, I feel grateful for his lack of judgement throughout this whole process and the calm he brings to my unique situation.

"Here, you'll need these, sir," he told me, passing me a small black flick knife.

"Thanks. Is the plane ready to go?"

Chen nodded. "Yes, sir. We need to leave in twenty minutes."

"Okay, have Marie pack Olivia's things."

He nodded before clicking his earpiece, already working through my demands. Once this was all over, I'd ensure that Chen would get a good enough raise that he could never leave.

I enter my room and find Olivia sitting on the floor against the bottom of my bed, her long legs out in front of her as she sits slightly forward because of her bound wrists. With her hair a wild mess, I knew she had fought Chen as he brought her to my room, and as suspected, she wasn't lucky to land another blow.

"Missed me, *Bella?*" I snapped as soon as her eyes looked up at me.

"Like a bullet to the head," she snarled back with quickness, still trying to free her wrists.

The zip ties were not my idea and I fucking hated seeing them around her small wrists, but she gave me no choice. As soon as she was pulled from Black's side, she began to lash out at anyone that touched her. It was like she only *needed* him.

It had torn away my last shred of patience.

I slammed my knees onto the carpet, twisting her onto her side before I forced her onto her stomach. Pressing her down with one knee to the center of her back, I grabbed at her bound wrists and pulled them back.

Olivia's spine bowed with the pain I was inflicting, but she didn't cry out. In fact, she barely made a noise at all.

Ice trickled into my veins. The power that I had only twenty-minutes ago, was disappearing underneath me... I could feel it with every act of defiance from her. I knew how to handle her when she was scared but when she was silent or angry, I faced new territory.

Fuck. I hated her power.

Removing my hand, I searched inside my pocket and grabbed at the small knife. With one quick flick of my wrist, I sliced through her zip ties, but kept her pinned down.

"We're leaving in twenty-minutes. Go get cleaned up."

Olivia hissed as she tried to wiggle away.

"I'm not going anywhere with you, not after what you've done," she snarled, pulling her hands to her sides, wincing as the cuts across her wrists caught the carpet fibers.

"Oh, but you are." I stood up and allowed her to sit up against the bed. "Zero options remember?"

She threw me a dirty look and tossed her hair. *Shit*, there were grazes across her wrists from the ties, bruises across her knees, and her dress was torn.

"There's no such thing as zero options, Luca, you should know that by now. I won't stop trying to leave you — I'll always find another way."

The truth in her promise stabbed me in the fucking chest. She knew just where to aim and how hard to drive the knife in.

Fuck, just as I'm holding on to the thinnest thread of sanity, she strips me bare and dips me in acid.

I grab her small wrists and yank her up with me, ignoring the hiss from her mouth and I push her into my bathroom.

The sooner we leave, the better.

"Is this what you want, huh? To keep me locked away for you and you only? Want me to be the perfect fucking slave who will drop to her knees at the mere sight of you?" She turns in my grip and slaps me hard against the face. I feel my cheek sting, but the pain is muted.

Her words always hurt more.

Flexing my jaw, I take a step back, forcing my inner rage to simmer into the soft glow of alcohol in my system.

I watch as she narrows her eyes at me, her chest rising and falling with each ragged breath. This time, there are no tears, she's bypassed the stage of fear and she's swimming in bravery.

Shame it wouldn't get her very far.

"You are nothing to me, nothing but a sick fuck with a god complex! Believe me when I tell you that I'll never want you, never need you and never—"

My hand reacted before my brain registered it was moving. I saw it around her throat, forcing her against the bathroom wall. Sneering into her, I pressed my nose into her cheek, resisting the urge to bite her soft skin.

Her gasp of fear does nothing to pull me back.

"Keep telling yourself that, Olivia. Maybe one day you'll start to believe your own lies, but in the meantime, you are mine and only mine. I'm the one in control here, not you. If I tell you to get on your knees, you will get on your fucking knees. Now do as you are told and get his blood off your skin and be ready in ten minutes."

"Get off me, you psychopath!" She tries to pry my hands away, but I press in warning.

"Ten minutes, Olivia."

CHAPTER THREE

Olivia Heart

I stand frozen, staring at the ruined white shower floor. Blood and soap mixes and drips from my skin. I'd never been squeamish of blood thanks to my mother and her love for medical journals that would be left around the house. As a child, I had been fascinated and would look at all the pictures, no matter how gross or revealing they were — it was my way of showing interest towards her work.

But now I feel sick.

My mother, whose face hadn't stopped haunting me since Luca's betrayal, had been the emotionally independent one of my parents. Although she was overly protective of my education, we never really had an emotional connection. She strived for perfection in everything, including me, and I always felt lacking next to her.

I would spend evenings being pushed into extra circular activities while she worked late nights. It had taken me years to realize that she was trying to fill my time, so I wouldn't notice her absence, but I always did. As an emotional child, it was hard to miss the mother that didn't turn up to your school plays or parents' evenings.

My father was my saving grace. He owned his own kitchen restoration business, would often work long hours, but would at least plan out weekends of fun for just the two of us. My father, also missing my mother, became my best friend as we took on new adventures together to fill that void.

Their death was something I would never get over.

Finding myself on the floor of Luca's shower, I wondered how different my life would have been if they hadn't died.

I wouldn't have met Luca and I wouldn't have given him that plane ticket. I'd be living in England, studying for the bar exam, and getting ready to find my place in the world. Maybe I would still be close to my friends from the university, following the normal social requirements of a woman my age instead of fighting them.

But instead, I had become a void of nothingness, sucking in darkness that had attracted an equally damaged person. Luca hadn't realized, but tying me to that chair and hashing out my painful history had also opened himself up to me.

The further I slipped out of his control, the harder it got for him to control his impulses. I was the only person who could take that away from him and I felt so stupid for taking this long to realize.

All he wanted was me and wouldn't stop at anything until I was his in body and soul. I'd seen it in his eyes when he forced me to make a choice, he wanted me to choose him. He wanted me to put him out of his misery once and for all.

But how could I when all he had done was lie?

Sucking in air, I realized I had fire in my belly for the first time in weeks. I can do this. I can hold on.

Anticipation energized me while I quickly dressed, choosing Luca's favorite color, and donning an all-black dress.

Even when Rum and Bones entered the room to take me, my mood continued to soar above their controlling energy. I didn't care that I was bundled into Luca's car, or that it stopped on his air strip. I didn't care that our next destination was a mystery. Didn't care that Black was possibly dead or close to it, he was nothing but a leech who had tricked me into caring for his wellbeing.

All I cared about was the plane doors and how they would trap me in with the people that had been ruling my life for far too long.

****

Luca's eyes do not leave mine as I'm forced to take my seat across from him by Chen. I glower right back, using my eyes to hurl every insult known to man his way.

A wall around me was building, brick by brick right in front of Luca. I knew he could see it forming because he was barely restraining himself in his chair. Aggressive energy bounced underneath his skin with every moment that ticked by between us.

I smirked, listening to the plane doors closing behind me. Belts clipped into place, but I didn't bother with mine. I knew it would piss Luca off.

Glowering with his near-black eyes, he leaned over and clipped me in, and for good measure pulled the belt tighter.

"Ironic, isn't it?"

"What is?" he demanded, leaning forward with enough arrogance to suffocate me. Normally, his dark stare would make me nervous, but right now I was fearless.

Another brick added to my wall.

I looked over my shoulder at Bones and glared. "That you think these idiots and your money will keep me by your side."

Chen glowered when I caught his eye next. Smirking, I turned back to Luca and leaned back into the fine leather seat, allowing the cushion to soothe my tense shoulders.

Luca leans forward, his body humming with unspent rage. "Be quiet," he demands, while rubbing his temples.

I closed my eyes. "It's sad, really. Especially, since you had to go to all this effort, and I still don't want to be by your side."

Too far. Shut your mouth.

Shut it.

Stop this.

I hear footsteps behind me and the plane tilts upwards. By the time I open my eyes, Luca is being held back by Chen and Red... just. He's bursting, desperate to get to me, but finally my guards do their job and steal away his control.

They choose now to protect me, not when he was forcing me to make a choice between my freedom or the one man who could give it to me. Now, when the venom between us was spilling out, they decide to step in. It's laughable, and so fucking unfair.

"Shut your mouth, Olivia," Luca hissed through my guards. He wants me to stop, to keep my venom to myself, but I want his final strand of control to snap.

I want to watch him pay.

I roll my eyes and ignore the pop in my ears. We're finally levelling out and high enough that it will be difficult to land.

"I don't think so. I'm done being quiet — done listening to you and your lies. You don't own me, Luca, or my voice."

"Olivia!" Bones hisses from behind me, placing his large hand on my shoulder. "Be quiet."

I shrug him off and shift forward — refusing his touch with disgust.

"Sir, please sit down. The seat belt light isn't off yet." The air hostess in the back with a dainty voice is ignored, but I'm not. All their eyes are on me but none of them are brave enough to shut me up.

I sigh before looking directly at Luca. "Twenty-minutes ago, you said I had zero options. Well, you were wrong, Luca, there's still one left in play."

Nobody speaks, but their silence is loud enough.

Luca pushes his way through Chen and Red who let him go and he towers over me. In three seconds, he falls from his throne and at my feet.

"What have you done?"

I traced my lips with my forefinger. "I've sent an email."

"Ah shit," Bones mumbled.

"Fucking hell," Rum hissed.

"An email?" I'm yanked up by the collar of my dress. Luca, who's a second away from combusting into flames demands, "What fucking email?"

A sarcastic laugh slips from my mouth. "Just an email with a few audio files and a little run down of our time together. Call it an *option*."

Chen barges by, desperate to get to his computer. Red pinches the bridge of his nose, trying to steady his breathing, and Rum leans forward with his head in his hands. Bones, for the third time since we met begins to sweat profusely.

Complete destruction.

It tastes so good to be on the other end of it.

But Luca is the one I'm focused on; his eyes are wild with an emotion I've never seen before; stricken with fear and pain. I devour the loss of his control, gorging on his fear with every second that ticks by until I'm close to being full.

Leaning into him, I capture his wrist that reaches for me. "Hurts, doesn't it?"

"Where? Where did you send this email?"

I ignore his plea and slip my hand to his watch. "In ten minutes, it won't matter."

Luca lets me go, turning away from me so he can hide. I settle myself back into my seat and enjoy the show as all five men begin to unravel.

They relied on their arrogance to keep them safe from me and now they were paying the price. Even though Black had turned out to be nothing short of a liar, he had given me an opportunity worth dealing with Luca's temper.

I'd had access to his phone, pretending to send my aunt a message in that small cubicle, but instead I had created a backup plan—a plethora of proof if things went sour.

With every moment that ticks by, I see the realization dawning on each of their faces. It's like every single Christmas wrapped up into one big fuck you event.

"Tell me, Olivia, tell me who you sent that email to or so help me I will—"

"You'll what!? Kill me?" I laugh. "Save your threats, Luca, you need me in your life, you've made that very clear these last twenty-four hours".

"Sir, there's nothing from Black's account," Chen called, his usually monotone voice now frantic while his fingertips swept his keyboard. "Or Miss Heart's."

I tut. "Of course, there isn't, Chen. Do you think I'd use an account you have access to?"

I turn back to Luca to find him in front of me, grabbing at my shoulders, imploring me to give him what he needs. My head sways, drunk on power.

"You're playing with fire, Olivia. I will find a way to make this go away. I always do so cut the shit and tell me who the email is going to?"

Even with Luca's hands suddenly cupping my face, his thumb gently rubbing my cheek, it wasn't enough to pull me out of the darkness. I was safe in my fortress; nothing could get to me here.

"Hmm, you know what, I don't remember who I sent the email to. It may have gone to Red's brother-in-law who works for the senate." I caught Red's eye and watched him shrink back. "Or did I send it to the school that Bones' daughter goes to?"

Bones swipes at his face but doesn't make a noise.

Luca's thumb paused on my cheek; his eyes were narrowing with every detail that slipped from my mouth. He knows that I have an arsenal of information now and he senses at any moment I could start spilling his secrets.

"Or did I send it to Rum's sister, the priestess?" I leaned into Luca's face, my hands smoothing down the hair at his temples. "Or did I send it to my Aunt Sarah?"

I could feel his muscles locking underneath his clothes. "I'll bury it, Olivia. I'll do what I have to." His voice was merely a whispered threat between us.

"Thinking about it, the email could have gone to all of them. I guess we'll find out in the next few minutes."

Luca took one last look into my eyes before ambling up on his feet. I expected his rage, prepared for it, but instead he calmly moved back to his seat and took out his phone.

Ignoring the distressed voice of Chen's team, he leaned back into his seat and closed his eyes. From this angle, I could see his pulse, hammering under the skin of his neck. His body realized the threat it was under even if his mind didn't and right now that was satisfaction enough.

"Chen, give Olivia your laptop."

"Sir?"

"Olivia needs it to sign into the account she used."

"I don't think so," I hissed.

Snapping his eyes open, he leaned forward and smirked. "You've forgot one important part of your plan, Olivia. If that email gets out, I'll make sure Dante puts a bullet between Black's eyes. You're not the type of person who can live with that on their conscience, you've proven as much. So, again, the choice is yours. Cancel the email or Black never makes it home."

Black, a man that had worked for Luca in keeping tabs on my work life, was once again in the firing line. A little voice that I often ignored told me to forget about him — that he deserved everything coming to him, but I reminded myself that I'm not a bad person and his blood could never stain my hands.

"He won't go home to his two children; they'll be fatherless just like you."

My armor doesn't flex in time at the new information. I didn't know Black had children; we didn't get that far. He had spent the little time we did have giving me the answers I wanted regarding Luca and my time.

Shit. I can't be responsible for this.

Is that why he wanted Luca's money? For them?

"Okay." I click my fingers for Chen's laptop, careful to compose my face. Surprise and distrust beams at me from all angles. Red in particular glares over at me, not bothering to hide his distaste for the situation I've put them in.

I knew Luca would call my bluff. Luca was smart and would never put himself in a situation without a plan B. We were very much alike in that respect. For me, it wasn't about winning or getting away, it was to show him just a fraction of the power I had in my arsenal.

He was right when he said he wouldn't let me go, but he'd discounted my tenacity to make his life hell in the meantime while I tried. That was the real option.

Chen's laptop was placed on my lap with two minutes to spare.

"You're doing the right thing, Olivia," Bones whispered from behind.

"Does your daughter know what you do for a job?" I snapped back, my fingers angrily typing in the password to my newly acquired email. "Does she tell her friends at school that her daddy is a kidnapper?"

"Olivia," Luca growled in warning. "That's enough."

I ignored him and found the email that I had set up in a rush. My hands had been clammy and had shaken during the setup of this email. I remember the swirl of emotions in the changing room. I'd never felt guilt and betrayal like it as I second-guessed my decision for a backup.

I looked over at Luca whose eyes demanded I press the final button.

"I could have left with Black the moment he found me," I told him. "But I wanted the truth from you first." I hit the delete button and listened to the sighs of relief behind me. "Now, I know you're nothing more than a monster who's incapable of honesty."

He narrowed his eyes in at me and leaned forward. Muscles bunched tight against his shirt, ready to burst through the fine material at any moment.

"I gave you the chance to my honesty last night, but you chose to get it from him. It was you who made the choice to break whatever little trust we had going."

I try my hardest to ignore the burn against my confidence. "You would have only given me half-truths and I wanted more."

I ignore the air hostess who nervously teeters next to me with the drinks trolley. Can she not read the plane?

I fold my arms across my chest. "Black warned me about what could happen if I came back."

He smirks. "And what did he say would happen?"

"That Chen would advise you to move me again."

I turned my head to look out of the window and into the darkness.

"I know now that Black was lying, and he was setting me up to get to you, but he told me plenty of secrets about you all. So, you can move me around the world, hire more guards, stop me from seeing my family, but I'll just find new ways to be free. And when I do, you'll realize it didn't have to be this way."

Luca didn't defend himself. In fact, I barely heard him move in his seat. Even without my eyes on him, I knew that he was looking at me, trying so desperately to contain the monster that didn't like being denied.

"Do whatever it is you feel like you need to, Olivia." I hear him shift in his seat. "It won't matter in the end because

I'll find you every time and you'll soon grow tired of running from me."

I scoff. "I doubt that very much."

CHAPTER FOUR

Luca Caruso

S hit.

Exhaustion feels like tar, weighing down on my limbs just waiting for me to succumb to the needs of rest. But right now, rest is a few hours away.

We've been trapped together for two hours in complete silence without a mere glance at one another. Even Chen and his men decided halfway through the flight to divert their attention to their devices — still dealing with the come down of Oliva and I's *situation*.

Barely functioning on the little energy that I have left, we disembark the plane to waiting cars organized by Chen.

I look out to the glittering tarmac with nothing but disdain. Paris, the city of love, fashion, and wine, greets me in the only way I deserve, with a hailing of rain and fog.

Joining mother nature's quest to punish me, Olivia glares over at an empty plane with AIRFRANCE emblazoned on its fuselage, unimpressed with our new home for the next few days.

I didn't have time to plan our next destination together. I needed to get us as far away from my mistakes as possible and I'd be a liar if I didn't admit that Paris probably wasn't the best place to escape to.

I had wanted to bring her here on different circumstances only days ago, to show her a different side of me — a romantic side. Fuck, how did we go from ripping each other's clothes off to this?

My head spins wild with regret.

Olivia was safe by my side once again, but now, she cannot stand to look at me, couldn't accept my hand when I opened her door.

Again, I'm locked out and stand floundering by her side.

I open my mouth to tell her what's going to happen from now on, but I can't bring myself to say the words that I know will tip her over the edge. Maybe once we're at the hotel and away from the many ears that follow us, I'll begin the claw back.

I'll start slow, buy myself enough time until her anger recedes into a place where she's more reasonable.

The car pulls us away, but I feel as though I left myself still stuck to my seat on the plane.

Olivia's words were ringing in my ears, reminding me of all my failures and taunting me. Of course, she had every right to protect herself after everything I had done, but she had owed me the chance to explain.

All I cared about was making sure she couldn't slip away.

The evil that lingered inside me only hours ago had left and now I was exposed to the uncertainty ahead of us. I needed a new plan and quickly before she slipped too far; but Olivia could cut me off every step of the way. And I would deserve it.

I pinched the bridge of my nose. A headache was looming, but I punished myself, trying to find the one single moment it went to hell.

Everything had happened so quickly and the thought of her not being in my life had cut me in half.

I'd seen her open up to me.

I'd seen her at my side.

And then I watched it disappear.

I couldn't risk it. I didn't want to go back to living on the edge of a knife, just waiting for someone to put me out of my misery.

Olivia was right; I'm a selfish bastard. I should have swallowed my fucking arrogance, been a man and told her the truth from the start. But it was done now, and the dust will have to settle.

She'll have to settle into her new life.

"Sir, passport control has cleared us," Chen confirmed, breaking me away from my thoughts.

"Good. Take us to the hotel."

At my side, Olivia took her hair down, gently running her fingers through her long tresses. It reminded me of the night of her cousin's wedding when it was my hands comforting her.

Now, my hands were not worthy.

I pulled out my phone, sending a quick text to Dante requesting an update on his one task—doing anything to distract myself from the misery sitting heavy in my stomach.

By the time we arrived at the hotel, the rain had picked up, thrashing down upon our already heavy shoulders. I'd tried to grab her elbow, bringing her to my side, but she was quick to step out of my reach.

A bellboy, armed with warm towels greeted Olivia from behind the white and gold marbled desk with a gloved hand and a smile. Olivia reserved her surprise and listened while he offered a warm drink, dry cleaning, and a personal shopper to replace her damp clothes.

"Non, merci," her words were soft and fluid, taking me by surprise. I had forgotten she could speak French; then I remembered she had been forced into the language by her grandparents when they tried to have her moved here.

Our bellboy's greedy eyes barely registered the men surrounding her and it pissed me off. Clearing my throat, I directed his attention towards showing us to our suite instead of drooling over Olivia, especially now that her dress was slick against her breasts.

The smitten bellboy instantly registered my face and flinched.

It wasn't polite to flirt with the owner's...er, captive?

"Bienvenue à nouveau M. Caruso, puis-je vous montrer votre suite?" *Welcome back Mr. Caruso, may I show you to your suite?*

I nodded, motioning for him to lead the way.

Chen and his team moved silently behind us, keeping their distance but it wasn't enough. Olivia was annoyed by their hovering, snapping at Red to give her more space when he bumped into the back of her.

Everyone was off their game today.

Bundling into the large private elevator, Olivia chose to stand by Bones, her eyes narrowing in at me when our eyes met.

"Monsieur, votre suite a été aménagée à votre gout." *Sir, your suite has been set up to your liking.*

"Merci."

Olivia sniggered. My French was not natural—in fact, it sounded harsh coming from my mouth. I didn't care though; Italian was a much more graceful, expressive language.

"Where is Francis?" I asked once we hit the eighteenth floor. Chen caught my eye as his team moved to the opening doors and out into their quarters.

Tomorrow, our debrief would be long.

The doors closed and we reached my private suite before the bellboy could answer me. Olivia couldn't keep the surprise out of her eyes as she carefully scanned our new surroundings. Unlike my home in Sicily, this was opulent and too much. The expansive space consisted of luxurious carpet, high ceilings, and antique furniture that had belonged to royals. The whole suite was big enough that if Olivia chose to push me out, she would have all the space she needed to do so.

The bellboy smiled with too many teeth. "He's on paternity leave, sir. Mrs. Adnet gave birth a few days ago to a baby boy."

Francis was my private butler who had looked after me whenever I was in the city. When he wasn't taking care of me or my family, he was looking after billionaires and their ridiculous needs.

A man that respected privacy.

"Quante stanze ci sono?" My French is rusty. I think Olivia asked how many rooms were in the suite.

"Tre, la signora Caruso."

Our bell boy had answered Olivia in the worst way. Olivia had suddenly gone from my captive to my wife, and she didn't like that very much. Thanking him through gritted teeth, she left us both in search of a bedroom without merely a glance back.

Already, she was seeking her distance.

I paid the bell boy for his service and asked him to organize a gift for Francis, all without asking his name.

There was no room for idle chit chat or niceties today. I wanted him out of our space and quickly.

Watching him scarper to the lift, hands full of cash, I looked around to see nothing was out of place.

My last visit here I'd been alone, ghosting in whenever business brought me to Paris. But now, I wasn't alone, my *wife* was somewhere in the suite, no doubt scowling at the romantic décor or plotting her next escape.

Brushing a hand over my face, I try to will myself to move from the spot I find myself glued to.

I need a shower and sleep.

I need her.

Or just for my world to stop fucking spinning under my feet for one second.

But I'm not so lucky to have such a simple ask go my way. There was a sound of glass smashing against the floor and then her voice, pulling all my attention back to the one person who made my life a living, breathing hell.

"Ow!" she yelps. "Shit — what the hell is wrong with him!?"

"Olivia?" I called, hearing my own voice echo off across the space. I flinch at the panic lacing its way around my vocal cords.

"I'm fine, it's nothing. Leave me alone, Luca!" she called back, but I ignore her.

She's not fucking fine until I deem her fine.

By the time I find her, she's in the main bedroom clutching her hand, trying to stop her blood from dripping onto the plush cream carpet.

The sight of her blood is enough to make my feet move until I'm standing in front of her, sizing up her wound.

I narrow my eyes, focusing on the cause of her injury. The crystal vase that's cracked into several shards sits in front of her bare feet- taunting me.

The bed just behind her is decorated with pink petals in the shape of a heart, stark against the crisp white sheets with its cheesiness making me cringe. Francis would never have done this to me, never.

I didn't think it could get worse until I saw the champagne cooling at the side of the bed, but it did. It always did.

Perfect. Just what we both needed when we could barely stand to be in the same room as one another.

"Are you deaf? I said leave me alone," she snapped.

I stuff my hands in my pockets, coming back to earth. "I would love nothing more, but you're bleeding all over my floor. Give me your hand."

I took a step forward and ignored her step back.

There was blood seeping out from her right hand, dripping down to her elbow. She needed to stop pissing me off and raise her damn hand.

Ignoring her flinch, I moved her away from the broken glass and to the bathroom, cupping her hand with mine. Before she could pull away from me, I pried open her fingers and saw the offending piece of glass stuck in her palm.

Every muscle in my body locked at the sight of the wound. Even something so small and superficial was my worst nightmare.

It's just a small cut, Luca.

She's not dying.

"Sit on the counter," I told her, while rummaging through the bathroom for the first aid kit, trying to distract myself from the visions of a seriously hurt Olivia.

"I can do it myself. I don't need your help," she huffed.

My eyes drank her in when I turned to face her. Her damp hair was starting to curl around her face. She looked angelic as she sat upon the marble counter, her big eyes regarding my every movement with suspicion.

"I know, but you're getting it anyway. Give me your hand, now."

"Of course. God forbid, you let me make my own choices."

She hissed as I yanked out the offending glass, but didn't pull her hand away. It wasn't so deep that I would have to stitch it.

I blister. "You're right, Olivia." I wipe her hand with alcohol, ignoring the heat from her skin. "I'm nothing but a selfish man that has stolen your choices away."

Looking up, I saw the skepticism blaze in her eyes, and I flared against the distrust. Had she forgotten already that she was the one who had betrayed me? That she had chosen to shut me out for a man that wanted only to use her?

I bite my tongue—hard, feeling the pain and using it to stop the detrimental words from spilling out of my mouth.

Just like that, I put the monster back in his box and silenced him.

I take a deep breath while examining the oval-shaped cut in the center of her palm.

"I'm a selfish man, but only when it comes to you." I rip open a Band-Aid and clean the rest of her palm with an alcohol wipe. "I can't let you go again, where you'll go back to shutting yourself off to the world and I'll go back to rotting in limbo."

She tried to pull her hand away, but I clamped tight and pressed on the Band-Aid "So no, you don't have any choices right now. Not until..."

"Until what?" she finally snatches her hand from mine, and our eyes meet.

I shook my head, torn between leaving and staying. I could tell by the way she was glaring at me that she wanted an argument, but it would end one of two ways.

I'd want to leave, or I'd want her, here on this bathroom counter where my desire would explode until there was nothing left of us both.

"Until you're willing to give me the chance to explain. Right now, neither of us are in the right frame of mind to be discussing this further."

"I'm starting to see a pattern here. Every time we get close to the truth, you shut the conversation down." She pushes me away and hops off the counter.

Again, she was calling me on my shit and leaving.

"Because you can't handle the truth, Olivia," I hit back sarcastically, following her. "Every time we get close... fuck! Look what you did last time I tried to be honest with you. You ran into the arms of Black."

Olivia turned around quickly with a fierce glare that could melt glaciers. "I didn't run into his bloody arms! He found me, and even if I did you have no right to tell me what I can and can't do. No right at all. How many times do I have to tell you this for it to get through that thick skull of yours?"

She poked me hard in the chest, trying to shove me away. Grabbing her, I pulled her into me, pinning her hands down by her sides.

"Stop it, *Bella*. Now is not the time to push me. I'm barely holding on to my patience as it is. We're done talking about this, okay? We need space and—"

"Time? So, you can plot and come up with new ways to make my life a living hell?"

Olivia was pushing down on a nerve I wasn't used to having touched. She wanted me to snap, wanted me to get angry so that she would have another reason to hate me, it was written across her face.

If I fell into her trap, she would only see me as the bad guy and use the monster against me.

Looking down at her, I realize the urges in me to scoop her up and take her to my bed were getting stronger with every glare and harsh word she threw at me.

Her anger was a siren's call to my libido, blowing on the flames with every sneer—and she had no idea of the torture she put me under.

I'm a fucking mess.

A mess that's turned on by her fury.

I hold her at an arm's distance. "I'm not trying to make your life difficult."

"You're just trying to force me to my knees where I'll have no choice but to obey, right? Be a good little bitch for the great Luca Caruso," she snapped, her words dripping with venomous rage.

She might as well have slapped me across the face.

My hands squeezed at her arms. "That's not what this is. You know it isn't, otherwise, you wouldn't have let me in, Olivia. We wouldn't have slept together if..."

"I made a mistake," she pulled away from my grip. "A stupid, stupid mistake in trusting you. The only reason we slept together was because I thought there was something redeemable about you, but I was wrong. So, fucking wrong"

The air in my lungs burned up and disappeared. My body seized into place, preparing for the final blow—the one that would bring me to my knees if she uttered the words.

But even with my body preparing for war, my eyes still glared hell her way, telling her that at any moment that fragile patience of mine will wear out.

"I trusted you, trusted that you were being honest with me, but it was all a lie. You kept me in the dark, filling my head with false promises just so that I wouldn't have the choice to leave."

She took a step back away from the hand I unknowingly outstretched towards her.

That's not true.

"I kept you in the dark because you couldn't handle it," I growled, pushing by her. "But my intentions were to always tell you the truth when the time was right."

With every blow she delivered, I found myself more and more desperate to silence her.

I need to get out of here.

"Of course, I couldn't handle it!" she yelled, following me. "Nobody in their right mind could handle being kidnapped by a psychopath and not knowing why!"

I turned and she was in my arms within seconds as I pressed her against the nearest wall. Olivia tried her best to wrestle herself free, pushing my buttons with every shove until I shook her.

"You knew why. You knew the moment you kissed me back." I was yelling back at her, trying to hold on. "I will never apologize for taking you. You were miserable, barely fucking living, so if you're expecting an apology, you'll be waiting a long time, *Bella*."

Fixing me with a deathly glare, she opened her pretty, fuckable mouth. "I hate you. Every single thing about you — I hate it."

I should have let her go, left this forsaken room full of lit candles and petals. Should have locked her in, but her sweet scent and temper had me by the balls.

"Good."

Smashing my lips to hers I demanded more than I should have done. I demanded her past, her present, and her future with my hands in her hair and my lips bruising hers.

My body set alight when her hands tugged at my shirt— viciously pulling me into her. I pour in my anger with my tongue, forcing entrance to her mouth, furiously devouring her bit by bit.

With every grab and bite, I felt the space yawning between us and the monster gaining advantage as it drinks in and fuels up on her anger.

I pull away, breathless. "Stop this now," I hissed against her swollen mouth. "Stop fighting me and give in."

She titled her chin up in defiance, her lips demanding I kiss them again. "No."

I snap and turn her around, pushing her up against the wall where she's safe. My hips pin her until she falls still.

I didn't want her hatred pouring into me. It's destroying me and feeding the monster. And if the beast that lived in me gained anymore advantage, I'd lose all hope of ever making her mine.

Moving her hair to the side, I ran my nose down the side of her neck, breathing her in. "Give in, Olivia. You know you can't fight what's happening between us any longer."

Her skin was flushed, her breathing labored and her eyes tightly shut. But she couldn't hide from me, not when I was the only man alive that knew how to read her body.

"Your body knows what it wants, what it needs, and that's me. So do your eyes, yet you continue to deny us both." Pressed tightly against her, I could feel her skin warm to me. "Give me what I want, Olivia."

The sweet sound of her gasp almost became my undoing.

I kissed her neck when all I wanted to do was bite.

"I'm done playing this ignorant game with you. It ends today, with me. From tomorrow morning, you will accept what is happening between us—do you understand?" My hand that had wrapped its way around her hair pulls her closer to me, exposing her neck.

Her barely-there whisper wasn't enough to stop me. "Why are you doing this?"

"I've been patient. I've given you your space, even tried to be honest with you, but you wouldn't meet me halfway. You've left me no choice, so now I'm taking all of yours."

"You can't just expect me to give in." She pushed back using her elbows, but I returned her, pressing her cheek flush against the wall.

"You already have. The moment you came back with Chen, the moment you set the timed email instead of just sending it, you made a choice." I kiss her shoulder. "You don't want to leave, Olivia. You just don't understand yet why you want to stay."

She hisses, but doesn't move, my words hitting raw nerves she wasn't ready for.

"You're wrong. I don't want you or this mess you've put us both in."

I laugh darkly, my mouth hovering by her ear. "Of course, you don't."

Before she tips me over the edge, I push myself away from her, turning on my heel and leaving the space that demanded romance not violence before she could get to me.

"Tomorrow, Olivia," I warned her, while pausing at the door.

Leaving to find relief in my own room, I told myself repeatedly that she would eventually understand; finally realizing what was happening between us would soon make sense. But the monster loved to push its insecurities onto me, whispering into my ear that this was all in my fucking head. That my black heart should begin to prepare for her constant rejection.

CHAPTER FIVE

Olivia Heart

F ire finds me in my dreams for the first time in years. I stand alone in the doorway to my childhood home with my bookbag and coat, viewing the slow destruction of my house as the flames eat greedily at its surfaces.

Frozen with fear, I do nothing but watch.

Ash begins to fill my mouth and smoke burns my lungs, but I'm silent—trapped against the source of destruction.

My thoughts are wild and frantic with panic for my parents, but my lips are glued together.

I know they're close. I can feel them, but yet, I stand at the door—frozen.

I silently scream for my legs to move, but they don't. I try to look behind to see if anyone on the street can see the smoke, but I cannot turn my head.

Red, angry fire licks at the carpet in front of me, eating the soft material and turning it into burnt plastic. Heat singes my young skin, forcing me to squint down the hallway until her scream wakes me.

I'm awake with both hands clutching at my throat, my nails digging into my skin trying to claw back the scream that left my mouth.

My skin is heated and clammy.

My covers go from comfort to suffocating in seconds. I rip them away from my legs, needing to feel cool air against my face instead of remnants of my nightmare.

The tears that I thought had dried up fill my eyes to the brim and spill into my lap.

Just breathe, Olivia. One breath. Two breaths. Three breaths.

Panic and fear loop around my ribcage, one-by-one, slowly and with malicious intent begins the torturous squeeze I know so well.

It's been years since I had that dream, but it forces all of the raw memories to the surface, and I want to forget. Forget the guilt that eats me for not being there even when I was a child.

Months after my parents' death, in the mess of my emotions, my brain had concocted this nightmare of me as a child, standing by as my parents turned to ash in our family home.

A cruel way of reminding me how helpless I'd been.

I'm out of the bed before I realize and opening the door back into the suite.

I can't be alone. Not when the squeezing around my chest is reaching the point of eye wateringly painful.

Every room is bathed in darkness, and it takes me a while to move through the vast space, ensuring my eyes have enough time to adjust without bumping into the furniture.

The first bedroom I open is empty and I'm careful to be quiet as I close the door.

When I open the last door, I know he's in there because I feel his energy calling to me from the middle of the room.

The relief I feel when I see him sleeping soundly, laying on his side, calms the shake in my hands. Even while sleeping he exudes power and aggression. I need it, him, to smother the pain roaming truant in my head.

I need him. *I need him.* This is too much to unpack right now so I won't.

I don't want him to wake, so I'm careful to pull back the covers only a little, holding my breath the whole time.

I ignore the small voice telling me this is wrong and listen to my heart instead. Tonight, what's right and what's wrong is outweighed by my need for comfort—the consequences forgotten.

I slip under the covers and push my back into him—sighing with relief when his naked chest touches my skin. I allow myself to relax just a fraction. The small contact however is enough to rouse him, and I suddenly feel his body freeze against me—the intruder in his bed.

"Olivia?" his Italian accent thickly coats my name.

I bite my tongue. I don't want him to hear the stress in my voice.

Hesitantly, I feel him lift his head from his pillow to peer down at me. Scrunching my eyes shut, I pray he'll not ask questions and just let me share his bed. We can return to our usual schedule of despising each other tomorrow when my hands don't shake, and my heart doesn't feel as though it's been through a blender.

He sighs softly before pulling me into him, wrapping his arm around my waist and anchoring me to his warmth. We fit so perfectly together, like pieces of a puzzle; and I hate that I need it.

I hate that I need him when I've never needed anyone before.

"I've got you," he mumbled against my neck.

The soothing of his heartbeat against my back promises me that he does. It doesn't take long for his promise and soft kisses against my skin to rock me back to sleep where I feel safe enough to return to my dreams.

****

It was hours later, when the sun was just peeking through the curtains that I find myself staring at the bedroom wall. Embarrassment had hit me as soon as my eyes opened, and the need for more sleep was long forgotten.

God, what's happening to me? I'd needed him so desperately that all that mattered was feeling his skin on mine and his arms around me. Amid my anxiety, my body pulled towards him, the one man that could offer the comfort I needed and left my feelings at the door.

I'd used him. That was all. I needed to feel his full control to stop the spiraling, because I knew if I went too deep there was no telling how long it would take me to find my way back.

Needing him was nothing but a self-protective measure.

Keep telling yourself that, Olivia.

I purse my lips, turning to peek up at him.

He's tan against the white sheets, beautiful and serene with messy hair and shapely mouth. He sleeps so peacefully with his arms protecting me — protecting what he's deemed as his.

I find myself admiring him, tracing across the edge of his jaw, feeling the stubble against the pads of my fingers. This is not right. I need to go.

Gently lifting his arm, I slip out of his bed and don't look back. I return to my room to shower, to scrub his claiming scent off my skin, while ignoring the empty feeling left in my chest.

Whoever had packed for me must have known the weather in France would be miserable because it was mainly sweaters and jeans. Assuming it was Marie, I'd make sure to thank her when I next saw her. That's if we go back to Italy.

Moving into the living area, I finally have time to appreciate the beautiful floor to ceiling windows that on a summer's day would warm the cream interior. The living room was soft with two cream winged back chairs with a matching chesterfield sofa. In the corner of the large open-plan room stood a black and gold grand piano, shined to the high heavens.

The room was beautiful and not what I expected from Luca. His usual taste was modern and clean cut, without color, unlike the feminine touch in this space.

Before my eyes could wander to the smaller décor, the elevator doors behind me ping open.

Turning, I was greeted with the bellboy that we had met yesterday. His cherub-like face and smile help me relax instantly.

"Good morning, Mr. Caruso has requested I take your breakfast order—is there anything you would like?"

My heart stalls at the mention of Luca.

"I'm sorry, I seem to have forgotten your name."

He smiles, forgiving my ignorance. "It's Jacques Arnaud."

I smile back. "Thank you, Jacques. I'd love an English tea and maybe some fruit; if you don't mind?"

"Of course, not, Miss Heart. I'll have room service bring it up right away." He turns to leave.

"Is Mr. Caruso joining me?" I realize how odd it sounds, but Jacques is my only outsider knowledge right now.

"Mr. Caruso left twenty-minutes ago for his meeting with one of your security detail."

I take a seat in the nearest winged chair. Knowing that Luca has left fills me with a strange urgency that I haven't felt before. But instead of over-analyzing, I smile at Jacques, so he doesn't have to pander to me any longer and can go about his day.

The rain that drizzles down the windows cannot distract me from the beauty I see in the distance. The Eiffel tower, in all her glory, stands proudly in the background glinting with strength and beauty.

Alice and I had visited the Eiffel tower years ago when we had begged our grandparents to take us. Alice had taken a million selfies in front of it, while I admired the magnificent tower and the people eager to climb to the top. Alice's frustration when my grandparents had grown bored of being her personal paparazzi was probably my second favorite part about the trip.

The girl could whine for England.

The elevator pings and my stomach rejoices. My glee is short-lived as I turn to face a woman that I've only ever seen once in a picture that was stored in Luca's phone.

Luca's sister, Aida, faces me in her Burberry coat, thick black tights, and heeled Prada boots. Her thick curls are coiffed neatly on her head so that the diamond earrings that drip from her lobes are given the proper attention they deserve.

Aida is beautiful and poised in high fashion—very much like her brother with matching sharp cheek bones and stunningly dark eyes.

"Hello, Olivia," her voice is brisk, her Italian accent coating the words that slip between her crimson lips.

I find myself standing, nervously twisting the sleeves of my sweater as we stare at each other.

"I'm sorry to intrude, but I thought it best if I finally introduced myself to you- may I take a seat?" She slips her eyes to the sofa and then back to me.

"Er yes, of course." I take my seat and she confidently takes hers, crossing her legs to the side like royalty.

Sensing my discomfort, she smiles. "Luca doesn't know I'm here yet, so you can relax. It's just us girls."

"Oh."

She laughs. "Well, I say he doesn't. Give those guards of his a few minutes and he'll be aware of my visit."

"Why are you here?" My question is abrupt, but she doesn't mind. I can tell by the way she watches me that she likes to get to the point.

Aida shifts in her seat. "I wanted to speak to you. Well, I wanted to check that you were okay. Dante has filled me in on yesterday's events and I didn't feel comfortable with what I heard. My brother was ignoring my calls, so I decided I didn't want to wait a moment longer to check in on you."

I don't reply. I'm too busy trying to process the fact that she's aware of her brother's actions, and my pathetic attempt at an escape. And that our fucked-up situation doesn't faze her.

"Are you *okay*, Olivia? You can tell me the truth. Whatever you say to me will be completely confidential."

"I don't believe that." I shake my head. "He's your brother."

And he hears everything.

"Yes, he is," she smiles softly, love shining in her eyes. "But he doesn't get a free pass for doing whatever he pleases because he's my blood—nobody does. If he's so much as hurt you, I'll happily put a bullet in his—"

60

The elevator doors ping open, and breakfast arrives, saving us both from the Caruso savagery.

"Perfect timing," she breathes, before turning to the maid that fails to hide her fear. "We'll take it to the roof, please." Aida is the first to stand up, teetering over me in her heels. She holds out her hand. "Shall we, Olivia?"

****

The roof was not what I expected. We wandered to our table under a hovering curved glass canopy that kept the rain and wind away. Flowers and greenery draped down from the walls and glass beams, cocooning us in nature while we still had the option to look out at Paris around us.

It was surprisingly warm with glass-orbed heaters placed in every corner of the roof, but no other guests have ventured up and I'm pretty certain it has something to do with the woman in front of me, and not the miserable weather.

"Do you like it? This roof was one of the main reasons I purchased this hotel."

"This is yours?"

"It's Luca's and my joint venture," she smirked into her espresso. "But I'm the one who's more interested in the hospitality side of our business estate."

I look around, enjoying the serenity that the space affords us. "It's beautiful up here, even in the rain."

Her eyes clock my hand as I move a piece of hair away.

"Your hand. What happened?"

I look down at the small Band-Aid that's peeling on my palm and frown.

"I cut it on a piece of glass," I told her, shoving my hand under the table. "I lost my temper last night when I saw my room was decorated with candles and roses. Stupid I know, but I was too mad to think straight."

Something about her eyes willed me to talk, to tell the truth, and it felt good to finally be able to talk to someone that didn't analyze everything I said.

"Luca really has lost his mind," she rolled her eyes. "I can see why that would piss you off," she nodded. "Especially, after yesterday's events…"

I gave my hands something to do by taking a sip of my tea. I couldn't think about yesterday, not when it had ended with me in Luca's bed.

"You tried to leave him again, didn't you?"

There was no judgment or anger in her eyes. In fact, she was perfect at masking her emotions—just like her brother.

"It's complicated."

"Dante told me it was when you learned the truth—that Luca had lied to you."

I didn't say anything. Instead, I let my silence fill the space between us hoping that she would understand that I didn't trust easily, nor was I comfortable discussing this.

Sighing, she leaned forward, pouring herself a glass of water before fixing me with a cautious stare. There was so much she wanted to know. I could see it swimming in her chocolatey eyes.

Welcome to my world.

"Eight years ago, I thought you were nothing but a figment of my brother's imagination. After his year of drugs and bad decisions, he returned to our Pa's deathbed a whole different person. At first, I thought maybe the drugs had finally got to him, that this mystery woman who had been kind enough to return him to us was just a figment of his overworked imagination…"

I'm transported back to the moment my eyes first landed on him in that airport. I'd recognized his pain instantly.

"Just to have Luca at the hospital was a miracle. Luca despised him."

I couldn't stop myself. "Why? Because of the business?"

Aida bit her lip before answering. "No, because he was a difficult man, Olivia. Our Pa was less about love and more about demands. You must understand our upbringing was not conventional, and Luca had to follow the family code. He was forced to accept his new responsibilities at the age of sixteen."

"What does that mean? What was he forced to do?"

She laughed, but I heard the anger. "What wasn't he forced to do?" she sighs before continuing. "A gun was placed in Luca's hand on the morning of his sixteenth birthday, and he was ordered to kill a cousin of ours who had been caught stealing. There was only one way to deal with this type of betrayal."

I imagined Luca's face as a young boy being forced to do the unthinkable. To have no control over his own actions, all to impress a man that wanted nothing but destruction.

I felt my mouth dry when my reaction to the death on his hand was muted. What wasn't muted was the pain I felt for Luca having to do the unthinkable without a single way out.

He was trapped against his will by people who should have protected him. Like me.

"Our cousin had stolen from the family and Luca didn't have a choice; our Pa would not let our cousin tarnish the family name. Having Luca take care of the problem was the perfect test."

I scrunched my eyes closed, trying to dispel the image of Luca being forced from innocent to monster.

Aida's soft voice still found my ears. "It was from then on that Luca pushed and pushed until he had the opportunity to leave the family, to take back the control he needed. For two years he was free to be young and wild, but then our Pa fell sick. It was our Ma that pulled him right back in after the funeral."

I opened my eyes back to her and she smiled warmly.

"Everything was black and white for him until he remembered a mystery woman in an English airport that didn't give a shit about his money or family's reputation."

"I remember he was upset and desperate. Aida, I just gave him my ticket so he could get to France."

"Well, it wasn't just a ticket to him. Don't get me wrong, Olivia, I didn't understand it at all until much later when I saw the affect you were having on his life."

"The affect?"

I'm trying to be present in the conversation, but my mind wants to focus on the new information Aida had willingly given. Luca had killed somebody. Luca was a murderer. His Black promises and threats were not empty anymore.

And I accepted this information without hesitation.

My moral compass was skewered. It had to be.

I'd met possible killers at work, even sought shorter sentences for some of them, but I had the guise that I would never know the truth about their cases.

But I know what Aida is telling me is true and it doesn't scare me.

Aida pauses, possibly sensing my inner turmoil. Was she worried that Luca wouldn't be happy with her divulging his secrets? Could she see that I wanted this information so badly, that I was practically on the edge of my seat?

Pull yourself together Olivia.

"After he took care of the business side of things, I noticed he was unable to settle, constantly on edge about something. Then there were sudden purchases in New York, a place we didn't care much to expand in. Dante, after much persuasion, finally confirmed he was buying everything around the woman he had met only once."

I remembered the folder he had given me the morning I had come around in his house. Remembered the burn against my pride at every microscopic invasion of my privacy.

"I still don't understand why he did all of that, but he couldn't come to me."

"It was to keep you safe and to give himself peace of mind — well that's what I've assumed." Aida picked up her espresso cup and sipped delicately, allowing me a little time to take it all in. "We had many enemies... well, we still do, but it took a while for Luca to keep them in check after our Pa died. Adding you into that mix would have given him a heart attack."

"You hear how crazy this sounds, don't you?"

Aida's laugh was small, but bright. "Crazy doesn't begin to cover it."

"It doesn't." I shook my head. "One minute, I'm living my life in New York, worrying about securing deals for rich criminals and the next, I'm being forced into a new life with a man who is full to the brim with secrets."

"Yes," she purses her lips. "Taking you like that was not his brightest idea, and I want you to know I do not under any circumstances agree with what he's done."

"Did you know that he was going to take me?"

"No, I didn't. I was always under the impression that he would go to you when the time was right, and I believe that would have happened if his hand hadn't been forced."

I find solace in the fact that she isn't involved in that part of Luca and my situation. This I can live with. But I don't buy for one second that he was never going to take me in the way he did—I'd seen as much in his eyes.

"There's so much more to this than meets the eye, Olivia, and I shouldn't be the one to tell you everything. I know you would appreciate it more if it came from Luca."

I nod in agreement. "I would, and he owes me that."

"He does."

She looked over my shoulder, smiling at a passing waiter and asked for two more coffees—her French immaculate compared to her brother's.

Settling back on me, her composure slipped from relaxed to formal, her shoulders tensing with the words she was preparing.

A few minutes had passed before she spoke again.

"I came here to check on you, and if I'm being honest, to meet the woman that has stolen my brother's heart. Please forgive me for being intrusive, Olivia, but there are some things I need to know before I feel comfortable enough to leave."

The coffees are placed in front of us—a chocolate heart stenciled on the top of each.

What is with this place and romance?

I dip my spoon in the middle of the heart and stir.

"Only if I have your word that whatever answers I give you stay between us. I've had enough of people digging into my life."

Aida didn't need to think about her answer. "You have my word. I'm not here to spy for my brother."

That was still up for debate. My trust would have to be earned.

"What do you want to know?"

"Do you feel safe?"

The question was not what I expected and for a few seconds, I froze.

"Yes, more than humanely possible. It's kind of hard not to be when you're surrounded by guards that keep you from the dangers of the outside world."

Aida shakes her head and I watch her curls bounce "No. I mean, with Luca, do you feel safe with him?"

"Sometimes," I grind the word between my teeth, feeling confusion swell and crest into my stomach.

She's careful to compose her face but I catch the worry that flashes across her eyes.

Across the table is a woman that loves her brother through thick and thin, but a sister who cares enough to step in to protect him from himself.

"You know you have all the power over him, don't you?"

I pause while picking up my drink. "I'm sorry?"

Aida smirks and I'm reminded of her brother. "Luca will do anything for you, and yet, you haven't used that to your advantage. I find it strange that you haven't used that yet."

I cough with shock, but she laughs cheerily at her bold assumption.

"You've slept with him, haven't you?"

I blanch and hurriedly place my cup down.

"Oh, this changes everything. No wonder he's losing his damn mind so quickly."

"It was before I knew the truth," I replied quickly. "I was confused and..."

"Falling for him," she finished, much to my annoyance.

I wanted to tell her it wasn't true and that I had made a mistake, but the look on her face told me she wouldn't believe me even if I tried.

Straightening up, she leaned forward across the table. "Even if what I think is happening is true, I want you to know, Olivia, that if at any time you want to leave you can."

It's my turn to laugh. Of course, she would try to lure me in with the promise that I could return to my life, but I didn't believe she had the power. Nobody did against him.

"I'm serious, Olivia. After recent events, if you and Luca cannot get through whatever this is, I will ensure you return to your life—whether Luca wants that or not."

I suck in a shaky breath. "He wouldn't let you. I'll be dragged right back to him."

"He wouldn't have a choice. We made a pact the day after your arrival that if at any time this got out of hand, I would take over. Why do you think he brought you here?"

Oh shit.

To hide me.

My options had gone from zero to one, but I didn't feel any elation this time. My heart was twisting with confusion instead, trying to hide from what it desperately wanted.

"But he knows you're here now."

She nods. "He does, and I can imagine he's struggling to contain his anger towards my visit," she laughs. "He's not the only one who can hire security to keep away the interruptions."

I look towards the exit of the rooftop bar and back to her—my mouth open with surprise.

"There's eight armed guards standing by in case any of them dared interrupt us. Don't look at me like that. I needed to make sure we would have time for an honest conversation." The coy smirk across her face tells me she's enjoying herself far too much.

"Is he with them? Is Luca downstairs now?"

"No, he's in a meeting with an old friend."

I picture Luca glaring over at Chen who would receive the updates from his team, and I try my hardest not to enjoy their possible misery.

"I'm serious, Olivia, if you want to leave you can and I'll take care of everything. You have choices now, but before you decide, I want you to be a hundred percent certain of your decision. If you choose to leave you will never see or speak to him again."

The pain that whips my heart doesn't go unnoticed.

"Luca wouldn't be able to let me go."

I picture him from last night, sleeping so peacefully in his bed knowing that I was under his roof. If I left, he would suffer. I would have all the power to make him suffer.

Could I do that?

"He's made a pact, Olivia, and in our family we take them very seriously."

I look out to the beautiful city of Paris and notice the rain has stopped for now.

"I don't expect an answer today. In fact, I need to leave soon if I want to make it home in time to pick Mateo up from school, but I'll keep checking in." She checks her Rolex before standing.

We leave the rooftop and take the short elevator ride to the suite. When the doors open, I'm greeted with an awkward standoff. Bones, Red, and Rum are standing together, glaring at the eight guards Aida had used to block the elevator.

Aida's men are dressed in black, the belts around their waists secured with vast weaponry. Unlike my guards, their expressions are unreadable.

"Stand down," she tells her men. "We're leaving."

They move out so quickly and efficiently towards the stairs, that they almost blur into one.

Turning to me, Aida leans in and places a kiss on my cheek. "Remember, Olivia, that you're the one who has all the control here. You just need to choose how you use it."

"I hope you're right," I tell her, feeling emotions swirl in my chest. "Thank you for coming and for being honest with me."

Aida smiles at me one last time before joining her security.

CHAPTER SIX

Olivia Heart

I heard Luca before I saw him. Harsh and fast, his Italian voice woke me from my accidental nap with a jolt. He'd burst through the elevator doors with his phone at his ear, his tie shoved in his pocket, and a look that could kill.

That was until he saw me sitting there, blinking sleepily over at him.

Ending his conversation with a short demand, he made his way over to me, his eyes scanning my face. "You're here."

"Where else would I be?"

"With my meddling sister," he replied tersely, as he took the chair across from me. I couldn't help myself; my eyes drank him in greedily. He looked so good when he was ruffled.

"I'm assuming from her theatrics today that you're aware of—"

"Your pact?" I leaned back away from his smell of cologne and rain.

He leans forward and buries his head in his hands. "Fuck, just one day. Is that too much to ask for?"

Yes.

"That's why you brought me here isn't it, to hide me away from her?"

He looks up at me with his dark eyes. "Yes. I needed some time before she got involved." Shaking his head, he stood up and took a deep breath. "I should have realized she would come; my family finds it very incredibly difficult to keep their noses out of my business."

"She's giving me a choice to stay or leave," I tell him, while standing up. The thought of my leaving hits the same nerve it always does. Luca goes from somewhat in control to alarmed in seconds.

A part of me wants to open my mouth to soothe him, but instead, the rational part of my brain responds. "She thinks I should give you a chance to explain, she said there's a lot more that I don't know."

I take a step closer to him and he steps back, his dark eyes penetrating right through me, trying to gauge my next move.

"There so much that you don't know. I'm not even sure where to start, Olivia. It's not just about spilling my secrets because I'll do that in a heartbeat. What I'm not willing to risk right now is losing that small part of you that doesn't despise the air I breathe. Once I tell you everything, there's a chance of whatever is here between us will become unrepairable."

"You don't know that." I take another step closer, but he hunkers down, his muscles locking into place—he doesn't want me to touch him.

The sting is strange and complicated, but I push by it.

"I'll listen this time and I'll try to keep an open mind— just please, tell me everything, otherwise…"

"You'll take Aida up on her offer," he blisters, raising an eyebrow my way.

My mouth dries and my heart stutters under his fury, but yet, my body yearns for it, demands it. I want to taste the truth that his aggression affords me.

Breathlessly, I all but whisper, "Yes."

"An ultimatum," he shakes his head. "Fine, I'll tell you everything you want to know, but I want two weeks to do so. This isn't something I can do in one conversation."

Two weeks is easy. I can do two weeks.

"You always want more time but... okay, fine. You have two weeks to tell me everything."

He suddenly looks exhausted, and he swipes down his face.

"You can't run, you can't make it difficult for Chen's team, and you have to give me your word that you'll try. If you can do all that for me, I swear, that if you decide that you still want to leave, I won't try to stop you."

I'm floored and filled with relief that the person across from me seems more human with every word that falls from his perfect lips. But a fissure of pain begins to wind itself around my heart with the mere thought of being let go by him once and for all.

He takes a step closer to me but, still doesn't touch me.

Air becomes nonexistent when I catch his scent again.

"Can you do that, Olivia?"

"You know I can."

Determination and unfiltered need from his eyes warms me from my toes to my cheeks. Leaning forward, he lifts his hand to touch my face but pulls away once he realizes. My eyes travel to the fingers that didn't contact my skin and back to him.

He's taking away his touch.

Why?

Frustration and neediness snaps at me, clicking its fingers, demanding that I touch him instead.

He shoves his hands in his pockets. "You came to my bed last night and then you left. Why?"

The blush across my cheeks begins to burn. When he's soft, when his words touch me with such need, all I want to do is bend to his will—to give myself over to him.

Honesty blooms, warming my chest. "I needed you."

And the intake of his breath tells me everything I need to know. I do have a hold over Luca. He's good at hiding it from me, but there's flickers of it between us, ready for the taking.

I open my mouth, but I'm cut off by the elevator doors pinging open and the sound of heels clipping against the floor. His eyes never leave my face, the unspoken words ghost across his lips as our conversation is cut short by new intruders.

"Bonjour!"

There are three women staring at us with big smiles, each with their hands full of garment bags and boxes. They are impeccably dressed, their makeup painted to perfection and their energy filling the room.

"What's going on?"

Luca smirks. "These ladies are here to get you ready."

Before I can speak, the tallest dances over with her straight raven hair and bright blue eyes. She looks like she just stepped off the runway.

"What for?" I ask Luca, as I sidestep her overly-eager hands that are trying to reach for my hair.

"We've been invited to a friend's charity gala. His wife, Katrina, has sent her team to dress you for the event." He shoves his hands into his pockets, pleased with himself while I'm boxed in by all three women.

It's like Alice's wedding all over again, but I let them lead me away, even with Luca smirking in the background. The sooner they dress me up the sooner I can meet these mysterious friends of his who may possibly be able to help decode parts of Luca.

So, I'll let him win this one.

****

The dress that hangs on the wardrobe door has been picked specifically for me by Katrina Belmont, fashion designer and wife to Theodore Belmont. I'm told, as my hair is smoothed and curled, that I'll be the first person to wear the beautiful gown, that it had never been presented to the public by the prolific designer — until tonight.

The gala, event of the year according to the small team around me, is a charity event where Mrs. Belmont auctions off her collections to support up-and-coming designers.

While my hair is harassed by curling tongs I stare at the emerald satin gown with a graceful one shoulder strap and fitted bodice that puddles into a seductive fishtail. It's completely breathtaking and I'm not sure I can wear it.

Even with my face expertly painted and with the help of my most complimentary assistants, I'm hesitant to slip into the fine material.

"Miss Heart you'll offend Mrs. Belmont if you don't wear the Alana gown." Serena, the woman with short blonde hair, smiles as she takes my hand.

"I'm not sure I can pull this off…"

She tuts at me before waving me off. "There's only one woman in this room that can pull this off and it's you, Miss Heart, now step, please."

Even when I step into the gown and her hands pull up the zip, I keep my eyes away from the mirror.

Instead, I watch the reactions of the women that have their eyes glued to me. Serena lifts my dress and helps me slip into the heels, while her colleague, Camille, touches up my hair—with a face full of glee.

After being doused in perfume, I'm pulled towards the mirror. They surround me, smoothing down the fine material to my skin, while I stare dumbfounded at the woman staring back at me.

"You will give that man out there a heart attack, Miss Heart." Camille, the makeup artist, smiles as she gently rubs my arms. I want to thank her for turning me into a goddess, but the words never make it to my lips.

Instead, I'm overwhelmed by a strange thought that crosses my mind. It's Luca and his strong hands around my waist before he unzips my dress and just like that, I'm transported back to the night we first slept together. The night he says I let him in.

I'd wanted nothing more than for him to touch me, I'll admit. And when he did, everything fell into place. But was that me letting him in?

It was good sex… no, amazing, mind-blowing, toe-curling sex, but was it enough to forgive him for everything he's done before and after snatching me away?

"Miss Heart, it's time to go."

CHAPTER SEVEN

Luca Caruso

I've been waiting for exactly forty-minutes, but I don't interrupt the work of Katrina's team, no matter how impatient I feel. Not when I hear snippets of happiness coming from her room.

Olivia's laugh is the most freeing sound I've ever had the privilege of hearing and right now it stills my impatience to see her. But it's rare that the angelic sound has come from something I've said or done. I flick through our recent memories together and find it difficult to locate a memory where she was completely at ease with me.

I stare down at her initial tattooed on my skin and punish myself with all the times I've upset her or made her cry. Focusing on all the times that the darkness inside of me had crawled its way out and wreaked havoc between us.

It's not the man I want to be.

I want to hear her laugh, to see her smile, to watch her happiness grow, but with every moment of our time together, I'm starting to doubt if I can be the one to give her that.

Our lives are being wrapped up together by vicious intricacies that seem uncontrollable, pushing out happiness, until it becomes nothing more than an afterthought.

Breaking me away from my tangent of dark thoughts, the sound of heels clipping against the marble floor and hushed whispers capture my attention.

I stand and wait, eager to see her.

The three women Katrina sent over are the first to enter before parting, their eyes brimming with excitement as they all beam over at me.

"Etre préparé." *Be prepared.* My eyes forget them, drawn to the one person that could bring the light into any room.

Olivia Heart shyly teeters into my space while nervously smoothing down her dress, bringing my attention to the curve of her hips.

My personal heaven stood in front of me in all her ethereal beauty and yet, she blushed when she looked at me. My unworthy eyes slowly drank every inch of her in; enjoying the shy seductress that didn't understand her true powers in that goddamn dress or out of it.

Shit. I wasn't worthy of even being in the same room as her.

I fortunately knew Katrina well enough to know that this dress was sent with the purpose of forcing me to soften to Olivia's recent betrayal—I'm certain of it.

In seconds, my walls of frustration and regrets fell around me and at her feet.

"Will you say something, please?" Olivia whispered, standing in front of me and biting down on her glossy bottom lip.

Fuck. I want to bite that lip.

I've been staring too long. I need to say something.

Could I trust that what I wanted to say wouldn't come out as a stutter? That I wouldn't feel like a teenager in front of these expectant women. Were there enough words to describe what I'm feeling?

"You look… beautiful, Olivia."

Smooth Luca, real smooth.

I wanted to say more, but the words clogged in my throat. They were too personal for the many ears in the room, so I had to hope that my eyes would say the rest.

"You don't look so bad yourself," she sighed, as she sauntered over to the ladies that had readied her to steal my heart, again.

My eyes pulled towards the hypnotic sway of her hips under the silk as she moved to hug them all.

Christ. Is she even wearing underwear under that tight silk?

"Thank you for all your help and for being so patient with me."

"It's been our pleasure, Miss Heart. Have a lovely evening and we hope to style you again the next time you're in Paris!"

After they finish saying their goodbyes, Olivia turns to me, her eyes brightening a little. "That was… an interesting experience."

"I'm sure," I breathe, trying to expel my urges to kiss her. It's been far too long since her lips touched mine.

I'm starting to feel the first stages of withdrawal.

Soon, my hands will start to shake, and the pain will become unbearable.

"I have something for you," I tell her. "I want you to wear these tonight with no arguments." Out of the pocket of my suit jacket I hold out a small red velvet box.

"Please, take them, Olivia."

She eyes the box with suspicion before gently plucking it from my hand and prying it open. Alarm springs within her eyes.

"I can't wear these earrings, Luca! They look expensive and—wait, are they butterflies?"

Embedded inside the last diamond on the drop is a tiny black butterfly, sitting inside a clear-cut diamond, just waiting to be accepted by her.

I watch as she lifts one of the earrings to the light, her face flushing delicately when she catches the tiny creature.

"Put them in," I tell her firmly. "Then we can go, and you can interrogate my friends."

"Thank you, they're beautiful and so… thoughtful." She passes me the box and begins to fasten them in her ears, right where they belong.

Chen has done wonders finding a jeweler willing to accommodate my last-minute request. They're perfect—just like their new owner who follows me to the elevator, her fingers touching my gift.

"How long have you known the Belmonts?" she asks me, once we're inside the elevator.

Electricity and heat flush through my body when I glance over at her. How the fuck am I supposed to keep my hands off her when she looks like *that*?

I swallow my groan.

I clear my throat of lust before answering. "I've known Theodore since I was fifteen. We met on his first day at school after he moved to Italy where his father was set to open a hotel business."

I remember this scrawny French kid who couldn't speak a word of Italian showing up at school with an attitude and a need to fight anyone who called him out on it. Theodore got into a fight on his first day with one of the bigger kids who had called him a frog-eating bastard. Once the big kid's friends joined in, so did I.

We hit it off right away once we realized we shared the same upbringing and the same urge to fight. It wasn't long until our families joined forces either.

"And his wife?"

We stop and step out into the foyer. I'm grateful because the tight space made it hard to concentrate on her questions. All I could think about was Olivia in this fucking dress, and how long it would take me to get her out of it.

If I guessed correctly, I'd say ten seconds.

Chen and Bones wait for us in the lobby, dressed in their dark suits, ready to blend in. I throw them a hard stare when their eyes land on Olivia with far too much appreciation to be strictly professional.

She's mine.

I take Olivia's hand, rubbing my thumb down hers.

"Theo and Katrina met at university—she was the only woman not fazed by his charms and tendencies to get into trouble. Theodore fell pretty hard, enjoying the hard time she gave him, and they married a year later."

Olivia glides through the foyer, gathering attention with every step she takes, but her eyes are on me. Where they should be.

"So, you all dropped out at the same time?"

It takes everything in me not to ogle at her ass as she gets into the car.

"Not exactly. Theodore left when Katrina realized Paris is where she needed to start her career. Theo and I only studied in England to get away from our families; we were never serious about our education or the country"

Our conversation flows with such normality that I don't want it to stop. If it stops, she'll retreat into her head and that's one place I can't seem to reach her.

Olivia looks at me, even in the darkness of the back seat she stuns me with her big doe eyes and pouty mouth that's covered in lipstick.

"Your friends, do they *know* about me?" her question is gentle, but I hear the intent behind it. Olivia wants to know how far my lies run.

Ah. We're right back at the edge of the abyss.

I look out of my window and focus on Paris, specifically, those moving through the streets without a single care.

"They do."

She gasps while trying to turn to face me, but her dress constricts her.

I'd like to constrict her in my bed, specifically her hands trussed up while I worshipped her body with the freedom my tongue craved.

"And they're okay with you bringing me to their highly publicized event?"

I catch Chen's eyes in the mirror, and he seems a little smug. An hour ago, he had warned me about the ramifications if tonight went badly, especially with all the press around, but he didn't understand- he never could.

"Yes, because they want to meet you, Olivia, and I'm certain we can go one night without the usual theatrics." I raise an eyebrow her way and she scowls. "We did it for your cousin's wedding, remember?"

She turns away, blushing I think. "We did, I suppose."

****

It's thirty-minutes later and I'm agitated, completely frustrated in my own clothes. My skin burns. My heart hasn't stopped pounding and my mouth is completely dry.

All because she hasn't said a word in thirty-minutes.

We arrive at The Belmont's estate where their magnificent chateau stands proudly, and it's so fucking French. My eyes scan across the house where light beams out from every arched window, highlighting the perfectly manicured gardens in front, looking for the owners of the estate.

Chen takes the long drive down to the main house that's currently buzzing with activity. There are cars stopping every few seconds at the front of the house, cameras flashing, couples and groups walking across the front gardens holding flutes of champagne. In true Katrina fashion, it's an over-the-top affair full of unusual people with expert tastes and large bank accounts.

Olivia carefully observes her new surroundings with apprehension, her hands gripping at the skirt of her dress. I go to take her hand, to offer comfort, but I stop myself.

"Is that—no it can't be—is that Bono?" she whispers, as we pull to a stop.

I look over her shoulder. "Yes, it is. Are you a fan of his?"

She scrunches her nose. "Oh, definitely not. Are you?"

I shrug, ignoring the tightening in my chest at how cute she is when she scrunches her nose. "Not exactly my taste," I tell her.

"What is your taste?"

You. On your knees.

Chen holds the door open for her, disrupting my intrusive thoughts of Olivia and me.

I'm quick to join her, my hand hovering on her lower back as I guide her towards the house.

Leaning in, I answer the question. "I prefer... the more aggressive forms of music. Anything that can drown out my thoughts."

Ah, deep Luca, too deep.

Olivia, as always, takes me by surprise as she smirks up at me. "I can see that. A little bit of Rock to—"

Just when things seem to be going smoothly, a flash of light streams across her eyes blinding her for a second. Blinking at the offence, she stumbles back, and I find myself reaching out my hand to pull her into me.

Fucking paparazzi.

"Mr. Caruso! Who is the lady? Is she your date?"

I shield her as best as I can, trying to ignore the fire her touch has ignited.

"Sorry," she's breathless. "The flashes caught me by surprise."

"Come on, let's get away from these vultures." Olivia's hand grips mine tighter as we take the stairs. Chen and Bones flank us, shielding us from the flashes that try to catch the woman at my side.

Once we're inside, my eyes find hers, checking that she's okay. A lush array of pink blossoms across her cheeks when our eyes meet. I instantly soften under her gaze, my urges to withhold my touch disappearing with every second that ticks by.

I want to touch her face, to feel her soft skin under my fingertips, to feel the world beneath my feet once more, but now is not the time to get lost in her.

"Sir, we should move, we're blocking the entrance." Chen butts in while still eyeing the paparazzi who are struggling to stay behind the black velvet rope at the bottom of the steps.

I growl in frustration while gently pulling Olivia to the side of the foyer.

"Can you do something for me?" I ask, my fingers tipping her chin upwards, so she has no choice but to look at me.

It takes all my strength not to lean down and press my lips to hers. All my goddamn strength.

I'm more certain now that I'm in withdrawals, and it's only going to get worse from here. Maybe we should head back to the hotel where I can lock myself in my room. Yes—I'll have Chen put her on a separate floor until I've got myself under control.

"It depends on what you're asking of me."

"I've asked a lot of you already. I know that, and I'm aware I don't deserve anymore, but for tonight, can we forget about everything? Can we just have one night where you don't run off and I don't have to drag you right back?"

She bites down on her lip, sending scorching hot blood to my crotch. Fuck. I'm in hell and she has no idea.

"Okay."

"Just like that?"

"On one condition."

There it is. The condition that will pave the way for this evening. Everything comes with conditions and strings with Olivia Heart.

My heart senses her leaning in and pauses mid-beat. "I don't want to be surrounded by guards tonight, Luca. I want to feel normal…"

The vulnerability shining from her eyes pulls me in like a weighted blanket. My urges to give her whatever she needs outweighs the darkness that whispers at me that she hasn't earned enough trust yet.

I know Chen and Bones are here to keep her from doing something stupid, but right now, I want normal just as much as she does.

Not taking my eyes away from her, I open my mouth. "Chen, you and Bones can take the night off."

"Sir, that's not a good idea—not with the paparazzi taking a keen interest in Miss Heart. We will leave you to your evening and take to the outskirts instead."

Chen is done taking our shit and even my glare cannot unsettle him.

Olivia's sudden smile beguiles me, her relief infectious, so much so that when she takes my hand I'm put at ease.

"I'll take it," she whispers.

I turn to Chen. "I'll call you when we're ready to leave."

He nods once before motioning for Bones to move with him.

Olivia wastes no time once they've left in securing my hand and pulling me further into the house.

We're just heading into the ballroom where guests are congregating when Theodore and Katrina spot us. Both are dressed impeccably well—Theo in his usual moody grey suits and coifed silver hair, while Katrina floated like a whimsy model who's just stepped off the runway.

Katrina moves with grace, taking her husband's hand as she eyes Olivia with complete and utter excitement.

Here we go.

"Heaven and hell are right on time, Theo. Who would have thought he would actually bring her?" She grins while leaning in to kiss my cheek. I watch from the corner of my eye, Olivia's surprise when she hears that Katrina is English, just like her.

"Hello again, Katrina. What has it been three hours since I last saw you?" I grumble, while throwing Theo a look of disapproval.

Theo sniggers into his whiskey, holding himself back so his wife can have her moment.

She turns to Olivia, dramatic as ever with her hand on her heart. "Olivia, it's so good to finally meet you. Thank you so much for coming to my little gathering."

Little gathering? There's around five-hundred people here, ready to shower her with attention. And she thinks that's little?

Olivia accepts her double air kiss with a shy smile "Thank you for having me and for this dress, oh and your team — that was really kind of you."

Katrina's eyes water at the compliment. "It was merely plain until you put it on."

Shit. I glare over at Theodore who smirks right back, loving that this is utter torture for me.

"As soon as I knew Luca was in town, I had to dig it out of the vault. I've been waiting for you to wear this dress for years and —"

Theodore finally feels the urge to step in. "Amour, come on now. Let Olivia breathe before you tell her all of Lucies secrets."

Really? Lucie? French bastard.

Katrina is not the slightest bit put off, instead she touches Olivia's arm and grins.

"My husband's right. I'm sorry, Olivia, I'm just so excited to finally meet you." She turns to glare at me. "Luca has told us so much about you that I feel as though I've known you for years."

I'm not sure if Olivia realized she had squeezed my hand, but the small gesture was enough for me to relax. I can't help the small smirk that graces my lips. Only days ago it was me comforting her in front of her family and friends.

And now she was offering her understanding.

"All good, I hope?" She's bright and friendly, trying to keep the conversation normal and away from the issues that hang over us like a dark cloud.

Theodore, the smug bastard, opens his mouth once again. "When it comes to you there is only the utmost respect and desire, Olivia."

Fucking French bastard gave me his word that he wouldn't make this anymore awkward for me. To fly and kick me over the edge he leans forward and winks at her.

I swipe two glasses of champagne off a passing waitress and pass one to Olivia, giving my useless limbs something to do.

I down my glass in seconds.

"These two are always pushing each other's buttons, which as you can see gets boring fast. Come on, I'll show you around and explain a little about what will happen tonight. Let's leave these two fools to it." With a roll of her eyes, Katrina forces her way between Olivia and I, taking great care to remove my hand so she can replace it with hers.

Olivia looks alarmed by the overly friendly woman who's keen to steal her away. But Katrina doesn't care. As both women leave the room, she tries to turn, glancing back at me, but Katrina soon takes her attention away.

Theo, sensing my urge to follow, outstretches his hand and holds me back.

"Let her go, she'll be fine with Katrina."

Of course, Olivia would be fine with Katrina. It was me who wasn't fine without Olivia.

CHAPTER EIGHT

Olivia Heart

Katrina is a ball of infectious energy as she whisks us away from the ballroom and into a corridor that's littered with guests eager to grab her attention. The woman that expertly diverts their attention is beyond graceful. A model with raven hair, high cheekbones, pale skin, and lips that would rival Angelina Jolie's. But her beauty isn't intimidating. Instead, she personifies warmth with every gesture or smile.

I don't know what I expected from the fashion designer, but this wasn't it. Maybe I'd watched too much reality television, but I thought fashion designers were supposed to be mean and moody?

"Keep going," she whispers with delight, as we dodge an attendee who's keen to talk to her about this season's colors.

I follow her lead, toward the back of her house where we enter a large, oval shaped room decorated in the finest of pinks. The space is graced with forty or more mannequins made of pure glass, their lifeless bodies wearing every shade of pink and lavender.

The ground that I suddenly struggle to walk through is covered in lush grass and daisies, bringing nature to my feet.

"This… this is beyond—I've never seen anything like this."

Katrina takes my arm within hers and pulls me over to a dusky rose dress that's an extraordinary vision of tulle and silk.

"This collection is one of my favorites. It's inspired by my sister who recently gave birth to a little girl. I wanted a collection that personified the power and grace women hold during pregnancy and childbirth."

"Do you have any children?"

Katrina smiles softly, her hands smoothing down the gown we're both admiring. "I will in just under four months' time."

My eyes divert straight to her stomach that is hidden in a perfectly designed dress that flares at the top of her hips.

"Congratulations," I breathe, watching her eyes beam with warmth. "You must be so excited?"

Katrina pulls me to one side when a passing group idles close by.

"Excited doesn't even begin to cover what I feel right now. I've been itching to tell our family and friends, but Theo is being his usual cautious self. He wanted to wait a few weeks after the gala, when my stress levels have returned to normal."

"He sounds very protective over you both." I smile.

She flicks her hair over her freckled shoulders. "He is, it's one of the things I love about him and well, his French accent, of course!"

The freedom in her girlish giggle is enviable. I can't help but smile right back at her.

"I see why Luca and Theodore are friends," I tell her, while moving through the room, heading towards the next where violins are playing a soft rendition of Anita Baker's Sweet Love.

Katrina takes my arm, pulling me into her. "They're both very uptight, but they mean well—especially Luca, even if sometimes he goes about it the wrong way."

I can see the twinkle of knowing in her eyes but force my questions to heel. I had promised Luca a night of normality, but right now it's me that craves it more.

This dress and I deserve a moment of peace.

We glide through the next exhibition which is bursting at the seams with white long-stemmed roses and scarlet red dresses. Each dress hangs delicately from crystal chandeliers, ready to be admired under the warm lights.

Fashion students and journalists are scattered in small clusters, whispering with delight at the collection named All My Love.

"Every dress that you see tonight will be auctioned off to the highest bidder. We specifically make one of each dress only. Our guests walk away with a piece of my heart and leave enough money to support a new designer. It's a pretty perfect deal if you ask me."

My fingers trace the top of a white rose in full bloom. "I don't know how you let any of these go, they're so beautiful, Katrina."

I see a faint blush pinking her cheeks. "It's a difficult task, but I remind myself it's all for a good cause. Come on, I want to show you something before the auction begins."

****

We stood in her private studio, away from the music and guests with just an awkward silence for company.

"Is everything okay?" My voice is tight when my eyes land on her. "Should we get back to your party?"

She bites down onto her ruby lip, biding her time. "Luca's told us everything, Olivia. I wouldn't feel right if I didn't check to make sure you were okay."

Embarrassment flushes my cheeks from the genuine care in her voice.

So much for one night of normalcy. I'm back to being captive.

"You sound like his sister," I tell her, as I flick through samples of cotton. "I'm fine, you don't need to worry about me."

Katrina offers me a seat and I take it slowly, trying not to crease my dress.

"I won't lie to you and tell you that I've understood Luca during recent years. I thought of him as nothing but dangerous and reckless until I saw it for myself."

My heart pauses. "Saw what?"

"The desperation he's struggled to contain while you were so far away. At events like this, he would be off on his phone or whispering with that security guard of his. When we noticed his visits became short and infrequent, I began to worry. It was like he was constantly on tender hooks and didn't want us to notice he was suffering. Theo tried his best to be there, even offered to take over your security team, but Luca couldn't let you go."

My feet had stood me up before I realized. It was hard hearing about this from a woman I barely knew, but she was keen to press on.

"What he's done is..." she slowly rises to meet me, her hands outstretched. "Is out of madness, but also blind, unrelenting love. His methods of showing you that are skewed but the sentiment is there. That man out there would go to the ends of this earth for you without a second thought for himself."

That word. That goddamn word.

Love.

Ice covered me once again, shielding me from the reality of what that word really meant for Luca and me.

Love is the most dangerous part of living. It forces you to give unwillingly, to weaken your shell in hopes that the person you trust won't shatter you into pieces.

I didn't have that trust in Luca.

Sensing my internal struggle, she continues. "Theo was exactly the same when we first met. Not as extreme as Luca, but he refused to let me go and did everything in his power to make me his."

I breathe hard at the comparison. "But you had a choice, right? Because you don't strike me as a woman to let a man make a choice for her."

"I did," she tells me quickly. "But if you take your history into account, remove all the ifs, buts, and outside influences, would giving Luca a chance be so difficult?"

Smoothing my hair down, I turn and divert my eyes to the tables that are littered with sketches and silk samples. "It's not outside influences that make it difficult, Katrina. It's the lies he's told when he's been given many chances to tell the truth. I understand, you're his friend and your loyalty lies with him, but right now he doesn't deserve a chance at my heart—not until he lets me into that head of his first."

I find myself gripping one of her sketches with a little too much force. The edge of the large design crumples between my fingers.

Katrina places a soft hand on my shoulder. "I understand. I do, Olivia. I just wanted you to know that he's not all dark. The light in him is worth seeing. I wouldn't be a very good friend if I didn't at least tell you that."

I turn to her, the sketch abandoned, to see the warmth in her eyes.

I had seen the light in Luca. It had wrapped me up into a cocoon of warmth and pulled me into him, until the darkness reached in and made an appearance.

"You're a good friend to him, Katrina," I tell her. "He's so lucky to have you and Theodore by his side."

Katrina laughs, catching me off guard once again with a wave of her hand. "Luca was right; you really are a queen of deflection. Come on, we've spent enough time talking about this. Let's go have some fun."

****

We find Theo and Luca at the head table, with their heads low and their voices even lower. I move towards him, watching him converse with his best friend. Even under the noise of a full quartet and hundreds of people, his voice finds my ears.

"Katrina not scared you off yet?" he whispered, as he stood to greet me.

If we weren't being watched by his friends, I'd have taken his hand within mine.

"Not yet," I said, as I took my seat, watching Theodore kiss his wife's cheek. Now that they were preoccupied with one another, I could see their attraction. Theodore was dark and intimidating, but protective over Katrina with every gesture. Katrina was light and airy, her hands stroking her husband's jaw with tenderness.

Even our fellow guests, nobody I recognized, at the table didn't dare to encroach in his wife's space unless he allowed it.

It was like watching Luca and I through a mirror.

A glass of champagne being placed in front of me disrupted my viewing and brought me back to Luca whose eyes watched me with trepidation. Tonight, right in front of me, the edge of his nerves were softening, but his body was still wound tight.

"Are you okay?" I whispered, leaning into him.

Confusion flickers across his face. "Yes, why?" his voice is brisk, but only for my ears as he leans into me, his mouth close to my ear.

Resisting the shiver desperate to ripple down my spine, I picked up my glass. "You wanted one normal night, but you're sat looking at me, ready to pounce. This works both ways."

He moves a curl over my shoulder, careful not to touch my skin, but I felt him anyway. "It does, but that's not why I'm looking at you like this, Olivia."

Under the table, his hand grabs at my thigh and I grip my glass, trying to ignore the heat spreading viciously up my thigh.

"I'm just finding it incredibly difficult to stop myself from dragging you from this room and finding a private corner where nobody can hear us."

My mouth instantly dries from his whispered intentions, and I find myself leaning into him for support. My body that is no longer under my control allows his hand to slip higher up my thigh.

I take a hasty sip of my drink, hoping the champagne bubbles will clear the fog of temptation, but of course, it barely touches the edge. With his free hand, he takes my glass from me, placing it back onto the table.

"Are you uncomfortable?" he whispers deliciously before placing a kiss on my naked shoulder.

Yes.

Memories of our bodies together spiral uncontrollably before me, switching my suffering from mild to unbearable in under three seconds.

That had to be a new record.

"You don't play fair," I hiss, trying to detach his hand from my thigh without drawing attention to us.

"Neither do you." He placed a chaste kiss on my jaw before removing his hands. "I was just checking to see if what you told me last night was true, that sleeping with me was nothing but a mistake. I can see now that you were lying."

I feel his victory swell around us as he leans back into his chair, completely and utterly relaxed while I try to regain my composure.

Sucking in a deep breath, I fixed him with a glare, but he smirked right back at me with pleasure.

"I was angry with you."

"So angry, but you still made your way into my bed last night."

My eyes caught those of Theodore, who had taken an interest in Luca and my conversation. My returning smile was tight but hopefully polite enough. Theodore nods once before redirecting his attention to one of his guests.

"It won't happen again," I mumble.

He laughs. "Of course, it won't."

CHAPTER NINE

Dante Caruso

I call Luca for the fourth time, and it goes straight to voicemail. Not only has he left me with his big fucking problem, but now he's all but disappeared into the world where only Olivia exists.

Shoving my phone into my pocket, I turn to face Black who is in and out of consciousness. He's been cleaned up; his injuries splinted and stitched, but his bloodied clothes remain.

I sigh.

I don't have the energy to deal with this right now. I need a drink and a woman to keep my bed warm. Not a fucking leech who is hell bent on destroying a part of my family for greed.

It always came down to fucking money.

I kick his shin forcing him to snap awake, a low hiss falling from his swollen mouth.

"Look who's finally awake," I drawl, while taking the seat in front of him. "Ready to carry on our little chat, or shall I come back when you've caught up on your beauty sleep?"

He better start spilling or I'll have no choice but to break Luca and my pact and up the interrogation. I'm not wasting another day breathing in the same oxygen as this cock sucker.

"I have nothing left to say. I've told you and your psycho cousin everything," he spits, dried blood cracking at the corner of his thin lips.

I lean forward, glaring at the man brave enough to slander my family. "I don't believe you. I don't believe that you allowed Olivia to come back for her passport when you could have taken her to the embassy. So, you can tell me the truth, or I'll just put a bullet in each of your knees—your choice."

And I would.

But only for Luca, so he wouldn't have to. I owed him that.

"You have ties in the embassy."

"We don't, and you know that." I reached into the back of my jeans for my Glock 26. "You came back for the money, didn't you? You hoped Luca had changed his mind."

He turned his face towards the door where four guards stood outside. My house was a fortress of men who would kill him on sight, and by the shake in his hands he knew that. And if he didn't the dogs would get him on the way out.

"Yes, I wanted the money."

I nodded. This I can deal with.

"Is this why you had secret files on Olivia, for blackmail?"

We had found a psychiatrist report in the back of his car, but his computer was where the real reports were. There were pictures, reports, and documents that hadn't been reported into Chen—and Luca was yet to see them.

I'd glanced over them briefly but there were cuttings of her parents' death, her birth certificate, pictures from her laptop webcam, and audio files of conversations between Olivia and her cousin Alice.

Then we found the files on Luca, which included sealed documents, destructive information regarding our family, and his involvement in Olivia's life right from the start.

"He destroyed my life the moment Chen assigned us to watch Olivia," Black started; his voice hoarse from screaming. "I hadn't signed up to be a fucking stalker. I was told it was for protection only, but he had me pulling her documents, scanning her phone and computer; destroying her privacy."

"You did it for four years." I lazily checked the magazine of my gun. "You were paid well for your services, until one day you woke up and wanted more. You don't care about Olivia, she's just your excuse to get to what you really want."

"That's not true! She's—"

"Your way to a fat payday." I stood up and pointed the gun down at his head, bored of this conversation and sick of the space he was taking up in my cellar.

"Isn't that right?"

"No! Look–please, put the gun down and I'll tell you everything you want to know."

"I already know everything. You're stalling, Black, and I have a date I need to get to so let's wrap this up."

"I'm not stalling, okay? The reason I needed the money was because I wanted to start a new life, to go underground."

"Why?" I pulled back the slide and heard the familiar click.

"Shit man, put the fucking gun down." He shifts back into his seat, but it's no good.

"Hurry the fuck up, Black. I have shit to do today."

"I needed the money to hide. I knew you two would come for me sooner or later. I needed the money to disappear for good."

My hand fell slightly, aiming at his center chest instead of his forehead. Black deflated right in front of me, ageing every second that I stared down at him.

"I spent hours watching her, and every day that went by I realized the severity of what I was doing. I didn't want to be involved anymore, didn't want to go to jail for a woman your cousin was in love with. I was going to use the money to hide and free her."

Shit.

It was worse than I had expected.

I knew there was something more. Call it a sixth sense, but I've always been good at sensing dishonesty in people and Black was a prime example. His actions seemed erratic at first, the cat and mouse chase nothing more than desperation but really, he was holding back until he had an opening.

Black was going to use Luca's money to steal Olivia away, all for himself.

I couldn't believe the fucking balls on the guy in front of me.

"I tried everything to stop it. I even tried to leave the team, but Luca wouldn't let me. He threatened my family and then it only got worse with the amount of time I was around her. When he took her, I tried to let it go, to put space between myself and the situation but I couldn't. She doesn't deserve this."

Anger made my finger itch against the trigger. "You don't know what she deserves."

He doesn't. He never will.

I had spent eight years around Luca to understand why Olivia was different.

"My blood itches when I think about what we've done to her. I haven't slept or eaten properly since they took her, haven't been able to forgive myself for being involved. If you put a bullet in my head, I know you'll be doing me a favor — that's how fucked I am."

There was no going back.

Luca's plan had been blown to pieces and the decision was now with me.

With the gun still trained on Black, I grabbed my phone from my back pocket and dialed.

Voicemail. Again.

"Olivia doesn't need a man like Luca controlling everything she does. She needs someone who understands her pain and how to make her see that she's allowed to be happy. Persuade your cousin to let her go."

"Shut your fucking mouth," I snapped, lurching forward, and pressing the barrel into the corner of his mouth. "You don't know a thing about her, or Luca, so shut your filthy fucking mouth"

"I know that she wishes Caruso had never taken her out of her apartment. He's fucking with her head and one day she'll see right through all the damage he's caused and there will be no going back for him."

I didn't need to hear this. My heart wanted to protect Olivia and Luca. They were so damaged that someone had to be there to keep out further harm; if that had to be me then so be it.

It's not like I would ever find someone to connect to like Luca had with Olivia.

I was far more broken to find deserved love.

Instead, all I could manage was a drink and a quick fuck with a random woman who could maybe keep my bed warm for a few hours. There would be no love story in my life, no woman to hold me accountable for all the bad shit I had done and would continue to do.

So, I would use the last piece of my soul to protect Luca who had protected me at the age of sixteen.

"You don't have to do this," he pleaded with me, as he pulled against the constraints biting into his chest and arms.

Chen and his team had cleared Black, leaving him with me while they moved Olivia, but this was no longer a simple pay off. No amount of money was going to keep Black away from Olivia.

Luca had left me with the task of guaranteeing his silence, but there was only one way to do that.

I recentered the gun and demanded he close his eyes.

"Please," he was begging, his eyes wide and frozen in fear.

Fury burned the back of my eyes. My finger began the slow squeeze—my heart speeding up with anguish and premature regret

"Dante, please, for fuck sakes man! If you pull that trigger, you'll have to live with the guilt for the rest of your life."

"Fuck," I yell into the open space, sweat dripping down my brow. "Just shut the fuck up and take your punishment like a man"

Black gasps, pulling in air through his bruised mouth. "I have a family, Dante. I have parents, and two young children. Please don't do this."

This guy was asking to be killed. Every damn time he opened his mouth the urge to press the trigger grew stronger.

I could feel it in my blood, swirling and tingling under my skin. His punishment was calling to me.

"You stupid idiot," I hissed between gritted teeth. "Why didn't you think about your children before betraying us?"

My opponent shifts in his chair, trying desperately to shrink away from the gun pointed at him.

"I did, that's why I'm in this mess. I thought about how I would feel if there was a team of men stalking my little girl." He shakes his head. "Let me go and remove the team watching my family and I'll leave Olivia and Luca alone."

"Not a chance."

I wasn't born yesterday. Black would disappear once again, waiting in the shadows for the ideal moment to take Olivia to get Luca's money.

"Well, isn't this fucked?" he spits blood at my feet, deflated and exhausted.

With my free hand I check my phone to find only text messages from recent hookups. It makes my blood boil to the top knowing that neither Luca nor Chen has taken the time away to return my calls.

I put the safety on and tuck the gun away, knowing I need more time before I decide whether to let this pig go to squeak another day.

With simmering rage, I move to him and kneel. "Look, Black, I very much want to put a bullet in between yours eyes and be done with this mess, but I need more than your word as reassurance."

It was a simple request. If he gave me what I needed, I would be kind and place him in the care of some of my most trusted men until he had earned his complete freedom back. If he didn't, I would spend the next twenty-four hours torturing it out of him until his body gave up and I could tell Luca it was an accident.

He spits a mouthful of blood at his side. "What more do you want from me?"

Looking down at the blood with disgust I move to stand over him. "If you try to contact either Olivia or Luca, I'll have your children removed from your family's care. I'll ensure that you never see either of them again. Agree to keep away and I'll agree to do the same."

"Yo-you fucking cunt!" he snarls, throwing himself forward. The chair he's tied to fumbles forward and he lands face first onto the concrete.

"That's me." I press my heel into the top of his spine. "So, do we have a new deal?"

CHAPTER TEN

Olivia Heart

So much was happening around us, but my eyes always found their way back to him. Luca attracted my attention like a moth to a flame, but I wasn't the only one feeling the effects of him. Women swooned over him, men forced their elbows in to try and talk business, but he never seemed fazed by it all. Instead, he would hold my hand tighter, taking great care to introduce me into his conversations.

Even when the lights dimmed, and the music faded to a soft melody, nothing could pull me away from him. I hated that his soft brush against my bare shoulder relaxed me. I despised that when he looked at me, I wanted to lean in and kiss him, to feel his lips on mine.

I should be telling the woman next to me, Allesia Delacor, diamond heiress, that my date to this event was in fact my kidnapper and I'd been held captive for two weeks. Maybe she would stand up and scream for her security to help me.

But yet, my mouth didn't yearn for freedom. It wanted something much more important.

While I sat, draining my champagne flute like my life depended on it, our table had turned their attention to Katrina who was sweeping the stage with her husband. Otherwise, they may have noticed the blush building across my cheeks from Luca's incessant fingertips that stroked the back of my neck.

I could demand he stops so that I can listen to Katrina welcome her guests, I knew that, but I know the empty feeling would return as soon as he removed his sinful touch. The same empty feeling I hadn't realized I lived with until he stormed his way into my life.

I bite down on my lip when he loosens his tie, exposing his neck. My mouth aches to place a kiss below his ear—to breathe in his scent and feel his warmth against my mouth.

Does he know that my body is no longer under my control? Can he sense that every cell in my body vibrates to the surface when he's close by?

I pull myself together, settling on quenching my new thirst with more champagne.

Why does this happen every time we're together? Why can I feel the tension building from my toes, desperate for the things I don't understand or have any experience in?

It's a constant itch that I'm scared to scratch.

Every second that ticks by, I feel my restraint slipping.

"I can feel you, Bella. Just relax, okay?" he whispers into my ear, while enveloping me in his clean scent.

I shift in my seat. "I'm trying," I hiss back, finding our proximity and the darkness unbearable.

He chuckles darkly. "Do you want to leave and find that dark corner, Olivia?" I hear the sultry suggestion in his voice, and my heart sprints into a frenzy. "I'll be careful not to destroy your dress this time."

I swallow thickly—images of his wicked hands having their way with this beautiful gown push me from melting to *needing*. "Stop it, you're not playing fair."

"I'm not, you're right, but I do know what would be very fair of me and that's easing your suffering."

My suffering. Those words have been uttered from his shapely mouth before. And I had let him tear at my dress and fuck me into submission.

That was before I knew the truth.

Before I realized it wasn't safe to trust him.

Shifting away from him, I put some much-needed distance between us and focused on his friends.

From the corner of my eye, I could see the disappointment on his face and allowed it to fuel my satisfaction, instead of the inferno of lust building between my thighs.

Like his sister had kindly pointed out, I had a lot of power over Luca and harnessing that would put us on an equal scale. I just had to work out how to keep control of my body when he touched me.

****

The auction moved incredibly quickly with people bidding for one of Katrina's beautiful creations. I'd watched two women, dripping in diamonds go head-to-head for her By The Fire collection that features tranquil blues and orange and blood red gowns.

Once their friendly bidding war ended, more women stepped up, with some pushing their partners to raise the stakes in hopes of winning a one-of-a-kind Belmont design.

Even Allesia had secured three pieces, much to Katrina's delight.

"Your friend is very talented," I mumble to Luca, who seems pretty bored with the auction. Especially with the gentleman with a handlebar moustache at his right, who's been trying to talk business all night.

"She is."

I fight the smirk threatening to out me.

Luca's sulking.

"What does Theodore do?"

Luca finally turns to me. "He's an investor. There isn't a type of business he isn't involved in, but he focuses mainly on state-of-the-art technology."

I look over to Theo who is whispering into his wife's ear and wonder if he's also involved in the darker side of business—like the man next to me.

"No, not like me." He's cold while he picks up his whiskey and takes a sip. "Theo comes from a family like mine, but unlike me, he found his way out early."

"You're close to being out though, right?" I ask him, trying to bring the mood back up.

Dark eyes burn into me, trying to catch an angle that doesn't exist. He sighs. "I suppose I am."

"Your sister told me today about your strained relationship with your father."

"Shit, Olivia." He grabs at my thigh under the table, squeezing hard. "Not here."

I blush. I had forgotten myself and where I was and the ears that could be listening.

"Sorry," I whisper, trying to undo his vice-like grip. "I forgot where I was for a second."

We've attracted Katrina and Theo's attention, but Luca hasn't noticed. Instead, with every second that passes his shoulders wind tighter, and I know he's not ready for the conversation about his father.

I press my hand to his face. "You're drawing attention to us. Please, let go."

"No," he growls.

Carnal need swims in his eyes, boring into me. "Kiss me," he demands.

I pause, but my mind doesn't. It jumps with glee, ready and eager to do as he asks.

"Yes, now. In front of these people," his voice heeds a warning that I don't want to ignore.

Leaning into him, I press my mouth hungrily to his, forgetting where I am and who sits beside me.

I feel his restrain barely hanging on once our lips connect. Under my hand that's slipped to his chest, I can feel his muscles coil, ready to pounce. But like all good things, he pulls away before either of us deepens the kiss.

Swallowing the whimper, I sit back into my seat, and catch my breath. I'm being punished. I'm certain of it. There's a devilish glint that sits in his eyes and I see now that he agrees with my assessment.

The audacity of this man.

He knows I'm struggling to fight the temptation that's building between us, and he still hasn't forgiven me for trying to leave. The monster that lives in him, wrapped around his soul, still seeks revenge.

Perfect, just perfect.

****

After dinner, Theodore had pulled Luca to one side, giving me the perfect opportunity to collect my unravelling thoughts. Excusing myself from the table, I left the ballroom where guests began to take to the dance floor in search of some relief that didn't involve dark corners.

I'd found myself drawn to the east wing exhibition labelled, "The Woman at Sea." There where twenty or so dresses, all in arrangements of style and shades of blue and greens, hanging from the ceiling. Each dress hung delicately from beneath a crystal chandelier ready to be plucked away at any moment by their new owners.

With every step, I found myself appreciating Katrina's fine creations that were not just made for a stick thin model. These dresses were for real women with real lives and bodies.

Fashion didn't seem so uninteresting anymore.

"Of all the people I expected to see tonight, you were not one of them, Olivia Heart."

I turn so quickly, that the bottom of my dress didn't have time to move with me and I stumbled forward, my legs twisted in the figure-hugging material. Clinging to William Adler, the man that was once my best friend and the person to have taken my virginity, I find myself staring up at him.

"Will," I whisper.

It had been so long. Will, with his short, dirty blonde hair and orbit blue eyes, had gotten taller and filled out in all the right places. The last time we had been in the same room together he was all limbs. That was seven years ago, and now he was all muscles with a chiseled jaw.

His wickedly handsome grin told me that some things hadn't changed, he was still the carefree man I once knew.

"Nice to see you, too, Olivia," he chuckled, while righting me back onto my feet.

"Sorry!" I laughed. "You caught me by surprise. What are you doing here?"

Will had gone from pale and weedy to sun-kissed and athletic. The navy suit that he wore, highlighting his broad shoulders, told me that he was doing well and taking great care of himself.

"My press group is covering the event." He smiled while pulling me to the side, allowing a couple to pass. "I'm just here to make sure everyone is doing their job and the Belmonts get the perfect write-up."

"Wait, you said press group — does this mean, you're on the board now?"

The last I heard from Alice, Will was managing a single paper which in itself was a huge deal. Will was always so driven, there wasn't anything he couldn't do once he put his mind to it, so being on the board wouldn't be a huge surprise.

"No," he chuckled, a faint blush crossing his lightly freckled cheeks. "I'm the CEO of the group now. I got rid of the board last year."

A low whistle fell from my lips. "That's huge, Will, congratulations. I'm so happy for you."

I go to hug him, but catch myself and awkwardly take a step back.

Polite as ever, he pretends he didn't see my outstretched arms.

"Thank you, Olivia, it's been a stressful few years, but it's been worth it. Anyway, less about me, Alice told me that you're now working in Italy?"

"When did you speak to Alice?"

Hurt flashes and sizzles deep in my belly. I didn't realize that they had been in frequent contact. Why hadn't Alice said anything? She knows I'm sensitive when it comes to our old friend.

"A few days before the wedding. I called to say I couldn't make it and she told me you had left New York for some big job opportunity."

"Oh…"

We stare at each other for a second, trying to fight the awkwardness that was trying to settle between us.

"So, Italy huh?"

I look up at him and instantly relax into his infectious upbeat attitude.

"Yes, they needed someone in their Italian office, and you know me, I can't stay in one place for long," I lie effortlessly.

Will stretches his hand and guides me away from a group who are entering the exhibit to begin the pack away.

"I do know that about you," he says, as we take a sofa on the edge of the room. "So, where's your date?"

Shit.

"He's with the host's husband." I bite my lip, turning my attention to the group who are clearing the room, all while trying to keep Luca out of my thoughts.

Leaning forward, elbows on his knees, he looks up at my face in the way he always did. "I'm not going to lie, Olivia, I was surprised when Alice said you had somebody."

I'm careful to mask my emotions before I reply, "Why's that?"

"You were never… interested in being in a relationship. It was hard to imagine you having a boyfriend. It's ridiculous I know, but I thought after what happened between us—"

I scramble. "Well, with these things you don't exactly get a choice, do you? Life comes at you real fast sometimes."

I try desperately to push away the last memory of Will and me, but it presents itself with cruel clarity.

We're lying in his bed, in his parents' home while the party downstairs forgets about us. Will smothers me with soft kisses, whispering against my skin about how happy he was that I'd given myself to him.

Our pact to give each other our virginities had started as a joke, until the day I decided I wanted to make it real.

While he basked in his high, readying himself to take me again, I was sinking lower and lower into a blind panic. Our friendship had catapulted into something serious, and his intentions became clear.

Will wanted me to be his girlfriend.

But I couldn't do it. The panic seized my heart with ice, not allowing another man to come into my life to just leave.

Before he could leave me, I left him. Pushing him away I scrambled, getting my clothes together, while desperately fighting off his worried hands. I remember telling him over and over again, that we were better off as friends but I could tell I had crushed him.

As I left, I decided to leave our friendship in that bed, where I couldn't continue to lead him on anymore or put myself in terrifying situations again.

"I wish I had the chance to speak to you after that night," Will interrupted, by placing my hand within his. "I had so much I wanted to say."

I looked down as his fingers clasped within mine. He was softly stroking my thumb, offering me peace.

"I know. I'm sorry for what I did to you that night. I didn't know how to deal with it all and I just needed to get away."

"I know," he sighed, before rubbing his jaw. "You forget I was with you through it all, Olivia. I knew you better than anyone. I just wished you had remembered that."

Will had been there through all stages of my grief and I had repaid him by taking his virginity and ghosting him. There was no apology big enough that could make up for what I had done or the cowardice that followed.

I squeezed his hand. "I'm sorry, truly I am, but I'm so glad you're here now so I can say it to your face. It's really nice to see you again."

He grinned, showing his perfectly white teeth. "It's nice to see you, too." He squeezes my hand once more.

"Did you bring a date?" I asked him, trying to steer the conversation away from the questions swimming in his eyes.

"No," he grimaced, dropping his gaze to our hands. "I've been too busy with work to find the time to date."

"I'm pretty certain as the boss you can shake off a few responsibilities to take a girl out." I shove his shoulder playfully.

Will grins before shaking his head. "You're right; I can, but if you see the women that want me you would understand why I don't bother. I'm just a walking bank account that they want to drain." He shakes his head. "Luca's lucky with all his wealth to have someone like you. After all, you've never been bothered by money or flashy things."

I freeze. "How do you know about Luca?"

Will stalls, his eyes moving from mine to the group of people in front of us. They're too busy removing the dresses and boxing them away to notice things had gotten very awkward between Will and me.

"Sources." He's careful not to catch my eye.

"So, Alice?" His hand in mine twitches and I take it as confirmation.

He finally catches my eye and I force a small smile. There in his crystal gaze I see us both as teenagers, hiding away from Alice and her invasive personality. How times have changed, now we're both adults that could not be further apart from one another.

"You know," he moves a loose piece of hair from my face, "You've changed so much, Olivia, but you're still the most beautiful woman I have ever seen."

I felt the urge to drop his hand and to pull away, but I didn't. I had done enough to hurt the person by my side that I wouldn't add this to the list.

"That's very sweet of you, Will but I'm —"

"Taken, I know." He knowingly smiles. "I'm very aware of the man that has taken you to be his."

Fear prickles at the back of my eyes, but I dismiss the feeling. I'm so used to being on edge, that I've mistaken simple kindness for something more.

Just as I open my mouth, I spot Luca entering the exhibit, shadowed by Theodore. I yank my hand away from Will's, but it's too late. Luca and his darkness had spotted us before we realized.

Will stands up with confidence, a gentle smile on his face as he helps me to my feet.

My eyes are on Luca and the aggression that builds within him with every step. Theodore behind him darts his eyes to the workers who are unaware of the tension unfolding and back to me.

"Who is this?" Luca barks, eyeing up Will with nothing but disgust.

I put myself between the two. "Luca, this is an old friend of mine, Will Adler."

I watch, with a front row seat as Luca realizes just who Will Adler is and see the jealousy ripple across his body. Of course, he knew who Will was, there wasn't an inch of my life that Luca didn't know about, but seeing them both together filled me with searing dread.

This was far too close for comfort. My past and future had met and neither of them looked like they respected the other.

CHAPTER ELEVEN

Luca Caruso

She's trying to kill me. She wants nothing more than for my heart to combust into millions of pieces so she can finally be free of me. If she didn't, she wouldn't have been sitting with another man, holding his hand with the world's most beautiful smile on her face.

My body had switched from human to monster, and it was the monster that reminded me who the fuck I am. I'm the one that stole Olivia away, the one who gets to hold her hand and be worthy of her smile — not this cock-sucking vulture that sees me coming and smirks.

I find it nearly impossible not to tear off Will Adler's face with my bare hands, but I manage... just.

"Looking for your next exposé?" I bark, taking a step forward and pinning Olivia to my hip.

Olivia looks from me to *him*, her brow furrowed with confusion.

Will, virginity stealer, holds up his hands. "I'm not in charge of the stories, Mr. Caruso. I simply make sure our papers stay profitable."

"Isn't the point of being in charge, to control what those do around you?"

Will's lips twitch to a smirk. "I prefer to give them their freedom Mr. Caruso, nobody likes to be stifled by rules." The smug bastard turns to Olivia, his greedy eyes gauging her reaction. "I can see I've taken up too much of your time, Olivia, for that I apologize. I'll leave you to get on with your evening."

Time you don't deserve.

Olivia is still bewildered between us, not realizing that Will and the papers he runs have a long history with me and my family.

"No, you haven't, Will," she smiles at him, again. "It's been nice catching up."

I inch forward in protest, but I'm stopped, forced back with the softest of touches.

"Luca," her delicate whisper softens my temper a touch. Our eyes meet and she warns me, demands with one look for me to calm down.

My body snaps to her command and I stall.

Theo steps around us both and opens his hands. "Mr. Adler, I'll walk you to the door."

Will casts me a smug fucking smile, his hands held up in surrender. "Of course, I don't want to cause any more trouble, Mr. Belmont. Please inform your wife that we have everything we need, and we'll be in touch soon."

His beady eyes find the woman that belongs to me. "Olivia, it's been a pleasant surprise seeing you tonight. I'll see you again soon, okay?"

Soon? What is with this Motherfucker?

Casting him an awkward smile that says, "I'm sorry about him," she utters her careless reply. "See you soon."

She will not.

Not in my fucking lifetime.

I lurch forward. "No," Olivia hisses, placing her hand on my chest now that she feels my muscles prepare for war.

My eyes, that are still free, have a mind of their own as they follow the man that thought he had the right to touch Olivia. If Olivia wasn't here, imploring me to back down, I'd have torn every limb from his body and dipped him in acid. Enjoying every damn second of it.

And that would have been just for taking her virginity.

As soon as Theodore and Adler leave, I turn on her. "What the fuck was that about?"

She glared, daring me to judge her. "Catching up with an old friend, Luca, what did it look like?"

Snaking my hand around her wrist, I pull her out of the room and away from any open ears.

"Catching up? Is that what you do with old friends, hold their hands in dark corners?"

We've made our way to the back of the house, stunned, but not stopped by the cold night air that wraps around us and clings to our rich attire.

Olivia storms at my side with ease, forgetting that she's in heels. "It was nothing but an innocent gesture. I haven't seen Will in years, and we were just talking!"

Years ago, when I had looked into Will Adler, I'd realized who he was but back then he was a nobody. Now he holds a media conglomerate that spent its time hounding my family and trying to expose our history.

I didn't care about the articles that his leeches would put out every few years, trying to stir trouble. I only cared about his connection to Olivia and why she had chosen to become a part of his history.

"Innocent gesture? There's nothing innocent about his intentions with you," I snap my teeth, warning her.

Olivia stops dead in her tracks, pulling her hand from mine. "Oh my god, your control knows no boundaries, Luca! Even jealousy has a grip on you."

I lose the last shred of patience and pin her against the house, shrouded in darkness from the ivory that hangs from a top window.

"You don't know a thing about what controls me."

She lifts her chin in defiance. "I don't because you won't tell me, and until you do, you have no right to be concerned about what I do and who with—so back off, Luca."

"It is my concern when the woman next to me is holding another man's hand."

Her eyes, even in the dark, taunt me. "I'm not yours to play with, Luca."

"Oh, but you are." I slip my hand to the base of her throat, allowing my fingers to hold her. This time she doesn't bother to hide her fear. "Every part of you belongs to me. Not that fucking simpering prick who tried to ruin you."

She flinches, instantly softening. "Stop it. You don't know a thing about him."

I slip my hand to the back of her head and pull back on her soft hair, arching her neck and disabling her view of me and my spiraling.

How dare she feel anything for the drooling idiot who didn't have the balls it took to stay by her side. How fucking dare she care for the simpering idiot.

"I know that the moment he took your virginity you couldn't bear to be around him. What did he do, Olivia? Did he steal it from you? Did he hurt you?"

She closes her eyes, succumbing to my voice. "No, he would never do that. Will's a good guy."

I can't take it much longer. I'm torn between tearing at her dress to get to her body or clawing at her mouth, desperate to rip the secrets she holds so closely.

I stare down at her beautiful face that was carved by God's hands himself, trying to find strength before I acted on my impulses. "Tell me what happened. Tell me why you ran away from him. I need to know."

Put my mind at rest or the multiple scenarios will continue to wreak havoc in my mind.

A lone tear slips from her right eye. "I pushed and pushed for it to happen between us, but I wasn't ready in the end. I was using him—trying to *feel* normal," she whispered. "It was me that took from him, not the other way around, and I know that makes me an awful person."

Shit. It's just as I expected.

"Do you feel that way with me?" I find myself tightening my grip on her hair. I can't bear to see her eyes when she tells me she regretted the moment we slept together, not again, not now when the words wouldn't be said in spite.

I can feel the bars on my prison closing in with every second that passes.

Say something, please.

"No," sighing, she expelled one of her secrets and kept the prison doors open for a little while longer.

Excitement and relief spontaneously catch fire and spread through my body. I loosen at her hair, allowing her to look up at me. "Why didn't you feel that way with me?"

Come on, Olivia, tell me the truth.

She wipes at her eyes, trying to drop my gaze and claim back her frosty exterior, but I don't allow it. I hold her face and press my lips to hers in a soft kiss.

When I open my eyes, she answers, "Because I needed you."

Her confession is a bright light in our otherwise dark situation, but before I can bask in the victory, she snatches it away.

She narrows her eyes and bares her teeth. "I needed you and I gave myself to you. I did something I've never done before only to find out you were not the man that I thought you were. You're my karma, Luca." She shakes her head, moves out of my stunned grip, and begins the walk back to the house.

No.

Fuck, no.

I join her step in two strides. "I'm the same person, Olivia. The same man that would risk his whole life to protect you." I force her to stop, grabbing her hand. "I have misguided you, I'll admit, but it was never to hurt you."

"You told me Black had sold my information to your enemies, Luca. That was more than misguiding me! That was scaring me into submission."

"He had, Olivia. Dante and I spent fucking weeks making sure none of the cocksuckers would act on it, but I didn't have all the information then. Look, it's not just about your submission—"

"You conveniently forgot to mention that nobody was coming for me after we slept together," she snapped, her small hands slapping mine away.

"I made a calculated decision that I don't regret. We couldn't track him down for days at a time, so we didn't know who else he was going to. It only takes one person to step out of line, to hurt you to get to me."

Olivia's cuts me off, "Why would they want to hurt me? I haven't done anything to anybody. I've kept to myself all these years. I kept myself safe!"

My stomach feels as though I've been stabbed as images of Olivia's lifeless body captures my consciousness.

"They would hurt you to get to me," was all I could bare to say.

And if they tried, well I would return to the life promised for me and kill them all.

"Luca!"

No. Not now Katrina.

Olivia sighs with relief and to my surprise takes my hand as Katrina approaches us. I'm not sure whether it's because my dear friend can be a little overbearing, or our conversation has scared her. Either way, her touch centers me back to the now.

"I will kill anyone that tries to hurt you," I whisper against her hair.

The sharp intake of her breath tells me she believes me.

"There you two are. I'm so sorry, Luca. I didn't know you and Mr. Adler had a connection." she throws Olivia an apologetic smile.

"I'm the one who should apologize, Katrina, I lost my cool there for a second. Hopefully, you'll still get your feature."

Katrina shrugs. "I'm certain I will, it's not like his papers have anything else to write about at the moment. Anyway, enough about that—Theo said you were leaving, so I came to see if I could persuade you both to stay?"

"Thank you for having us, Katrina, but I think it's best if we leave," I tell her, ignoring the confused look on Olivia's face.

"Always so serious, Luca," she chides me with a grin, before leaning over to Olivia and placing a kiss on her cheek. "It's been so nice to meet you," she beams. "I hope you enjoyed tonight minus Luca's outburst," she raises an eyebrow my way.

I roll my eyes.

Olivia laughs. "I did thank you, and thank you for this beautiful dress. I'll make sure to return it back to your vault."

Katrina waves her away. "It's yours, Olivia. You're the only woman who could wear that dress, so please accept it as a gift."

Olivia pulls her into a hug, thanking her with a warm smile.

My dearest friend moves to me next, places a kiss on my cheek and whispers, "Don't fuck this up or you'll have me to worry about," before leaning back with a wide-toothed grin.

CHAPTER TWELVE

Olivia Heart

Theodore and Katrina had been nothing but gracious to me and their guests, taking careful consideration to shower as many people with attention as they could. I thought by meeting them I would get a better sense of who Luca was, and I did. He was a complicated man with numerous issues, but he was very much loved without judgment from his two best friends, and that told me a lot.

He isn't just a monster that has boundary issues and an insatiable need to control everything. He's also a man that holds enough good in him to be worthy of friendship.

Relief spreads underneath my skin at seeing the man who can be soft and kind, who cares deeply about those that he loves.

"You're quiet," he interrupts my thoughts.

"I'm just thinking about your friends—they worry about you a lot."

He looks away, ashamed, I think. "They don't need to worry about me."

The look of love in Katrina's eyes told me differently, she cares for him like family, sees past his darkness and focuses on his light.

I want to ask him if he knows about Katrina's pregnancy, if Theo has confided his own worries to Luca, but decide against it. It's not my secret to spill between friends.

I drop my voice so Chen and Bones cannot hear.

"They miss you, especially Katrina; she mentioned tonight that your visits would often be cut short because you were always on edge about something."

Surprise paints his handsome face, but he doesn't try to hide it this time "I haven't been the most attentive friend I'll admit, but they understood. They knew that my priorities were elsewhere."

In New York with me to be exact, that's what he said with his eyes, but not with his lips.

"How often would *they* update you?" My eyes find the backs of Chen's and Bones' heads.

Luca leans down, his large hands lifting the train of my gown so he could slip my heels off. His grip around my ankle dominates my senses, sending a familiar wave of warmth to my center chest before I can stop it.

What the hell was that?

"As often as I needed. There would be days where it would be once in the morning and then there were days where it was every hour, on the hour — whatever I needed."

Chen cleared his throat in front, but we both ignored him.

"What could you have possibly wanted to know, Luca? I'm pretty certain I was either at my desk obsessing over some case or in my apartment."

Luca pinches the bridge of his nose, dragging in a deep breath. "I needed to know that you were safe, at all times. Some of the clients you interacted with would be a cause for

126

concern. I'd have your security run background checks on them all and ninety-percent of the time they weren't even worthy of breathing the same air as you. But that feeling wasn't as bad as the nights you would go running."

He tilts his head back against the leather head rest and closes his eyes.

"I felt like my chest would explode when they would tell me you were running around your local park," he whispered his confession for my ears only. "I'd pace my house for the whole thirty-minutes of your run until I'd get the message you were safe in your apartment."

My nightly runs were as frequent as the criminals that entered my office. With my headphones in and solid ground underneath my feet, I would push myself past my limits and free my mind of dirt, lies, and criminals.

It was my way of cleansing away the dirt.

"Every time?"

"Every damn time." He opens his eyes back up to me. "I'd tell myself you were safe with your guards, that there were enough eyes on you to keep you safe, but nothing helped with the urge to go see for myself. Then there were the nights where you would be followed..." He turns his head to look at me, flickering anger melting away at his softness. "I sat on a runway in New York at three am in the morning once, with the only thought of storming your apartment and demanding you stop."

His laugh is a mix of arctic cold and a dull warmth, showing me a fraction of his struggle.

"That would have been... strange."

He laughs, dragging a hand through his short hair. "It would, but maybe I would have slept that night."

A crushing weight that I had never felt before begins to press down on my chest. Images of Luca all alone in his house steal me away from him. I picture him trying to fight his desperation while I carelessly flitted my safety at night.

I felt selfish and undeserving of everything that he had done for me. What man would give their every waking moment to a woman that doesn't know he exists? How much strength would it take to trust that those you employed would protect the one thing you held dear?

Even with his darkness and his often-fraying temper, he would still put me above all else. On that pedestal that I didn't deserve to be on.

Curiosity got the better of me and I turned, giving him my full attention. "What would they do to the men that followed me?"

Bones in front sniggers and Chen turns to glare at the side of his face.

Luca was blunt without apology. "They would do as I ask."

I squint, trying to decipher his vague reply. Luca sighs as though my mere question is far too painful to answer.

"They would incapacitate their abilities to rape—"

I hold up my hands. "I get it," I wheeze, trying to dispel the bloodied images that had taken up space in my head. But the saving grace was the little voice in the back of my head that reminded me of the pain and life-changing misery I had been saved from.

I'd been saved from my own naivety by his money and guards, protecting me from the evil that lurked in every corner of this earth. How could anyone ever repay that? How had I been so ignorant of the favors of his darkness?

Luca brushes a nervous hand through his hair, and I realize I want to touch him, to use my touch to apologize for my nothing short of bratty behavior.

For what feels like the first time, I listen to my heart. I unclip my belt and slide over to him, ignoring his glare at my now abandoned seatbelt.

"What are you doing?"

"Shush." I lean up and run my hand through his hair, raking my nails across his scalp as I go. Tenderness and the need to care for him are stronger than my need for any more secrets. It can wait, after all, we have two weeks together before I make my decision.

A soft hum of appreciation vibrates in his throat when my fingers trace across his jaw line.

"It seems unfair that I slept soundly while you worried about me for all those years," I tell him, my eyes travelling to his mouth.

His eyes flicker with contentment. "I wouldn't change it. If my life has to be on a knive's edge to keep you safe, then so be it."

"No," I gasped, holding his face. Luca's eyes fully open to me, swimming in confusion. "That's no way to live. I don't want that for you, Luca."

"What else am I supposed to do?" He gently pushes me to the side, before quickly leaning over and clipping the belt around me.

I glare at his hands that have taken me away from him. "Ease up on yourself."

And me.

He looks to Chen and Bones who are awkwardly trying to distract themselves from our conversation by talking about sports. I ignore them both. We're so close to what I need, and I can't let it go because there's people sharing our space. I grab at his hand, bringing it to my lap, imploring him to look at me.

"Please, Luca, I don't like the thought of you barely having a life because of me."

"I came to terms with this a long time ago, Olivia. I realized the moment I laid my eyes on you that my whole world was shifting to center around you. I've been put on this earth for you and only you. Call it crazy, call it psychotic, call it whatever you will, but there's a reason I haven't been able to forget you."

He turns to me, his eyes mirroring that of a man in great pain. "You own me, body and soul and I'm man enough to admit that to you. But you refuse to let me in, to own you back in the way that's *fair*. That's my problem to deal with not yours."

My world spins on its axis and then flips. Desire and confusion begin to unfurl its tentacles and wrap its way around my pounding heart, squeezing until I'm breathless.

I look at the man who burns in hell for me. "I don't want to own you," my voice is barely a whisper between us.

"I know, and the unbalance of it all is what kills me." He turns his head, removes his hand from mine, and puts up a wall to protect himself from my rejection. Again.

I'd hurt him. Burned him. Dismissed him. And left him twice, all in the space of two weeks. My chest ached to comfort him, and my words mangled, failing to form some sort of verbal resolution.

Calling to me like a beacon of light, I stare at my initial tattooed on his skin. The symbol, the promise to not marry anyone but me—he was all mine whether I wanted him or not.

Ownership. The act to possess something and deeming it yours completely. The word tastes ruthless on my tongue, just like the man at my side who wants nothing more than to dominate my life completely without apology.

Could I do that? Allow myself to want him, to be with a man that had no boundaries, whose darkness still stood in the middle of us? And in turn take everything that he has and make it mine?

****

We stand in silence as the elevator climbs the hotel. Chen and Bones don't meet my eyes as they step off, but I can tell they're glad to be free of us. And when we arrive at the penthouse it seems Luca wants to be free of me too.

I watch him pull his jacket off as he storms away without a glance back.

Dread fills me as I watch him go.

Has he had enough of me? Maybe my hand holding with Will had been the nail in his small coffin of patience...

I wait for a few moments, hoping he'll return, but my hopes are squashed when I hear the faint click of his door closing from the glittering hallway.

Kicking off my heels, I make my way to my own room with my heart in my throat.

The unknown had always haunted me from the moment my parents had died. One day, I had everything I needed in life then suddenly I didn't. My parents were gone, my childhood home partly destroyed and grandparents who wanted me to forget, to be a normal child were clawing their way in.

My whole life had been ripped and shredded in a single morning while I took my math test, worrying that I'd fail, and my mum would force me into extra tutoring.

But that wasn't the life I lived now; that young, terrified little girl had grown up. My aunt had protected me, provided me with enough love that I could focus on my studies and find my way back to the land of the living.

Luca had taken over, providing stability for me for eight years in the shadows, and had never left me, not once.

I thought I was protecting myself by ignoring the soul sucking grief tied to my life but instead I languished in purgatory — between good and bad. But now my need for self-preservation was damaging the one person who would go to the end of this earth and back for me.

Luca was risking more than his sanity and that was already weighing on him heavily, he was also risking his whole life. He knows there's consequences to the protective measures he had put in place and then my kidnapping. He knew if he was caught, he could go to jail.

Yet, he put me above all of that.

No... I can't do this anymore. We can't spend our time going around in these circles.

I turn, ignoring the small voice that demands I stop and make my way back across the suite until I'm in front of his bedroom door.

I knock once.

He opens the door in just his suit trousers.

Words on my tongue crumble away into infinite dust. Glorious is the only word to describe the man who stares down at me with apprehension and exhaustion.

I want to run my fingers across his shoulders. Lick the dip just above his abs. Bite his neck. Kiss his lips. Pull his hair.

Own him.

Let him own me.

It's an exciting prospect that I don't yet understand, but I'm open to exploring it if he'll let me in.

"Olivia?" my name floats from his mouth like prayer, and I blush.

Does he always have to look so damn good?

I step into his room and close the door, using the door handle to keep myself upright.

His eyes darken, his Italian accent thick and sexy as it rushes to my ears. "What are you doing, *Bella*?"

He steps closer, towering over me, but I don't shy away from him.

"I'm here to talk, Luca. I'm not leaving this room until we've finished our conversation."

He steps back, irritation hardening his jaw. "What happened to our night of normality?"

I push by him, ignoring my urges to touch his smooth chest and I make my way to his bed. The black bed sheets glint under the low lighting of his room, holding so many promises.

"The clock struck twelve ten-minutes ago." I shrug before reaching to my side where the zip of my dress sat. Gently I tug, releasing the material that clings to my skin, all under the heated gaze of Luca.

"What do you want to know?" He stalks towards me, but stops, keeping me at arm's length where I can't persuade him with my touch.

I feel the irony burn between us. He had persuaded me with his touch the night before Alice's wedding, when he had pinned me against the bathroom sink and made me come for him. Coached by submission with his skilled hands and filthy words of persuasion.

But I don't have that luxury… but I do have...

A plan begins to form, and determination warms me from the inside.

I stand up, my eyes on his, as I begin to slowly undress, removing the one strap slowly.

He hisses through gritted teeth, hands balled at his sides, but his depthless eyes never leave mine. Luca wants to watch. "If you take that dress off, Olivia, be warned, there will be no talking tonight—just your screams."

I pause, regaining my breath he had quickly snatched away with filthy promises. "Can you not multitask?"

He glares, fire burning in his eyes. "Are you challenging me?"

Bravery touches me. "Yes." I let go of the strap that keeps the dress to my body, letting it fall gracefully around my feet into a puddle of emerald green.

Luca's eyes lock onto my face, desperately trying to keep them from wandering down my body where he knows he isn't safe. But I decided to let mine wander, to appreciate his chiseled pecs that were moving quickly under the strain of desire.

I was quickly becoming drunk on my new power.

"Look at me, Luca," I demand softly.

"I am," he rasps, suppressing his needs, but the lick of his bottom lip gives him away. He wants to taste me.

I take a tender step forward. "All of me."

With one hand, I touched his cheek, trailing my finger from his temple to his mouth. He shudders into my hand before grabbing my wrist, holding me in place.

"Olivia, you have no idea what your touch does to me. No fucking idea. Please, stop *this*."

I look at him from under my lashes and whisper, "No."

He growls, pressing my hand against his crotch, against his bulging erection that strains against his trousers. I gasp under his forced hold.

"This is only half of what your touch does to me."

I'm barely breathing under his heady glare, but our tour of his body continues, tracing his lower stomach until we reach his center chest. I feel his heartbeat thrum against his ribcage, mirroring a hummingbird desperate to escape its cage.

I bite down on my lip.

"My heart feels as though it will explode at any minute. Can you feel it?"

Feel it? It's practically jumping into my hand.

Wanting to be owned and protected.

I'm breathless in my reply, "Yes, I can feel it."

"From the moment my eyes found yours, I had no choices anymore. Olivia, you own my heartbeat, thoughts, dreams, my desires… you own me. Every bit of me, do you understand?"

His mouth suddenly hovers over mine and I'm desperate to close the gap—to feel him claim me once again. I want the freedom his kisses offer me, to forget the mess around us and to give into my cravings.

"I tried to forget you." He slips our hands to the band of his trousers, placing my fingers to rest on the waist band as he unzips his fly. "I did. I tried to move on, to ignore the emptiness I felt—"

I cling to him once his trousers drop and this time it's me that doesn't have the courage to let my eyes wander.

"But it was impossible to forget the girl who saw right through me and made the pain stop with one fucking smile. I had a taste of freedom with you, Olivia, one moment of pure relief that stole my heart and sunk me into an addiction."

The air around us was heavier now, smoldering until I couldn't breathe.

"You would call to me at night, haunting my dreams with your eyes and your sweet voice. Every moment away from you I was sinking further and further into the empty, Olivia, without a way back to the surface."

The way he said my name called to the urgency I felt between my legs. My body was hot and cold. Hard and soft. Heavy and light. Nothing felt as though it should when he smothered me like this.

Hazy and breathless I swooned into him, licking my lips with desire.

Please kiss me.

Eyes still on mine, he dug his fingers into my hips and began walking me back until my spine connected with the cool wall.

"I knew I would drown if I didn't do something," he tilted my chin back up when my eyes began to wander, "and then I remembered you telling me to pay your kindness forward, so I did. I gave it to you, the one person who didn't want anything from me, who had no expectations." His lips brushed mine, teasing me.

"I wasn't in the right space to come to you, I wasn't ready, but what I've done for you all these years has kept my head above water."

"I'm grateful for everything that you've done for me, even if I don't agree with some of your... methods," my voice was barely audible now that his fingers traced the top of my breasts. "I want you to know that."

I've lived relatively free, protected, with all my needs met while he suffered in my shadows, lost and alone to the feelings he now spills between us.

How had I not realized this before? Am I that damaged that I cannot see another's pain?

My urgent kiss against his lips catches him by surprise. Luca freezes at my forwardness, his lips barely moving against mine.

I pull away unsure of his rejection but determined to be honest. "All this time I hated that you had stolen me away from my life." I slid my hand into the waistband of his boxers, careful to keep my eyes on his as I pushed them down.

I can't have anything between us.

Not anymore.

"You weren't living, Bella. You were simply existing," he growled, pushing me back into the wall with his hips and brandishing me with his cock.

I gasped at our connection. "I know t-that now."

"Do you?" His hands claim my hips, steadying me from dizzying lust that had taken control of my limbs. "Because you seem quite eager to get back to the life that rewards you with nothing but loneliness."

My mouth dries now that his temper flares into our building inferno of lust. But I don't have the time to pull back when his hands slip from my hip to my core, claiming me with infinite control.

"Luca," I gasp, trying to see through the stars that cloud my vision.

His fingers slide through my wetness, swirling, and teasing against my clit without further warning.

"Do you think I wasn't aware of your loneliness because I was so far away, Olivia?" He forces me to look at him before pushing his index finger into me in one claiming glide, not allowing my eyes to close against his sensual assault.

"You could be a million miles away and I would still be able to *feel* you."

I mewl pathetically, desperate for more as I cling to his biceps.

Where had my control disappeared to? How did he claim back control so easily without me even realizing?

I don't care. He can have what he wants. He can have me for the rest of my life.

I arch my back, wanting more, wanting him to stop, needing my racing thoughts to hold. "You knew...you knew..."

"I did." He pinches my nipple without mercy.

My body is aware of the mix in signals, but doesn't know how to respond; the violent pinch against the sensual slow dip of his fingers makes it difficult for me to focus.

"You came in here to steal my secrets." He presses his body against mine, suffocating me in his heat. I feel his breath against my ear. "And now I'm in the mood to oblige, Miss Heart. What else do you want to steal from me?"

Oh, *God*. I don't know anymore.

I don't even remember my own name when he bites down on my neck, his teeth sinking into my skin distracting me from the wanted invasion of a second finger.

I cry out from the mini explosions of shooting stars trying to escape my womb. Breathless and a millisecond from falling to pieces I try to push away.

Luca grips me harder. "I'd spend hours at a time, imagining you like this, just for me—completely at my mercy. Fuck you're so hot when you let go"

My hands reach the nape of his neck, sliding up his scalp where I tug at his hair. I'm desperate, begging him for the release that he's teasing from my body.

"I can't take this an-anymore." I fall into his chest, but he doesn't relent. He pushes his fingers in and out, fast and hard. I struggle to stand, my digging into his arms with my nails, halfblooded moons appearing across his skin.

He bites down on my shoulder before whispering, "Neither can I. Every time you leave me, I feel as though I'm going to—"

He runs his nose up the side of my neck, breathing me in, nipping my ear. "Become nothing but a man who failed at securing what's rightfully his. I can't let that continue."

His words brush against my skin with force, and he stalls his fingers on the cusp of my orgasm. Before I can claw back control, he slips away from my body with cruel intention glinting in his eyes.

My mouth pops into a flustered O when he places his finger into his shapely mouth, sucking slowly with a wounding smirk. His groan of satisfaction is vicious.

Tears pool and overflow.

Shock and embarrassment burn me when I see that we won't be taking this any further tonight. We're right back at square one and this time it isn't me running.

I glare through the pool in my eyes. He's keeping me on the edge as punishment, it's there swimming in his victorious smirk.

"You bastard," I hiss, trying to push him away.

He barely moves. "Now you'll *understand* what it's like to feel so fucking vulnerable and desperate, Olivia."

"You're punishing me!?"

Dipping under his arm I free myself and grab his shirt that lays across his dresser. Angrily, I put it on, haphazardly doing up random buttons in a desperate attempt to hide my nakedness.

My pride is bruised and battered from my own stupidity. Luca couldn't have hurt me even more if he tried and now the scent on his shirt coats my skin, reminding me of my failure.

"How could you do that!?"

"You said you wanted to know more about me, Olivia," he taunts. "This is how I've felt all these years. And now it's worse because you won't admit what's happening between us. I won't do this anymore—you need to be honest with yourself before I'm honest with you."

My heart, that only seconds ago breathed fire, was now slowly being smothered by the ice-cold water he had poured on it.

I feel his taunting presence behind me, and I ignore him. I won't let him have the satisfaction of seeing me cry.

I keep my head low, focusing on the plush carpet beneath my feet. I open my mouth, waiting for my retort to form but instead I'm left dumbfounded and confused.

I lurch forward, grabbing the door handle and yanking it open with little to no grace. He doesn't follow and I'm grateful because it doesn't require two of us to complete the walk of shame back to my room.

Back to the room where I'll spend the rest of my night burning in embarrassment and lust.

CHAPTER THIRTEEN

Luca Caruso

Black and the fucking mountainous issues that bastard had caused was still at the forefront of my mind. Dante had called this morning to inform me that Black had been let go on a private airfield just on the outskirts of Sicily to a new team. But even with the leech's promise to forget Olivia and me, there wasn't much certainty he would adhere to it.

Dante, the night Black had sent that note to Olivia, was the first to suggest we kill him, and Chen was second. Dante's vendetta was out of loyalty to me, Chen's was out of betrayal for going against his whole unit. Both men were out for the taste of his blood and rightfully so. Now, I was second guessing whether denying them was the smart thing to do.

If this was eight years ago, I wouldn't have batted an eyelid at their suggestion, hell, I would have done it myself with a smile on my face. But I'm not that man anymore. I'm not *him*.

The only way to control this now was a new team Dante has tailing Black and his family for the next few months as an insurance plan. If he steps out of line, I'll have to revisit my no-death policy and kill them all.

"Sir, Miss Heart's cousin hasn't stopped ringing her phone. How would you like to proceed?" Chen interrupted my breakfast from the table over.

Looking up from my laptop, I squinted into the sun. Paris had brightened up considerably and the sun beamed down at us on the rooftop bar, rays bouncing off the glass tables.

"Take it to her."

"Do you want me to wait by her side until she's finished?" He stood up and straightened his tie.

If it was up to Chen, he wouldn't allow Olivia the freedom to speak to her family, as far as he was concerned, she couldn't be trusted.

"No, she's fine to speak to her alone." I take a sip of my espresso, trying to get back to my emails when I realize he was still standing there. Chen was good at his job and thorough. I would never be able to fault his cautious side, but right now I needed him to just do as he's told.

"Take the phone, Chen," I ordered.

Nodding sharply, he turned on his heel and made his way across the roof, careful not to attract attention from any fellow guests. It was times like this that I envied Chen's ability to blend and disappear into crowds of people.

Once he had gone through the door, I turned my attention back to the emails that continued to pour in. A deal to purchase a hotel in Barcelona was about to sour now that they were aware of my identity. My shipping company was having regular spot checks by local authorities causing my customers to itch, and my sister was trying me by 'checking' in on Olivia and me after her visit yesterday.

Just when I thought it couldn't get any worse, an email from Jack Veen my IT consultant popped up.

To: LC@CEnterprises.com
From: JVeen@Veenconsultancy.com
Subject: Hard drive contents
Today at 09:45

Mr. Caruso,
I've received Black's laptop, but I'm going to need more time. The hard drive has an anti-tampering system that I'll need to get around before I can access the files. Regarding any emails, same goes for those. There's several on the system that are encrypted so I'll need to find the cipher key.
Give me twenty-four hours and I'll send you over what I've got.
Jack.

Anti-tampering? Cipher keys? Whatever they are, they've purposely been put on there to keep us out. Black had been specifically chosen by Chen to run Olivia's IT security because he was an expert at remaining hidden, but Black in person was reckless and greedy.

I'd be surprised if he had anything on the laptop worth knowing.

Forwarding the email to Chen, I asked him to speak with Jack in the morning to work out whether Dante's cautious plan was for the best.

****

I'd spent one agonizing hour on the phone to my sister, Aida, who was nothing but smug after her impromptu visit yesterday. Once she had gotten over herself, and I warned her to stay out of my business, we began discussing our new joint venture in Barcelona which she was going to salvage. I ended the conversation comfortable knowing she was taking care of the issue and packed up my things and headed back to my suite.

I'd only gotten halfway out of the elevator when Red stopped me.

"Sir, have you seen the papers this morning?" He pointed his large, overly scarred hand towards the coffee table.

Glancing over, I saw one paper displayed open in the middle, a large photograph of what looked like Olivia and I on the right-sided page. I dropped my belongings on the sofa and scooped up the paper.

Olivia and I were at the bottom of the steps together, she was looking at me with her big doe-like eyes, her mouth slightly parted in surprise. She looked like a smoldering beauty standing next to me, an angry uptight bastard.

And then I saw the headline.

Luca Caruso dernière compression. Combien de temps celui-ci va-t-il durer? *Luca Caruso's latest squeeze. How long will this one last?*

The article went on with its slanderous lies, accusing me of having been with multiple women over the years — using and dumping them when I grew bored or to avoid settling down.

Where the fuck do they get this shit from?

I could barely contain myself when I read the prediction that Olivia will only last by my side a few weeks until I grew bored with her.

Screwing up the piece of shit article, I flung it across the floor and rounded on Red. "Has she seen this?"

Red eyed me with a practiced calmness. "With her breakfast this morning, sir"

"Cazzo" *Fuck.*

After dismissing her last night and now this, I was certain she wouldn't be able to stomach the sight of me. Would it be too much to be offered a break in the shit show that was slowly becoming my life?

I didn't have time to wallow, she entered the room with Bones and Chen, both hovering at her heels while she spoke on the phone.

She barely glanced my way while taking her seat by the coffee table where the paper once sat.

Today, she was all heaven in a pink shift dress and black fuck-me heels that highlighted her perfectly long legs. I tried to push the devious thoughts of what she looked like under the fine material, but it was no use.

"He was pretty sure about it... Yes, he said that he had spoken to you a few days before the wedding."

"She's on the phone to her cousin, sir," Bones mumbled, joining Red and I as we stared over at her. "Hasn't said a word about the photograph."

I didn't have to turn to know that Red and Bones were finding this predicament of mine hilarious. Never in my life had the press gone after my personal relationships until now, and I was certain it had something to do with William Adler.

Cock-sucking bastard with his upturned nose and pompous accent. What the hell did Olivia see in him all those years ago? He reeked of desperation and the need for her approval.

Wiping a hand over my face I was about to head to my room when Olivia's sharp curse caught my attention. Bones twitched to move to her, his hand reaching for the phone. Red took the door, ready to evacuate us, and Chen took his spot in front of me, preventing me from going to her.

"He needs to mind his business, Alice!" she hisses. "No, I don't care that he's our grandfather, if anything that makes this worse." Olivia's shoulders braced, ready for impact. "If he spent less time meddling in my life, I might actually be able to stomach a conversation with him."

Glaring at her guards I motioned for them to disappear, and quickly. Olivia's mood had gone from cold to arctic in seconds and they were making it worse.

I positioned myself behind her while they left, barricading in her temper in hopes of containing it.

Turning her back on me once again, she walked to the window and my shoulders sagged. Fuck, it was like torture being so attuned to her every emotion. I was a puppet on strings, being pulled from one extreme to another. I'd long given up trying to control myself around her. It was useless. There were forces beyond my control that worked to keep me by her side and fighting them was futile.

I know I should leave so she could talk to her cousin in private. And there was work still to be done before it was time to return to Italy, but my feet kept me planted behind her. Always needing to tend to her.

Olivia sighed loudly, pushing a hand through her loose hair.

"Look, you should be enjoying your honeymoon right now, not worrying about him or his ridiculous opinions. We'll talk about this another time, okay?"

Alice must have agreed because Olivia's body softened. I watched her shoulders dip, her breathing settle, and more importantly I felt the spikes around her temper recoil back into place.

Finishing up her conversation, she bid her cousin goodbye, promising to be better at calling her back and demanding that Alice send photos of her honeymoon when she could.

Turning to me she stole my breath; she was fresh faced with a faint blush residing on the top of her cheeks from her temper. I was cocooned in the smell of coconut and jasmine—her scent that strangely reminded me of home.

Olivia was my home.

My lighthouse… but right now the light was off.

"I'm going out," she told me, her voice soft as velvet but her intentions as hard as steel. There was so much tension left in her body, but I didn't know if it was from my denial or her private affairs. "I'll take Red and Bones."

I bristled. "Where are you planning on going?"

The last time she took her guards, she had tried to leave me.

"Shopping, sightseeing, out for ice cream—I don't know, but I'm going out. I'm not spending a day couped up when Paris is on my doorstep."

I couldn't help it; I smirked at her challenging stare. She was still pissed and frustrated with only one way to get back at me and that was trying to leave.

Two can play that game, Miss Heart.

"I'll take you."

"Don't you have work to do?"

I smirk. "Yes, but it can wait."

Over my shoulder I shout for Chen. Appearing out of the shadows, he caught my eye and nodded, ready for instruction.

"Olivia and I are going out. I'll need the keys to the McLaren. Can you have it waiting out front in two?"

"Yes, sir. I'll have the team tail behind in the SUV."

"That won't be necessary," I told him firmly. "I'll call you if you're needed."

Again, like clockwork, Chen stood forward to protest my decision, but one look from me and he let it go. We have had many arguments, but he knows this is one he won't win. Under my watch, she had never disappeared so if anyone was qualified to keep an eye on her it was me.

With shoulders wound tight and his temper at a boiling point, Chen disappeared down into the staff elevator to prepare for Olivia and my day.

Olivia watched our silent argument, but didn't interrupt, not when she was still surprised that I had dismissed her guards without a second thought.

I held out my hand for her to take but she ignored it, forgoing my touch, and made her way to the elevator.

I stepped next to her, gauging her ever-changing emotions, and realized quite smugly that, unlike last night, my touch was the last thing she *needed* right now.

I lean into her, my lips brushing her ear, "Something wrong? you seem awfully... tight today."

So tight, it's all I can think about.

She tilts her head away, fighting me. "Nope. Nothing's wrong with *me*." I hear the breathlessness in her reply and see the blush creeping across her cheeks. Her innocence that paints her beautiful skin calls to me, testing me... for just one taste.

The elevator doors open just in time, and we enter the small space. The air crackles and hisses with unfinished business against my skin and from the way she fidgets I can see I'm not the only one feeling it.

I'd been an idiot last night to have dismissed her attempts to talk. At first, I'd been impressed as she waltzed into my room, confidence brimming to the top, but then I realized she only wanted early access to my secrets.

Her impatience had pissed me off.

I was furious with her. She was using the powers she had, to get what she wanted without a care for the repercussions. I'd realized her intentions the moment her dress dropped, and I knew I had seconds to claw back my self-control and to barricade myself in against her prowess.

Otherwise, I would have dropped to my knees and worshipped every part of her, spilling my secrets until I lost myself, becoming nothing to a woman that doesn't understand me.

Now, as she leans back against the glass of the elevator wall, all I can think about is fucking her in this tiny box where I can watch her come from every angle.

Do it. Take her now.

"What did you think about your little exposé?"

My lust disintegrates sharply.

Ah shit. The article.

"Nothing but bullshit," I throw her a look, warning her to tread carefully.

She glares challengingly my way. "Try spending your morning explaining that to your family."

Perfect. Just fucking perfect.

"I take it your grandfather is finding it most difficult?"

The elevator doors ping open into the marbled foyer. I don't ask or wait for her permission as I take her hand in mine. I delight in her shiver, but don't let it get to my head.

It could be a shiver of disgust.

It's busy this morning in the hotel but we don't need to weave through the guests checking out. People move out of the way, keeping their distance as we head towards the front doors that are opened ceremoniously for us.

"I've never cared about what he thinks," she told me, titling her chin in defiance. "And I'm not going to start now."

I resist the urge to kiss her. "Looks like we finally agree on something, because I don't care what he thinks either."

I don't. If the man only knew a fraction of the truth, he wouldn't be easily swayed by pathetic lies written in some has-been paper.

"You know the truth. That's all that matters," I tell her.

She's thoughtful for a moment, biting her bottom lip as she looks up at me. "That's true," she agrees, finally for the first time, but looks away before I can grasp it.

Her eyes track my McLaren convertible spider that Chen carefully drives to the front of the building. It's menacing as it crawls panther-like to a stop in front of us. The black bodywork beams under the sun's glare with malicious intent, but I don't spend time relishing in its beauty.

Olivia raises an eyebrow my way as the doors slowly lift above the car. "You have a thing about fast cars, don't you?"

I smirk. "I do. Ladies first." I guide her into the seat that is low and close her door once she's in.

Chen hands me the keys, but not without a final plea etched across his face.

I choose to ignore him.

Slipping into the driver's seat, I slip on my belt, hit the ignition, and pull us away from the hotel.

The car's speed soothes the edge of my frustration and I relax into the seat, letting the leather mold around my shoulders. At my side, Olivia is a completely different story. From the outside, she's calm as she peers out of the window, but I can feel the frustration building inside that mind of hers.

I should feel guilty for edging her last night, but right now I'm far too smug.

"Forget about the article," I demand.

She turns to me. "I'm not thinking about the article."

I touch the peddle, dropping a gear as we hit traffic. I forgot how much of a pain driving around Paris was.

"Are you thinking about last night?"

Because I have been. I still am. Every time our eyes catch, I remember the sweet taste of her on my tongue.

Her blush is delicious, but her honesty more so. "You seem very pleased with your cruelty, Luca," she twists a strand of hair between her fingers.

"Some lessons are crueler than others."

She scoffs, turning to look out into the streets of Paris. "I didn't expect a lesson, I just wanted to talk to you, to understand our situation better."

"With your body?" I snarl.

Her shoulders tensed. "Yes," she snapped. "Yes, I did, but haven't you done the same to me?" She shakes her head, filling the car with the scent of coconut.

"You were defensive straight away, Luca. I only wanted to tell you that I understood in parts why you had done the things you have—that's all! I wasn't there to trick you into spilling everything."

She understood? She understood... she had accepted parts of me? I don't understand.

I wanted to look at her completely, to look into her eyes and search for my answers, but the traffic was clearing, and we needed to move.

Her voice is softer when it returns to my ears. "I get why you did what you did last night. You wanted me to feel what you have felt for all these years."

She stops and our eyes meet.

"And I do feel it. You're right, I'm not honest with myself when it comes to you. But it's not because I don't want to be, this is all new and," she takes a deep breath, "you took everything that I knew away and expected me to understand with little to no information. You've known me for eight years Luca, but I have only known you for a few weeks. I need time..."

I grit my teeth from the overwhelming feeling of regret that tries to engulf me. "It's hard to find patience around you."

We're close to our first destination, but I slow the car, not wanting to rush this conversation. We're finally getting somewhere and it's a safe place to be, much safer than using our bodies to torture one another.

Olivia's smile doesn't reach her eyes. "We both need time."

I want to ask her why she needs time, but I'm afraid of the answer. Afraid that the time she needs will lead to her taking up my sister on her offer and Olivia will cease to exist in my life.

That one, cruel, but quite possible option starts to crumble away at my confidence in making this work between us. I know letting her go will destroy me. There is no way of going back, not now that I've had a taste of her and our life together.

My choices are simple. I either open myself up to her and expose every sin I've carefully hidden over the years or go to the final and last extreme.

Either one has a 99.9% probability of ending in disaster.

CHAPTER FOURTEEN

Olivia Heart

Paris.

The city of love.

Well, that's what a gentleman screamed at Luca and me while we were getting out of the car. Dressed in an all-black suit, the street vendor saunters his way over, carrying a bunch of individually wrapped red roses and a huge grin across his face.

I cringe away, always hating these awkward situations in tourist spots and stand behind Luca, who doesn't seem the slightest bit bothered.

"For the beautiful lady, sir?" He holds out a rose to Luca who seems unimpressed by the flower dangling in his face.

The vendor stumbles back under Luca's intense gaze, suddenly aware that he may have bothered the wrong man, until Luca pulls out his wallet.

"One isn't enough. I'll take them all."

The vendor leans forward, not hearing him correctly. "Sir?"

"I said I'll take them all. They are all for sale, correct?"

"Oh yes, yes sir!"

What?

Luca pushed cash into the vendor's hand and scooped the roses and pressed them into my unexpectant arms. At least three of them fall to the ground as I try my hardest to keep the rest in my arms.

"What are you doing?" I squeak.

"Buying you roses," he tells me, a smirk on his face when he sees that I'm blushing every shade of pink.

"Sir, this is too much," the vendor tells him, while trying to give back half of the cash.

He's right; this is way too much for my heart to handle.

Luca waves him off. "Keep it."

I stare down at the at least sixty roses in my hand, confused by the man whose body screams violence, but heart whispers romance. How can he flip between two extremes so quickly?

Just last night, I tried to show him that a small part of me was beginning to understand what was happening between us, but he rejected me coldly, demeaning me to suffer from the unfinished magic from his hands.

I'd gone to my room in tears, angry and embarrassed that he had turned the tables and doused me in karma. He'd punished me for pushing, for trying to open myself up to him and my head had spun with confusion.

This endless loop of right and wrong held me hostage more than he ever could. I'd tried to fight the rage infused lust that still echoed in my body, tried to ignore the deep pull of a sparkling orgasm, but my own hands betrayed me.

I'd finished what he started but found no satisfaction from the dull orgasm.

My body gave me a few seconds of peace before the furnace switched back on to full heat. A slow and torturous torrent of thoughts began to build, forcing their way to the forefront of my brain, of Luca and everything I wanted from him.

I'd wanted his hands in my hair as he kissed me breathlessly.

Envisioned his handprint brandished against my ass and the sweet sting from his smack—a pain I'd never felt before.

Hands taking their place around my throat as he slipped into me inch by inch, claiming my body with his, all while forcing me to watch my own submission.

The urgency I felt in my heart and between my legs had left me breathless and in tears. Once the tears had dried up, disgust overwhelmed me at my new secular tastes I had developed in the short time of being by Luca's side.

Was I turned on by his rejection? Is that what this was? Wanting something I couldn't have… or was I, like he had said, now experiencing what it was like to feel so fucking vulnerable and desperate?

"You know I'd love to stand here all day and watch you, Olivia, but don't you want to see Paris?"

I look up to find him smirking at me, his hands in his trouser pockets. His smirk drops a fraction when our eyes meet, and I worry that he sees the thoughts so plainly in my gaze.

"Something the matter?"

Of course, he *sees* them. He put them there, tattooed them over every rational cell in my brain-corrupting me.

I push forward, ignoring his question and raised brow. "Can you open the car, please?"

He pops the front boot with the button on his key, takes the roses from me, and empties them into the tiny compartment, filling the small space instantly.

Once he returns to me, I do something that neither of us expect, and I ignore the voice in my head telling me no. I launch myself into his arms and kiss him.

Not because I want to.

Because I need to.

My mouth catches his and the fire that burns brightly in my stomach hisses and explodes, sending shrapnel of lust into every vein. Every cell in my body sings with euphoria for him, betraying my confused soul once again.

I expect to feel satisfaction when his tongue licks at my bottom lip but it's not enough. I want bruises. Bites. Teeth to clash.

I want him.

I don't want romance from his hands that are softly cupping my face.

I want the heaviness in my heart and limbs to disappear. Urgency between my legs to recede and my body to heed back to my control where sanity exists.

Luca groans into my mouth when I grab his tie and tug. I can't think straight with his taste in my mouth and his hands gripping tightly against my hips.

I tug harder.

This is all your fault, all of it. Look at what you're doing to me. Infecting me with your darkness.

He's the first to pull away, surprise and confusion glittering back at me "Fuck, Olivia, what was that for?"

I touch my lips resisting the urge to groan. "A thank you for the roses," I lie, breathlessly.

He cocks his head with suspicion. "You're not a very good liar."

I know.

I look away and gently part out bodies. We've got ourselves a little audience at the coffee shop across the street and having my unravelling on show makes me uneasy.

What's happening to me?

"I'm not lying. The roses were sweet… and I wanted to thank you for them."

He takes my hand, as if sensing my struggle at the attention we've gained, and we begin walking towards a small square littered with chess players and resting cyclists. Towering in the background is the Eiffel tower in all her glory, partially blocking out the sun and providing shade for the tourists that idolize her.

"You're welcome, but that's not what that kiss was about. I felt your frustration and needs, Olivia, burning against my lips."

I look away to hide my sizzling blush and focus on the chess players to my right instead who are locked in their battle. Just like me… facing my own battle against my control that seems to be slipping through my hands and right at his feet.

Luca chuckles darkly. "I can still feel them now."

Check mate.

My barely-there restraint splinters into anger. "You must be so pleased with yourself."

"I am." He stops and turns me to face him with enough intensity to make me cower. "Of course, I'm pleased, you're finally beginning to understand what I feel for you every day. And when you finally reach your breaking point, when you reach the same mountain top that I'm on, you'll understand everything."

Insatiable hunger, anger, and pain radiate from him as he lays out the new map for me to take. And with careful eyes he watches me to see if I'm ready to forgive him for stealing me away and forcing me to face the mysterious bond that keeps us together.

I don't know if I'm strong enough.

If I can be the woman that lets go of her pride completely.

I just don't know.

All I know is that I've changed in these short weeks, and there's nothing I can do to stop it.

I shake my head, trying to free my mind of its confines. I look around the square and exhale a tiny bit of frustration. We need to talk about something else, something normal or I'll jump him again.

"I came here when I was sixteen with my grandparents and Alice and not a single thing has changed."

"That's not true, you have."

I bite my lip at the hidden message beneath his words. "I'd spent the whole trip wishing to be alone because I couldn't stand to be around Jack, now I can see what a waste that had been. This place is beautiful."

I laugh, remembering his constant remarks for me to smile and to enjoy myself like a 'normal teenager,' but I was still dealing with a lot. My parents had only been dead a year and those feelings of grief had coated me like a second skin. The last thing I wanted was someone breathing down my neck, trying to force me to fit his standard of normality.

Luca's hand squeezes mine. "At your cousin's wedding, Jack made a point of telling me about the death of your parents and that you were very much still fragile about it."

I bite the inside of my cheek, trying to ignore the word fragile that bounces around my head like a ball with spikes.

"He's wrong. There is nothing fragile about you, nothing at all. You've spent most of your life protecting yourself and that takes a strength he'll never understand."

I look at him, and even though his words are soft his body is not. He hears the contradiction in his own tone and braces, knowing I could call him out at any moment.

"I've always had a problem with control and authority figures."

I hope he hears what I'm trying to convey.

He drops my hand as a small boy on a yellow scooter zooms between us, squealing with delight as their friends try to catch up on foot.

Luca and I snap back together, walking in sync by the chess players and the small audiences enraptured by their games.

"You're not the only one."

"What?"

He pinches the bridge of his nose, stress radiating from him. "I'm a hypocrite, Olivia, always have been, always will be. I'd fought the same control your grandparents had put on you with my own family, but instead of pushing back, I became infected with the need to control everything my way—to never feel that powerless again."

We stop by a small body of water that separates two large grassy banks. He's hard as steel with his hands in his pockets while glowering at the water in front of us. He's gorgeous with the sun beaming down on him, lighting up his honeyed skin in a way that makes my mouth water.

Jesus. Is there any part of him that I don't find attractive?

Words bubble and spill from my mouth. "Do you want to control me?"

I need to know so badly that I forget to be embarrassed.

"Yes," he exhales, as though it causes him great pain. "I want to control you, but not because I want to take anything away from you. I need to control your safety, your finances, your health; because without you there is no me. It isn't a case of stripping you of your happiness and freedom because I want to give you that, but I need this structure in place to feel sane. Do you understand?"

I return to stare at the water, scared to see the honesty in his eyes. Sometimes getting what you wished for is downright terrifying.

"You could've had anyone, Luca, and you chose the most damaged person to want. I don't know if I can do this with you. I don't know if I can accept this for what it is."

Why did my mouth betray me? That's not what I wanted to say... at all.

He freezes at my side, and we turn to face each other. Painted with aggression, he spits out his words. "And what is it, what is this to *you*, Olivia?"

I bite down on my lip, looking at my feet. "You uprooted my whole life and tore down the walls I had placed around me for a reason. This whole time you've tried to force me to accept this and," I waved the space between us, "protected yourself. You know everything about me, and I barely know you. You have to see how unfair that is?"

Who protects me from you, Luca?

He pulls me to him, his hands slipping to my face. "Like I said before, I won't apologize for taking you. I can't. You need me as much as I need you and that doesn't constitute an apology. I'll admit that I haven't been as open as I should, but what do you expect when you shut me out every time I try?"

"I didn't last night." My index finger traces across his chest before dropping to circle the buttons on his crisp shirt. Luca's breathing changes under my touch from normal to harsh.

My eyes are not brave enough to peek up at him from under my eye lashes, so I focus on his chest and the taut muscles beneath his crisp black shirt.

"I needed you," I whisper, "but you decided to punish me for trying to talk to you. You were so mad at me, but you forget I'm new to all of this and to you."

I push the hand between us and remove myself from his grip before the memories of last night take control. Right now, I needed strength more than I needed to revisit that painful memory.

"We have two weeks before I make a decision. Please don't push me away anymore. Give me what I need, and I'll promise to keep an open mind."

He doesn't like the space I've put between us; he teeters on the edge of decimating it with his frustration, but I hold him in place with one look.

If he touches me at this moment, I won't be able to hold myself back. I'll fall so fast with no way of getting back up.

"I've told you; but now I'll promise you. I will tell you everything you need to know."

CHAPTER FIFTEEN

Luca Caruso

I'm rewarded with the smallest smile.

"I know you will." She takes my hand and pulls me away from the small body of water we had stopped by.

Even such a small connection enthralls me and forces me to forget the ultimatum hanging over my head. In seconds, Olivia has worked her magic and forced me to drop my tension and be present. She doesn't realize it, but there's magic in her touch and I'm very much under her spell.

We spend our morning in a comfortable silence, grabbing coffee and making our way around The Trocadéro like the couples that surround us do. But we're different to them in every single way, we don't sightsee or take pictures to reminisce later in our lives. We're sitting side-by-side, close, but not touching, just trying to have one moment of normality together.

My mouth opens many times, itching to tell her how we're made for each other. How the universe had put her in front of me for a reason and no matter the paths taken I'd have found her one way or another.

But the monster delivers his usual blow. I begin to question the tiny possibility of never meeting her and the repercussions of not having her in my life. I'd have turned into the one man who could make my blood run cold. No, I'd have been much worse than him.

I'd have been nothing but a blood thirsty savage.

I'd have bathed in the blood of my enemies instead of just overstepping them like he had. I'd have let the monster that's clung to my soul since birth out of his cage so he could fulfill my birthright.

My body count would be in the thousands with no redemption possible. My country of birth would have been in ruins under my greed and there would be nobody to stop me wreaking havoc.

But her.

I sighed, snapping myself together. "Come on."

"Where are we going?" she asks softly, pushing away her hair that had been captured by the gentle breeze.

"I'm taking you to lunch."

****

We didn't need a reservation at Girafe, a picturesque restaurant with calming cream banquettes, marbled floors, and traditional French decor. My name bypassed the need for a reservation, and we were moved to the rooftop where the Iron Lady waited in the distance.

Paris's skyline glittered prettily in front of us and soon the sun would be right above us. I didn't want anything getting in my way of viewing Olivia, so I had the waitress move us to a private spot in the corner.

Sensing my eyes on her, she turns to me once the waitress leaves to get our drinks. "Is there anywhere you aren't known?"

I lean back into my chair, enjoying the way the sun burnishes her hair and highlights all the warm tones. "There are a few places left where I'm still unknown."

"Do you like it? Do you like being recognized?"

"No."

She bites down on her lip, possibly distilling whatever burning question she has, and then takes a sip of her water. I watch her carefully, enjoying her delicate fingers circling the lip of her glass. She eyes me with caution, waiting for me to speak, but if she wants her answers, she's going to have to work for them.

This is the only way I see this working.

"Is that why you have Chen?"

I grit my teeth. "Yes, Chen is my personal security."

Our conversation is put on pause as our waitress places two glasses of Merlot on the table. I don't even remember what I had ordered. I had been too busy watching Olivia stare into the Paris skyline.

Olivia sips the wine and smiles up at the waitress, "c'est parfait merci" *It's perfect, thank you.*

Jesus. Fucking. Christ.

Her confidence in a foreign language pulls straight at my crotch and I shift uncomfortably in my chair. I'm almost glad she cannot speak Italian because if she did, I'd be in serious trouble.

"How did he become your personal security?" she asks when the waitress leaves.

It's a long story and one that I'm not willing to share completely.

"Theodore hired him."

Surprise paints her face. "For you?"

I wipe my face, trying to distill the urgency to wrap this conversation up. "Yes," I growl. "He thought I needed the help when I took over my Pa's business estate."

Truthfully, I needed Chen. I had enemies building faster than I could count when I started clearing out the bad business decisions my Pa had made. Just having that one person watching my back meant I could be more efficient in executing the many heads of the snake.

"Dante wasn't enough?"

I laugh, cutting through the tension I alone had created. "Dante is quick to violence and would lay down his life for me, but he's also hot headed and tends to think last."

A ghost of a smile dusts across her mouth. "He's very quick with his women, too."

Too fast. My cousin hadn't ever settled with one woman, never experienced the calamity that a relationship could provide. Instead, he pushed anyone away that tried and fucked his way out of having to settle down.

"He is, but it's not his fault. His own family put the same expectations on his head as I had on mine."

"And what where they?"

Ah fuck. The only person to blame for this avenue of conversation was me. I'm not ready to go there with her, not when I can't control the outcome in front of all these people.

I make a quick decision. "To take over the family business."

It's true and it's enough.

"You and Dante together, how would that work?"

Jesus, the questions never end. No wonder she had been good at her job, the woman could get blood from a stone.

I shrug. "It's tradition in our family for the men take care of things."

166

"Aida mentioned that your sixteen—"

"No," I growl. "No, we will not discuss *that* here. Do you understand?"

She leans back away from me, fear ghosting her face, but she soon recovers and tilts her chin in defiance. "But I know. I've known for a few days and look; nobody can hear us. What are you so worried about?"

What?

What?

My center of gravity all but disappears. Hot sweat begins to build at the back of my neck and my muscles lurch into defense mode. I look towards the exit and begin calculating how long it will take me to get us out of here.

Olivia grips the table until her fingertips turn white. "Aida told me, Luca, she told me that you had to... take care of a person that had stolen from your family," she dips her voice, "that you had no choice."

I didn't.

I never had a choice.

The moment I was born, I had been condemned to a life of greed and bloodshed. Not even my mother's sweet nature could protect me from the man that raised me to tolerate the smell of death under my nose. God rest her soul, but she had been so fucking blinded in love that she hadn't noticed how fucked up her children had become.

"That's the real reason why you have to control everything around you, isn't it?"

"Stop," I warn her.

She nods quickly, submitting to my final warning.

"I'm sorry."

I look up from the table, right into her. "Why are *you* sorry?"

"I shouldn't have pushed you to answer that, you weren't ready... but I wanted to hear it from you."

I lean forward. "And?"

She sucks in a shaky breath. "And now I know."

She hasn't screamed at me, thrown her wine in my face, or tried to run. Instead, she looks at me with a clarity twinkling in those moss-colored eyes.

"I've killed people."

I have. Many people. Not just that one.

Her face doesn't change, but my fear does. It plummets so quickly into my stomach, that I feel breathless. This isn't what I expected, and I don't know how to wade these unknown waters with her.

My enemies could learn a few things from Olivia—the woman has a perfect poker face.

"I know," her voice is liquid, filling my ears.

I flare. "So, you can accept that I'm a murderer, but not that I want you? What the fuck is wrong with you?"

Her gasp only infuriates me more. Everything about her is fucked up, and I don't have the patience right now to work my way through the puzzle pieces that are her emotions.

I'm caught off guard and cornered.

Again.

"Don't lash out at me," she bites out the words with enough venom to match my own. "I haven't judged you, so I expect the same courtesy in return, Luca."

"You should judge me."

Picking up her drink with delicate fingers, she swirls her glass with utter calmness I've never seen from her before. It steals my breath and makes my skin itch.

"My last client was a teenage boy who had sexually assaulted a drunken girl at a party. He said he didn't do it, but I saw the truth." She narrowed her eyes, anger burning in her irises. "He had no remorse for what he had done, and I had to spend my time brokering a deal for him—for this predator that knew daddy's money would take care of everything."

She picked the glass back up and sipped, her gaze flitting between me and the skyline—wondering whether to continue.

"If you had the choice to pick his punishment, what would you have chosen?"

She tilts her head and I watch as the sun catches the green in her eyes, turning them almost see through. I see the internal battle begin before me and feel that she's pulling away, cautious as always.

I lean forward and snatch away her glass, placing it down and taking her hand. "What would fit his crime?" I demand.

She looks down at my hand and shivers. "There's no going back for a man like that, Luca. The only punishment to fit his crime would be death."

And there it was.

Olivia's web of darkness that had been calling to me all these years, like a siren's call, over and over again. Her infliction was the blackest of blacks, and it sits against her perfect soul, stark and waiting patiently. All I can hope is that it's for me.

Fear steals the power in my voice. "And me? Is there any going back for my crimes?"

Her palm against mine tightens and she finally looks up at me and I hope it's me she sees and not him. "Are you the same man that did those things?"

"No."

I'm not. I'd spent eight years making sure to keep my blood thirst in check. All for her, so that if by some miracle I would be redeemable.

She doesn't realize it, but as she stares at me her thumb traces soft circles on my hand, soothing the tension over and over until it recedes.

"Have you ever hurt someone who's innocent?"

Innocent?

Had any of them been innocent? No, of course, they hadn't. I'd dealt with murderers, thieves, rapists, and abusers in my line of work. None of them had redeemable qualities or an ounce of guilt.

I pull her hand to me and place a soft kiss across her knuckles.

"Never and I wouldn't. Those days are over and have been for a long time."

Throughout my history, I had lost myself and swam in the blackness, enjoying the freedom, but my moral compass of right and wrong always remained whole. I'm proud that my Pa couldn't break that out of me, no matter how hard he had tried during my childhood.

"But I won't lie to you, Olivia. I say those days are over, but if anyone ever tries to hurt you, I will not hesitate to kill them—whether you remain by my side or not."

Whether she remains by my side or not...

The thought alone is worse than death—it's rotting in limbo, suspended where time continues.

How can I go back to an existence where she isn't by my side? I feel the familiar waves of dread wash over me and the not so gentle ache yawns open.

Her intake of a shaky breath brings me back to the now and I notice she hasn't recoiled away in disgust.

"If someone tries to hurt me, Luca, they're not innocent, are they?"

I smirk. She understands. "They are not."

She removes her hand from mine and picks her glass back up. "I won't take away your choice to deal with those people in the way you see fit, if that situation ever arises."

The not-so-subtle message floats above our romantic setting and lingers like a dark cloud, just waiting to burst and clear away our sins.

Whether she realizes it or not, Olivia has just given me her consent to protect her without judgement, and I find it a difficult task to stay in my seat. In ten minutes, she had stolen away one of my secrets and replaced in with a stamp of acceptance.

In ten minutes, she had looked right into the eye of the monster and accepted him for who he was now.

"Always in your head," she slips from her seat and stands up. "Relax, I'm just going to freshen up." A ghost of a smirk graces her lips and I know she's smug. She knows I'm still reeling from our conversation.

Leaving me to my thoughts, she exits the rooftop without a glance back.

A waiter appears and I distract myself by ordering for the both of us. I don't give it too much thought, instead I opt for the Blue Lobster linguini and another bottle of red.

The red wine does nothing to soothe the urgency crawling under my skin as I wait for her. So, I decided rather than suffer, to do something about it.

CHAPTER SIXTEEN

Olivia Heart

I'd left him to gather myself, but it was taking longer than I had expected. I'd spent the past five minutes staring at myself in the mirror, trying to steady my beating heart that was far too keen to return to him.

Needy.

I felt so irritatingly needy for the first time in my life and hated every part of it.

I gripped the white and grey marble-top counter and bowed my head, ignoring the woman in the mirror who I didn't recognize, who was flushed with foreign desire. She was starting to get on my damn nerves with her erotic yearnings and demands.

She was clawing at my walls, ready to taste more honesty that the man upstairs was willingly sharing. She wanted the molten desire to finally spill over so that I would have no choice but to give in. I could feel her pushing, whispering that there was no point in fighting anymore — I'd already lost.

"Damn it," I hissed, pushing away from the counter. "Get yourself together, Olivia."

I smooth down my hair and take in a deep breath. I can do this. I just need to put my guard back in place for a few hours, get what I need, and then by the time I tire we'll be back at the hotel where I can hide away in my room.

Hopefully, my door has a lock.

I pull open the door, ready to face Luca again, and only to be pushed back into the bathroom. His hand covered my mouth, stopping me from screaming in surprise while his dark eyes promised me salvation.

My guard fell before it had even reached the halfway point.

Slowly, we retreated into the bathroom—the only sound was my heels clipping against the floor.

Heat travels from my lips until it pools in my lower stomach.

"Be quiet, Olivia," he growled.

Those three wicked words took a knife to my heart and cut out the rational part before discarding it quickly and replacing it with thick desire.

"What are you doing?" I whispered, as he removed his hand from my mouth.

You know what he's doing. You want this, you want him…

"I'm apologizing," he closed last night's disaster by smashing his lips to mine. Picking me up faster than lightning, I had no choice but to wrap my legs around his waist and submit into his stronghold.

Ferociously, he attacked me, dominating my senses with bites, licks grabs, kisses, and the formidable creature inside of me matched his intensity. There wasn't a part of me that hadn't burst into life under his touch, not one single part that didn't want him.

I felt sweet relief for the first time in hours.

Kiss by kiss, bite by bite, he was stealing my sanity.

I groaned when my back reached the wall, his hips digging into mine.

"Can you be quiet for me, Olivia, or do I need to cover your mouth?" he demanded; his voice hoarse with lust.

His tongue licked up my throat until he reached my ear where he bit down, sending an explosion of stars to dance in my vision.

"Yes," I moaned, grabbing at his hair- tugging, needing him to sate the ache between my legs. "I can be quiet."

Liar.

He hissed, moving his hands between us, slipping up my inner thigh until he reached the barrier between us. I felt a single finger press against me and saw the power spread across his face.

I was soaking already and he was incredibly pleased with himself.

"I'm going to put both of us out of our misery." He bit my bottom lip before licking into my mouth, tasting the wine we shared. "But when I get you back to the hotel, I'm going to show you what it's like to be truly fucked — understand?"

I squeezed my thighs around his hips. "Yes, I understand," the soft words that fluttered between us gave him everything he needed.

"Keep your legs around me." He pressed his trouser-bound cock against my core, creating the most pleasant friction where I needed it the most. I rolled my hips with a moan — demanding more.

Luca smirked against my mouth. "Shush now." Without warning, he slid my underwear to the side, yanked down his own zipper and pushed his cock into me with no remorse.

I cried out, forgetting my promise of silence as he pushed inch-by-inch, claiming me completely with delicious torture.

The fullness of his cock inside of me sated the fire only briefly, until he thrust his hips upwards, hitting my sweet spot with devious intent. He knew me, knew what I needed before I did.

"Shit, you're so wet, *Bella*."

And it's all your fault.

All of this.

He growled into my neck on a harsh thrust, losing himself in what I was offering him—my forgiveness and understanding. I held him, my moan slipping between my lips, echoing into the space around us and breaking my promise to be quiet.

Luca kissed me long and hard, dipping his tongue into my mouth... He was relentless in his rhythm, searching and demanding my orgasm that was rippling uncontrollably already.

With every spark of my looming release, he stole more from me without mercy. And I let him.

I yanked at his hair and bit down on his lip.

He growled into my mouth and slammed upwards, nearly toppling us both into the marbled tiles, but it didn't matter. Luca pulled me back down and I cracked and splintered into shards right in his arms as my orgasm exploded between us.

I cried out and bit down on his shoulder. My bite took hold of him, and he arched his neck with his eyes tightly shut. Groaning and hissing, I was allowed the gift of watching him unravel before me. I'd never seen him so lost and free at the same time, never witnessed such beauty until now. The groan that stuttered through his lips would stay with me for the rest of my life.

I expected relief and pleasant exhaustion to sweep through me, like it had the first time we slept together, but this time, I felt nothing but an uncontrollable hunger for more.

Luca caught my lips and kissed me softly, pulling away to look at me.

Shock glistened freely in his usually guarded eyes. "Why are you crying?" His hands were soft this time as he stroked my face, lovingly bringing me back to him.

I touched my face, feeling the tears that had spilled onto my cheeks. I don't know why there were tears or why I still feel so desperate. Even if I did, I don't think I could answer him. How would I explain what was happening without sounding like a total headcase?

I smile while wiping away the evidence. "I'm just a little overwhelmed. You caught me by surprise, that's all."

He pulls back as gently as he can, he slides out of me, zips up his trousers, and helps me back onto solid ground. If my heart still wasn't trying to beat its way out of my chest I would have been impressed by his strength.

He combs a hand through his ruffled hair. "There's more to it, but here isn't the right place for that conversation. Let's go, our food should be at our table."

"Um, can you give me a minute?"

He looks confused until he realizes why I need a private moment.

Luca leans in. "If I had my way you wouldn't be allowed to clean away what we just did in this *very* public bathroom." He kisses my cheek. "I'll wait outside"

"O-kay."

He doesn't see the way my mouth falls open, like a mouth breathing idiot as he leaves, and thank God. I've spent far too much time blushing today under his watch.

I quickly clean up, trying to ignore the need for more of what we just did in this beautiful bathroom, and return to him.

Without another word, he threads his fingers through mine and pulls us both out of the dark hallway. While we walk, I begin the embarrassing task of straightening my dress and smoothing my hair with one hand, hoping that nobody noticed or heard us.

Of course, we're not that lucky this time. A passing waitress winks at me as she saunters by, but Luca doesn't seem to notice, or he doesn't care. Nothing and nobody seem to faze the man that holds my hand.

Well, except for me.

I seem to faze him a lot more than I should.

****

Luca takes off his jacket as soon as we get to the table and reclines into his chair. Every muscle in his finely toned body relaxes while we're served with exquisite food and more wine by a waiter who, by the blush on his cheeks, must have been caught up on the staff gossip.

But I no longer care about that, I'm too busy watching him, wound tight by every movement that he makes. Something as simple as the way he clutches his glass has me yearning to snatch away the object and replace it with my hand.

The wine does nothing to dispel the inferno that's rearing back into full power, and if anything, it makes it worse. My inhibitions are already in tatters and the alcohol supplied will surely make them stay that way.

The food, though I'm certain it tastes good, barely registers against my taste buds, they're too busy savoring the taste of him—committing him to memory.

Is this what he meant by, when I reach the same mountain as him? Is this how he's lived his life for eight years? If it is then I want out, I'm not strong enough to live on the edge of withdrawal constantly.

"It will get easier once you accept it," he tells me, after wiping his mouth on the cream napkin.

"Accept it?"

"That I own you." He's unapologetic, leaning back into his seat, giving me the most perfect view of him. "If you don't, the urgency you feel pumping around your blood will only get worse. Every one of your senses is already wired to accept me—so is your heart. But if you keep denying your mind, Olivia, you're going to be miserable."

There was no malice or manipulation in his tone, just a simple offering of advice.

I sucked in a deep, shaky breath. "What have you done to me?"

He laughs. "I wish I could take the credit for it, but unfortunately I can't. All I know is how it feels and there's no use in fighting it; trust me, I've tried for years."

I push away my near empty plate and look out to the city of Paris.

Maybe Luca's right: once I stop fighting the attraction between us, I'll be free of the helplessness I've felt since the moment he stole me away and I'll be able to think straight.

Oh, the days when my life was simple and easy. My only worries were making sure I closed deals for my clients, ensuring my boss looked good and that we maintained our high-profile status. But that had offered me not a shred of happiness, instead it made it easier for me to use work as a Band-Aid to the loneliness.

I turn back to find him watching me, his face hidden behind a mask of control. I love that look.

"I want to go back to the hotel."

He raises an eyebrow, a smirk threatening to grace his shapely mouth. "If we go back now, you'll submit to me, to do with as I please. Are you sure that's what you want?"

A shiver ripples across my sensitive skin while the new sensual creature inside of me squeals with delight. We're an atomic bomb of nerves, lust, and anger, but she doesn't care, she only cares about his seductive promises to ruin us completely.

Clenching my jaw, I murmur, "Yes."

CHAPTER SEVENTEEN

Luca Caruso

Complete control. It's mine for the taking, dangling right in front of my face and fuck it feels so good. Olivia's acceptance came at me hard and fast, right from the moment I had uttered the words about ownership. It had spoken to the dark side of her, corrupting her innocence, and I didn't feel an ounce of guilt for it.

Every part of her was mine.

We were finally evening out.

I'd demanded the cheque and left a tip big enough that they would focus on the money rather than what Olivia and I had done in their restroom. And if it didn't, I could care less. We would never see them again.

My attention was focused on getting Olivia back to my hotel where all my dreams could come to fruition. Every thought burned brightly against the forefront of my mind, where I planned on bringing her to her knees, to clear her of the last few locks around that heart of hers. When I'm done with her, she'll only be able to focus on our future and not the past that drags her down.

She wanted to understand what was happening to her and I would take her there, to show her how this obsession started, and if she accepts it, I will show her where it leads.

Olivia's silent at my side, almost too quiet, as I pull the car away, but I understand this time. It was a lot for her to come to terms with, and my demands to know what she was thinking would have to wait. Her body would tell me soon enough.

I took the backstreets, avoiding traffic that was starting to build in the city and hit the gas. We were five minutes from the hotel and from getting what I wanted and there was no chance I'd be stuck in traffic.

"Is that Chen?" Olivia asked, leaning forward to look at her mirror.

Following her gaze to the black SUV speeding up behind us I tried to get a good look at the driver, but the sun was glinting off the windshield, preventing me from seeing him clearly.

If that motherfucker had been trailing us all day, he was dead. I'd specifically demanded he stay behind.

"I think so."

Hitting the call button on the steering wheel, I was put through to Chen's number.

He picked up on the second ring.

"I told you to back down," I bark, squeezing the steering wheel with frustration.

"Sir?"

I didn't have time for this shit.

"Why the fuck are you following us? Didn't you hear me when I said your presence wasn't required today?"

"Sir, we're still at the hotel," Chen's voice muffled through the speakers as he began to move.

Olivia turned in her seat, trying to get my attention, sensing that something was wrong.

Squinting in the rearview mirror, I try to discern the license plate. Dread washed over me now as the SUV was gaining speed, narrowly missing a few pedestrians trying to cross the street.

"AVV-655-QC," I snap.

"Running it now. We're on our way—keep the line open, sir," Chen's voice echoed throughout the small space. I hit the paddle, taking us up a gear, and the car snarled into action.

"What's happening, Luca?" Olivia's voice was etched with fear, but I couldn't look at her. "Who are they?"

"I don't know," I told her, ignoring the urgency spilling into my blood "Hold on."

A tight bend was up ahead, and I'd have to slow down to take it. I'm going to lose speed, but hopefully, I can pick it up once through the curve.

Fuck it.

I coast and we slide into the bend at high speed, nearly losing two wheels. I corrected the steer and hit the gas, pushing the car to move. Olivia grips her seat belt that's tightened against her chest and hisses.

My eyes slide to the glove box in front of Olivia. Was there still a gun in there? Could I get to it without freaking her out?

"Chen, what's happening?" Olivia demands, her eyes frozen ahead.

"Don't say a word, Chen," I glower her way. If she freaked out now, I wouldn't be able to concentrate.

I hit the break and we slid around a second corner, burning the tires while I fought the steering to keep the car on the road. I hit the paddle and dropped a gear, ready to hit the gas when we lurched forward with a bang.

Olivia yelped and clutched her seat tighter.

"Fucker," I growled, allowing my eyes to slip to the mirror.

"Two in the front, another two in the back," I snapped into the open space, hoping the connection was still live between Chen and me.

I didn't have time to plan my next move, Olivia's scream caught me by surprise and the steering wheel slipped. We were hit again, but this time it was on her side.

We careened violently onto the side street, so viciously, that I lost my bearings on the road. My vision disappeared into blackness when my skull connected with the window. From what felt like seconds, my car snarled up into the air, leaving solid ground, twisting, and smashing us back down onto the road with a steel-crunching slide.

Glass shattered and the roof crunched in around us, boxing us into our new death trap.

"Sir!?" Chen yelled, crackled through the speaker.

Acidic burning and the taste of blood spread throughout my mouth and nose while I hung helplessly.

My eyes frantically searched for Olivia who was hanging suspended by her seatbelt, her eyes closed and her face obscured by her hair that was covered in blood.

"Shit! Olivia, Olivia! Come on, wake up!"

The car that had hit us screeched to a stop just up ahead, cutting off the street. Black boots stepped onto the ground, and they began to part into formation.

Panic swelled and burst open into my chest as I scrambled for my seat belt. Pushing the button, I fell to the roof of the car, right onto my shoulder with a groan, but the pain would have to wait. I leaned down into the glove box that had popped open on the crash and yanked out the Glock.

Clicking off the safety I pointed it through Olivia's broken window and fired at the first set of legs I saw.

"Fuck," my target screamed, as it fell to the ground, clutching his leg.

Sliding back the chamber, I fired again, hitting him center mass.

I turned back to Olivia. "Olivia!" I shook her, but she didn't move.

Tires squealed up ahead and I knew Chen and his men had joined the fight. Two more shots rang out with people screaming around us.

"The girl! Get the fucking girl and let's go."

Two new sets of boots were seconds away from reaching Olivia's side. I pulled back the side and fired and hit one in their left thigh. A scream echoed between us, and I waited until he stumbled before me.

I slide back again and squeeze the trigger, watching the man in the mask fall back from his bullet to the head.

"Sir, we have the rest cornered. Stay in the car until you're clear," Chen's voice rang through the car.

"Get a fucking ambulance," I yelled, reaching up to Olivia's neck and searching desperately for a pulse. Her skin was clammy to touch and her pulse, barely there.

A bullet whipped by her window, and I launched myself at her seatbelt, forgoing the rule of not moving her.

I pressed down on the button, and she fell down into my arms.

Rubbing her arms, desperate for the warmth to return to her skin, my shaking hands checked her for injuries.

"Come on baby, wake up. Come on, Olivia, open your eyes."

A set of boots reached her window, but didn't stay standing for too long, three bullets tore through them, and they fell at my feet.

Focusing on Olivia, I scanned her whole body, looking for the blood that was covering her face and chest. But I couldn't find where it was coming from.

Shit.

"Sir, are you both okay?" Chen was the first face I saw as he dropped to the ground, his knees covered in blood. His pitch-black eyes landed on Olivia, and for the first time, I saw dread coat his features.

"Where's the ambulance?" I yelled, cradling her face.

"It's a minute out, sir." Bones dropped to his knees and began tearing at the door. Red and Rum joined him, ignoring the dead bodies bleeding out at their feet.

Their one goal was to secure Olivia's life, and right now she was trapped in a box of steel with me, and from the suffocating smell could start burning at any minute.

"Olivia, wake up. Come on, wake up for me, *please!*" I stroked her face that was losing its color with every moment that slipped between us.

All I could think was internal bleeding and how quickly the injury could take her away from me. A minute was too long. I could lose everything in a minute.

The door yanked open, and without a second thought Chen leaned in and stole Olivia away from my arms. Once her weight was supported, he stood up, turned away, and disappeared from my view.

I crawled out of the crumpled metal that was once a car with the help from Red, but my eyes stayed with Olivia who swayed in Chen's arms. I stumbled to follow, barely managing on my feet as I watched the ambulance and police scream their way towards us.

****

The drive to the hospital was agonizingly slow as a team of paramedics worked on Olivia. They were all over her, clipping her neck into a brace, her fingers to a monitor and trying desperately to wake her.

Nothing could have prepared me for the hopelessness I felt sitting at her side, holding her hand, praying to anyone that was listening for her to survive.

When we entered the hospital, her team turned into a small army of nurses and doctors. I was pushed backwards as they wheeled her into a private bay and told to stay.

From the spot they left me in, I watched as they began tearing at her dress with scissors, exposing her to the many eyes that searched her for injuries. Pitch black bruises covered her chest and abdomen where the seat belt had held her.

Nothing could have prepared me for watching a stranger put his hands on her lower stomach, pushing down on the already vicious bruises that painted her skin.

Olivia lay there in her underwear, completely exposed, and the irrational part of my brain wanted to cover her, to protect her modesty from their invasions. I lurched forward with the intent of smacking their hands away when Bones and Red grabbed at me and held me back.

"Sir, let them work." It was Bones in my ear, his gruff voice barely registering. "She needs them right now."

A doctor pushed through, placing an oxygen mask over her mouth, and began demanding her vitals from the team that was working on her. Their French blurred, my brain too slow to translate, but I knew they were worried about the blood that covered her and why her blood pressure kept bottoming out.

A nurse turned and pointed at me.

I looked down and saw it was me that was bleeding. A chunk of glass was wedged in my right bicep, sticking out at an odd angle, trailing blood behind me.

"Focus on her," I growl. "I'm fine, just make sure she's okay."

A nurse putting an IV into Olivia's arm took a quick step back when Olivia's wrist twitched to the sound of my voice. Opening her bloodshot eyes, I watched them widen as she peered up at the team around her.

Her right hand reached out towards me, and I saw that she had two broken fingers.

"Olivia," I called, my heart in my throat.

Her breath fogged up her mask in pain as she tried to lift her head to search for me.

The same nurse that had fit the IV rushed to me, dragging me by the arm and into the room. The nurses and doctors separated, making room for me briefly before they got back to work.

"Parlez-lui pendant que nous travaillons." *Talk to her while we work.*

"Olivia, stay awake for me, okay?" I whispered, kissing her forehead while her eyes rolled. "Hey, keep your eyes open, okay?"

Please, don't leave me here Olivia. I need you.

My hand smoothed away her bloodied hair.

"It hurts," she gasped. "E-Everything hurts."

The pain in her voice pulverized me to a pulp. "I know, baby, but the doctors are going to give you something for the pain. Just stay awake, okay?"

She groaned when the doctor stuck her foot with a needle. I couldn't bare it, couldn't bear to see her this way, but my eyes glued themselves to her where she couldn't slip away.

Olivia's heart monitor whirred into life behind me, and the thumping of her heart had me by the throat. It sounded harsh and unnatural, fighting for survival.

I couldn't breathe.

"Monsieur, nous devons l'emmener pour un scanner." *Sir, we need to take her for a CT scan.*

"I'll come with you," I told the nurse, but she dismissed me, pushing me away from Olivia whose hand dropped limply from mine. Another nurse stood wanting to tend to my injury, but I couldn't allow it. I ignored her and followed Olivia, who had been covered with a sheet and wheeled to the closest elevator.

The doors opened and everyone ushered in, but there was no room for me.

"Sir, let's get you fixed up. Chen will be here to debrief us soon." Red obscured my view, his hand outstretched as though he was trying to corral a wild animal.

The elevator doors closed, and she disappeared into the belly of the hospital — alone and scared.

What if it's the last moment I see her alive?

I bypassed Red's hand, shoved through a set of double doors, and walked until I found the stairs. Yanking open the door, I threw myself into the cold empty space, gulping down air into my lungs.

Everything hit me at once. The smell of Olivia's blood under my nose, the piece of glass still in my arm, and the sound of her scream echoing over and *over* again in my ears. I couldn't hold on any longer, my heart detonated with wild fury.

I barely felt the pain across my knuckles from slamming them into the wall. Nothing could pull me away from the agony of Olivia's battered and bruised body that sat in my mind's eye, a reminder of my failure to protect her.

This was my fault. All of it. I was fucking reckless and now the woman that I loved was broken and alone.

Slumping down the wall, I ignore the blood that was still pouring down my jacket. My bleeding could wait.

Holding my head in my hands I felt adrenalin turn to exhaustion, adding its cruel weight to my limbs.

If she leaves me, I won't survive.

A world without Olivia isn't worth living in.

****

Theo was the first to find me, shrouded by darkness in the stairwell. He moved silently towards me, careful to keep his distance from the feral animal I had become, and took a seat at the top of the stairs.

"I've cleared you and your team with the authorities. There will be no questions asked," his voice echoed into the space. "We're trying to trace the identities of those killed, but it could take a few days."

No. That was too long.

"I'll find out who they are before then." I heard my own voice and how empty it sounded.

Theo sighed, rubbing a hand through his greying hair. "Do you have any idea who it could be?"

The question hung between us.

I'd spent an hour torturing myself, creating lists and completing my own background checks into those with enough balls to try, but I came up empty. The Mexican cartel wouldn't care, the Lithuanians still required my services, and the Russians didn't know about her. Everyone else didn't have the resources or the care to track and hunt us down.

"I don't," I grind the words between my teeth. "But when I find out I'll slaughter everyone involved. I'll not stop until everyone's dead."

The hissing inside grew louder in agreement.

Theo turned on the step, regarding me coolly. "I'll be right at your side Luca. Whatever you need, I'll be there with you"

"No. You're out—I'm not dragging you into this, not when Katrina's expecting your child"

His face remains remote, but the twitch of his right eye tells me I've caught him by surprise.

"She told you?"

"Yes."

He squares his jaw. "Katrina will want me to help."

"I don't want you involved."

What I had in mind would not only pull Theo back in, but he may not leave. I wasn't going to have that on my already heavy conscience.

Theo narrowed his eyes at me, and I knew we would be revisiting this conversation. "You need to speak to your men and get your arm looked at. You're pissing blood everywhere." He grimaced over at my sodden jacket. "Olivia's going to be out of her scan soon and she's going to need you on your feet."

I scoffed darkly in disagreement. Pushing back up the wall until I stood on two feet, swaying for a second from the blood loss that was finally getting to me.

I raged at the loss of control over my own body. "They didn't want me. They wanted her, they wanted 'the girl,'" I spat out the words that were acid on my tongue with disgust.

He stood up; his eyes glinting malicious retribution. "I know, that's why you cannot deny my help. If this was Katrina, you would be the first one to step in to help and don't try to deny it, Luca—we both know I'm right."

The smirk across his smug fucking French face pisses me off. Just like it had from the very first moment we had met. He was just as stubborn and ready for a fight then as he is now, with the only thing changing between us is the women we care about.

"Fine."

****

I entered the floor and was pulled into a small room where a doctor and nurse pulled out the offending glass and stitched me up. Luck had its way of torturing me today, because all I suffered was a wound to the arm, bruise to the left side of my face and a sore collarbone.

I'd demanded an update on Olivia's injuries, but neither of them knew and neither of them could look me in the eye.

So, I turned to my team of men to distract me.

We all met on the floor Olivia would be placed on once she was out of her scan. Chen, still covered in our blood, stepped forward and bowed.

"What do you know?"

Bones took a seat behind Chen and held his head, muttering to himself over and over, but I couldn't focus on him. His ramblings were already irritating my frayed patience.

"The men that attacked you are all dead, sir. Military trained from what I could tell at the scene." Chen reached into his suit pocket and pulled out his phone. "I searched the vehicle alongside the police, and this was waiting on the backseat."

He swiped his finger across the screen once. It was the leather back seats of the SUV that had driven into us. There were leather restraints built into the seats, enough to pin her wrists and ankles down.

"And this." He swiped again to an open box with one needle. "We think it was a tranquilizer, sir."

"Fucking pricks," Red hissed, turning away from us to glare out of the window.

My muscles coiled tightly, ready to fight as I stared down at the single photograph. Whoever wanted Olivia, wanted her bound, knocked out and completely at their mercy.

My fingers twitched to crush something, anything until I felt Theo's hand on my shoulder.

"Could this be Black, do you think he finally got someone to listen to him?" Theo asked.

Black? Could he have secured an enemy big enough to pay him off and to get to me? The perfect double-cross... but I doubt it, he was irrational and greedy—not to be trusted by those who worked in our business.

Chen's eyes caught mine, his loyalty to only address me was admirable but right now I needed answers. I nodded for him to move on.

"It's a possibility."

"It's definitely fucking him." Bones stood up, his eyes wild with fury. "He's the only one it could be. We should have killed that cunt when we had the chance."

He was right. I should have, but my silent promise to Olivia, to be a better man, had stopped me from executing him. I wanted to laugh, that single unspoken promise to be a good man didn't mean shit if I couldn't protect her.

"Relax," Chen snapped at his soldier. "Keep a level head."

I was with Bones, there would be no relaxing until the person responsible, the scum at the top, took their last breath.

"Chen, keep digging. Speak to Jack about his laptop and tell him we need the files now," I barked my orders. "I want around the clock surveillance of Olivia's room and up the security around my family. And Chen, speak to Dante, tell him what's happened and tell him to see if anyone knows anything. If this isn't Black, I don't want to be caught off guard."

"Excuse me—sorry!" a young female nurse with fiery red hair interrupted me, clutching a clipboard to her chest. "Mr. Caruso?"

I turned, forgetting what I needed from my team. "Yes, that's me."

She smiled softly. "Miss Heart has been placed in her room. A doctor will meet you there shortly to discuss her results."

Results? That meant there were problems. A possible head injury, internal bleeding—

I exhaled a breath, cutting myself off.

"Is she okay? Is she awake?"

The nurse, clearly uncomfortable by all the expectant eyes, threw Theo a sheepish smile, clearly not allowed to give me much more information.

"Miss Heart is in and out of consciousness, that's all I can say at this time. Please follow me and I'll take you to her room."

****

I wasn't prepared to see her this way.

It took me eight steps to be by her side. I counted them, trying to distract myself from what I was seeing. But when I stopped by her bed, I had no choice but to look. Dustings of bruises covered one side of her face and her beautiful hair was matted with my blood, stark and ugly against the pillow.

She looked so fragile laying there against the white sheets. My eyes took the treacherous journey of scanning her body. There was an IV stuck in her arm and a pulse oximeter clipped onto her right index finger. On her left hand, were two broken fingers that had been splinted and wrapped up.

I fell into the seat at the side of her bed and swallowed thickly.

How had she gone from strong and beautiful to damaged so quickly? Why couldn't it have been my body that took the brunt?

I'd trade my body for hers.

"Mr. Caruso?"

I didn't have the strength to stand up to face the doctor who entered the room with the nurse from earlier.

"Yes." I looked at Olivia, wishing for her to wake up so I didn't have to face this alone.

"I can see you've had your injury tended to—that's good." He looked me over, pity in his pale blue eyes. He was a lot older than me with his pale skin, light hair, and weathered skin, but he brought a sense of calm which I could appreciate.

"Olivia," I demanded. "Is she going to be okay?"

He briefly glanced at her. "We've stabilized her blood pressure and the CT scan came back clear, which is good. We've had to splint her fingers and assess the bruises on her neck and torso for deep contusions, but so far these look okay. We were worried about possible cracked ribs, but she's in the clear for those, too."

My eyes scanned her sleeping face. "Then why isn't she awake?" I growled.

Why aren't those deep forest green eyes open for me?

He smiled again. "Shock, Mr. Caruso. Miss Heart's body has experienced a great trauma and she has a lot of healing to do. We will continue to monitor you both through the night so if you need anything please call one of the nurses."

I didn't feel an ounce of relief. Even when I carefully took her hand in mine, her cold skin only reminded me of the risk I had taken today. I should have taken Chen and his team. We should have had a border of security with us at all times, so we weren't such a fucking target.

But I'd gotten lost in my arrogance, forgetting that nothing good in my life would ever come without danger following me.

And when Olivia wakes up, I would have to face the rejection in her eyes when she realized that I had done this to her. My selfish, destructive desire had put her in harm's way and I'd failed to protect her.

She would throw the little trust we had built together away and take up my sister's offer to return to her normal life where kidnappings and crashes didn't exist.

And I couldn't blame her.

"I'm so sorry, Olivia."

CHAPTER EIGHTEEN

Olivia Heart

A single Swallowtail butterfly landed on the pad of my fingertip, trusting me explicitly with its fragile form. Its black wings and yellow veins glistened in the sun as I admired its fine beauty. The delicate creature fluttered under my admiration, but didn't spread its wings to fly. It wanted to stay with me a little longer.

"In some cultures, that's a sign of rebirth," he whispered into my ear, as I sat with my back against his chest.

We were back in The Butterfly House, enveloped in its warmth while sitting on the moss-filled grass.

"Somebody's been researching them," I teased, my eyes still on the creature content enough with its new landing spot.

He chuckled while rubbing his nose up the side of my neck, his warm breath sending delightful shivers down my spine. "That right there is the aftermath of shedding a physical prison, where a damaged soul can be reborn into freedom."

The Swallowtail dipped its wings in agreement.

I whispered back, "It is?"

His arms around my waist pulled me closer, his voice soft and gentle, caressing me into his warmth. "There's freedom waiting for us, Olivia."

I tried to turn, to face the man whose words danced across my skin, but I couldn't turn more than an inch.

"We'll both be able to fly the moment I am yours."

"But you are mine," I tell him. "I understand what that means now."

The butterfly that sits on my fingertip lifts with its wings, angles down, ready to leave.

The hands that held my waist pull away, his chest that warms my back disappears, and the energy that he protects me with melts into the floor.

My eyes, pooling with tears, watch as the Swallowtail decides the heartbreak is too much to bear and takes flight.

Leaving me all alone, where space no longer holds the same comfort it once had, I stare out into the void with only one choice to make.

CHAPTER NINETEEN

Dante Caruso

P ick up, pick your fucking phone up you piece of —"

"Sir?"

My temper bursts between my lips. "Do you have eyes on Black?"

The line muffles for a second. "He's in his room under guard, sir"

"Put him on the phone. Now."

The line goes quiet until I hear a door open, and slam shut. The sound of boots squeaking against wooden floor echoes into my ear. Black and the team I have set up are in the halfway house in Belgium, waiting for the new team to switch in and take him back to England.

I put the phone on loudspeaker and wait, trying desperately to ignore the hammering of my heartbeat in my ears. Only ten minutes ago did I get the call that Luca and Olivia were in the hospital after an attempt at taking Olivia.

"Is he awake?" I hear Joshua, one of the men assigned to Black's surveillance, demand.

"Just go fucking in, will you?" I hiss down the phone. "Get him on the fucking line or so help me I'll come down there myself and slit all of your throats for wasting my time."

199

"Sir," Joshua mumbles, exasperated.

I hear the sound of Black's door being opened and Josh calling out to him, but there's no return.

I hunch over the phone, glaring seven bells of hell at the device.

"Ah shit."

Every fiber in my body snaps to attention as I yank up the phone.

"What is it?"

Joshua breathes down into the phone. "It's best if I send you a picture, sir."

I don't need a picture to tell me what's happened. Black's dead. Olivia's in the hospital and Luca's an hour away from self-destruction.

My phone buzzes and I find myself opening the encrypted picture.

Tied to a chair, bound, and gagged is Black with one single bullet wound to the head. The gag in his pathetic mouth is a tight roll of money, English money with one word carved in his forehead.

GREEDY.

I don't flinch against the violence in front of me.

He deserved to die, but it should have been by our hands, not by our new enemy.

"Sir, did you get it?"

"You have a rat," I snarl into the phone. "Find out who it is and take care of it. You have one hour."

I cut the call, sent the picture to Chen, and launched the phone into the empty fireplace where it cannot deliver any more bad news.

CHAPTER TWENTY

Olivia Heart

I open my eyes slowly into the darkness.

Under my nostrils is the smell of antiseptic and blood. It overwhelms me and makes me feel sick. Pain radiates in my left arm from the wires and tubes sticking out and attached to what looks like an IV bag. Everything feels so tight and wrong. I'm cold, but burning up at the same time.

I feel slow, dazed, and there's an awful taste in my mouth.

It's completely quiet, except for the constant beep at the side of me, and worry begins to trickle in. Where am I? What's happened? Where's Luca?

Taking in a deep breath, readying myself to sit up, I flinch — there's a sharp stabbing pain radiating underneath my ribs with every movement.

I remember my scream as Luca's car veered into the road and then nothing. Just fuzzy blackness.

Pulling my hand to my side, I try to stem the excruciating pain, but my fingers scream at me, too. I hold them up and see they're broken and have been splinted.

Fear coats my skin — what else is broken? Did Luca make it out safely?

Oh God.

A flicker of him leaning over me, covered in blood, shoots to the front of my conscious, but it could have been a pain hazed dream.

"Luca?" I whisper into the darkness.

I listen carefully, expecting to hear his voice, but all I hear is my heartbeat speeding up on the little annoying machine at my side.

Where is he? Is he hurt?

I hiss through gritted teeth while clutching my side. I force my body to sit up, ignoring my screaming pain receptors and the thumping in my skull that tell me to lie back down.

In the corner of the room, I see him, eyes closed, leaning forward on his knees with his hands together. Is he praying? Is it that bad?

"Luca?" I wheeze painfully with a dry throat that tastes like pennies.

His head snaps up and glossy eyes reach me through the darkness.

He's okay, he's safe, and in one piece. But his energy is different, he's cold and distant, lost in his head while tense eyes scan over my injuries.

He jumps to his feet, startling me, and suddenly he's standing over my bed.

"I'm okay," I whisper, masking my face so he doesn't see the true pain I'm in. "I'm still here."

I reach out to touch his hand, but he flinches away. I try again, but the pain under my ribs stops me from reaching out. Tears glass my vision while rejection fills my heart to the brim. I feel useless to prove to him that I'm still here and that the woman he stares at isn't a ghost.

His voice finally reaches my ears. "Your hair—it's covered in my blood." He's void of emotion, robotic, and cold.

Dark eyes scan the top of my forehead, disgust creasing in the corner of his tired eyes. I itch to touch my hair, to see how bad it is, but I'm too busy looking at the bruises on his face and the bicep that's bandaged.

"It will wash away."

He snarls in disagreement. "Your fingers are broken; you can't wash that away."

I know. I can feel my bones aching under the tightly wrapped splint.

I try to take his hand again, but he moves away from the bed and drops his gaze, settling to glare at the door. He wants to leave; he cannot stand to see me this way and it cuts through me like a hot knife.

"And the bruising…" his chest rises and falls with aggression that's leaking into the room.

My eyes widen and my head throbs from such a simple action. Was I more injured than I first thought? Was there another injury to add to the list that he was too scared to tell me about?

Is that why he wanted to bolt?

I looked down at the ugly green hospital gown that covered most of my body. Possibly a blessing in disguise now that I realize just how much this was affecting Luca.

I licked my dry lips. "Everything will heal in time, Luca."

He shakes his head and takes the seat next to my bed. When he finally looks at me it's only for a fleeting second.

Do you not want me now that I'm damaged goods?

Anger splits me away from my pain. "What happened? Why are you being this way?" I demand, gripping my sheets with fury.

His hands curl, gripping at his jeans. "We were hunted."

That was it. Three words, but it was enough; I remember the moments before the crash. An SUV snarling at the road behind us, desperate to stop us from making it back to the hotel.

Hunted.

Hunted by who?

Luca stalked his way over to the edge of my bed. Gently taking my head in his hands while forcing me to look him in the eye, but I don't have time to enjoy the burn of his touch. "They wanted you. They wanted to take you away from me, Olivia."

I don't have time to control the fear in my voice, desperation steals it away. "Who did?"

For the first time, I see fear reach in and steal away his dominating rage. He doesn't have to say a word, it's written across his face. Luca didn't know who wanted to kidnap me. And now I understood why he couldn't bear to look at me.

His worst fears are coming true—he doesn't think he can protect me.

"Black's dead."

I recoiled from the bomb that he dropped "What did you just say?"

Luca's grip tightened in my hair, too tight for the headache that still pounded viciously under my skull, but I didn't have the strength to tell him.

"Whoever he was working with knew he was a liability under our watch. Left him with a bullet to the brain and a mouth full of cash."

I dropped my gaze, not wanting Luca to witness the fear that had gripped my heart with both hands.

"Someone accepted his deal, didn't they?"

I looked back up from under my lashes. Luca's fear switched to barely containable rage in seconds. I watched the monster take control, wanting retribution for the injustice I had caused by letting Black free.

Any normal person would have been scared, but I sighed with relief. This was the Luca that I knew and trusted.

His jaw hardened. "Whoever accepted must have expected Black to hand you over, but when that didn't happen…" he laughed darkly, remembering my betrayal. "They decided to take him off the board so that he wouldn't run his mouth. They needed him dead so they could make their first move"

My mind raced and my body became too hot.

My heart monitor cuts through the tension with its obnoxious screaming pulling away Luca's attention.

I didn't need the loud beeping to tell me that I was about to have an anxiety attack, the searing pain in my chest was enough.

"Stop," he snapped at me. "Stop it right now." He shook me by the shoulders, but the pain didn't register in my ribs this time.

I look away, trying to drag air into my lungs, stretching my ribcage to work without mercy. It didn't work. My attack was taking over, building with the menacing need to suffocate me.

Black spots coat my vision and I begin to lose him.

Chaos and pain ripple, burning me for being stupid, and try to force me back into the shell of safety.

Bursting through the door to save me from myself, three nurses dressed in red and white raced to my bedside. Their hands touched my clammy skin, trying to soothe me while their French blurred into a haze of requests.

An oxygen mask was thrust over my face, and I gripped it with all my lasting strength. Gulping in the new air, I focused my eyes on the man that now stood at the bottom of my bed, drowning in self-hatred and guilt.

I didn't want to see it, the loss of control in his eyes. That wasn't the man I was falling for, not the man that I needed to make this right.

"G-get out," I snapped at him, pointing at the door, wanting him away from me.

A nurse tried to push me back onto the pillows, but I fought to stay upright. Even if it felt as though I'd been impaled by shards of glass, I wanted him to see what he was doing.

"Get him out. Please. I don't want him in here!" I yelled at them, hoping they would understand my request.

Clutching the mask tighter to my face, I gulped down large doses of oxygen.

Luca took a step forward, trying to stop what was about to happen, but the nurse closest to him stepped from the bed and held out her hands, pointing towards the door.

"Monsieur, s'il vous plaît laissez." *Sir, please leave.*

****

A few hours later, I had expected to wake up to an empty room, but Bones was sitting in the same spot Luca had occupied, flicking through a magazine with disinterest.

"Morning, Olivia," he smiled too brightly, too fake for someone who was usually gruff and distant.

Pushing myself up, I propped myself up against the pillows. The pain across my body was dulled, almost too distant to register thanks to the new drugs they had given me.

"Why are you here?"

He avoids meeting my eyes and focuses on the French vogue in his bear-like hands. "Protection and well... Mr. Caruso didn't want you to wake up alone."

I sigh while rubbing the sleep from my eyes. "Is he still here?"

He laughs. "Did you think he would leave?"

I don't answer him.

Bones drops the Vogue. "He's in the waiting area, pacing the shit out of the floor and trying his best to not lose his mind." He picks up another magazine and begins carelessly skimming its pages.

Looking around the room I'm in, I notice it's not the usual hospital room you would find yourself in after a near death experience. Its large space and comforting décor make it as comfortable as a hotel room with sofas tucked on the far left of the room.

"How bad was it?" I mumble, while looking over my shoulder to the bathroom.

I need to look at my body, desperately. I want to see the damage for myself and the reason why Luca couldn't stand to be in the same room as me. But I don't know if I trust my feet to get me there.

Sensing my discomfort, Bones stands up and holds out his hand. I blush, throwing off my blankets and scooching slowly to the edge of the bed.

"Real fuckin' bad. I have no idea how you both got out of that one. The car was a mangled cube of steel by the time we got to you."

I take his hand and groan at the overstretching of my ribs. The drugs they had given me must be wearing off. Looking down at the IV that connects me to a little stand, I pull at the needle and yank it out of my skin.

Bones groans, "Hey, take it easy, okay? That shit makes me queasy."

His eyes are brimming with worry as he pulls me forward and off the bed. I bite down on my lip—the pain is much worse standing up. All the blood rushes to my bruised joints, burning and stinging.

"Does my family know I'm here?"

He helps me with the first step, but I sway on my right side and lurch into his chest. Crying out, I snatch as his bicep, digging my nails into the muscle as I try to stay on two feet.

"Shit! Olivia, let me go get a nurse to dose you back up."

I growl, "No, just give me a minute. I need to find my balance."

Peeling away my grip, without needing to ask, he places his arm around my waist and steadies me without pressing onto any sore muscles. His time dragging wounded soldiers out of battle has come to my benefit.

I catch my breath and look up at the man with the marred face and baby blue eyes. Bones, even with his faults, is a kind man that has put up with my shit and never once called me out on it.

I wonder if he has this much patience with that little girl of his that lives in America.

He sighs and takes a small step forward, taking me with him. "Your family doesn't know you're here; they think you're on a business trip. We think it's best they're kept in the dark until we know more about the people who wanted to take you."

I balked. Bones was talking freely… without needing permission from Luca. And he reminded me that there was someone out there who wanted to get to me, someone who didn't mind inciting painful injuries to do just that.

"We're bringing extra security in for you—it's just a precaution before you get all uptight about it." He grins, like hell isn't erupting around what's left of my shattered life.

"I don't understand. Why would they crash into us if they wanted to kidnap me? They could have killed me… or was that the plan?"

We're at the bathroom and I'm surprised at how big it is in here. There's a large shower in the corner with a small glossy-white seat that I can sit on when I no doubt struggle to stay upright.

Bones' face becomes the perfect mask of nothingness, reverting to his post as my guard and Luca's employee.

"I don't think they wanted to kill you. It's more than likely they were hoping to push you off the road, but the speed of Mr. Caruso's car would have made that very difficult."

Not wanting to think about the people who were out to hurt me, I step out of Bones' hold and grip the bathroom sink. Looking up at myself in the mirror, I fight the urge to cry.

It's not that bad. It just looks bad… once I've showered, the color to my skin will return and I'll look somewhat human again.

Thick, purple-red blood coated the front of my hairline and had spread down to my left ear, right down to the matted parts of my hair. Knowing that it wasn't my blood made it so much worse.

"What happened to Luca? Is he okay?"

"A few bruises here and there and a piece of glass pierced his bicep, but they've taken care of it." Bones was gruff behind me, trying to avoid my eye in the mirror.

"Is he really okay or are you protecting me on his orders?"

He smirks. "He's good physically. Mentally, he's ready to kill someone."

Looking down at my neck, I see peaking just underneath the collar of my hospital gown, the beginning of a seatbelt-sized bruise. The mottled rainbow of green, blue, and black against my skin told me that the bruises were only going to get worse.

But at least his injuries were minimal.

"Do you need me to get a nurse?"

I shake my head. I wanted to do this alone. "No I'm okay. Can you shut the door?"

He shuffled his feet, unsure. "I don't think you should be alone, Olivia. What if you fall and crack your head? Mr. Caruso will cut my balls off and present them to you as earrings if you do..."

I tilt my chin towards the red cord hanging down, close to the shower. "I'll pull that if I need any help."

He nods and closes the door gently, leaving me to begin the process of assessing my injuries and cleaning up. I'd be here a while, but I hoped by the time I was done I'd feel a little more human and less like a victim.

CHAPTER TWENTY-ONE

Luca Caruso

Pacing outside of her room was the only thing that kept me from exploding into smithereens. Aggression and hatred licked at every part of my body, burning me over and over until all that was left was ash. I was beyond reproachable as mixed emotions pumped and coursed through me. I was barely hanging on to the man I needed to be for her.

Black was dead.

Someone on my payroll was a mole.

Olivia was badly injured and beyond pissed at me.

I hadn't meant to lose myself with her last night. My intentions were never to cause her further pain, but as soon as those eyes of hers found me in the dark I knew how close I had been to losing her.

I had died a million times waiting for her to wake up.

And when she did, I couldn't believe she had come back to me, couldn't believe that when she looked at me, I saw relief and need. She needed me, needed a man who couldn't keep her safe.

I laughed to myself, much to the fear of the woman sitting at the nurse's desk doing her best to ignore me; the man that had paced a thousand times in front of her desk.

With my luck, she'll call psych.

All I wanted was for Olivia to accept me for who I was and now that I had it, I didn't fucking deserve it. It was my fault she was in pain; it was my fault that I had led her to a path where she was repaid in broken bones and bruises.

"Sir." Bones nodded, as he stepped out of her room.

"How is she?" I ask, dreading the answer. Hating that he wasn't watching her.

"Stubborn as ever, but okay. The doctor is going to come in and check her over once she's had her shower."

A shower? On her own, in her condition?

Visions of her falling and cracking her head halt my anger. God damn it, she wouldn't want my help, but I don't have the strength to leave her alone. I need to have eyes on her, to always make sure no more harm can come to her. And it's not like I can ask her guards to step in.

Fuck, I would slaughter them for just looking at her.

"Rum's gone to pick up Dante from the airport. Can you find out his ETA?" I ask, with my hand on her door.

"Yes, sir." He throws me a look of confusion, but doesn't question my sudden change in attitude. If anything, the guards around me have gotten very used to the flit of emotions and have learned to adapt.

I open the door to her room and hear the shower running. I cross the room without pausing. Grabbing the door handle, I'm in two minds whether to go in; would she want me in her space after last night? Could I be in her space when every mark reminded me of my failures?

I open it anyway.

In front of the small bathroom mirror Olivia stands completely naked, her hospital gown puddled at her feet, admiring her survival.

All conscious thoughts trace the curves of her body, engraving every part of her against my heart and mind. Even covered head-to-toe with bruises, she's the most breathtaking woman to have ever been created.

If anything, she's a piece of art that I hope to admire for the rest of my life. Lured and struck in the heart once again, I watch her as she moves her hair to fall over her shoulders.

In the fogged-up mirror, lost in her own thoughts, slim fingers trace the bruises across her chest. She doesn't see me, watching her, desperately wanting to kiss every injury, every scrape on her skin until they disappear.

She doesn't see the man behind her that's so close to getting down on his knees and begging for forgiveness. Or the man that wants to leave and begin the hunt for those that have brought us here.

"Olivia," I call her name.

She looks up and finds me in the mirror but doesn't shy away. "I'm going to shower."

I hear the unspoken words 'and you cannot stop me.'

I step forward just as she turns around. Her injuries demand that I fall into a pit of self-loathing, but her eyes snatch my attention away, bringing me back from the edge.

There's a warning waiting for me, if I can't be strong for her then I need to leave.

"I'll help you. Here, take my hand."

She doesn't reject my touch, even though I'd deserve it if she did. We move to the shower that's big enough for the both of us and I help her up the slight step.

Humidity clings to my skin and lust pounds forcefully into my every vein, but I reject my urges and focus on my one goal: making this right.

Without removing my clothing, I step in behind her, making sure that if she falls it's into my arms and not the cold tiles. Placing a hand on the bottom of her back, I guide her towards the water. The spray catches her front, and she moans, her head falling forward into the rainfall.

"The pain…" she hisses. "I need to sit down."

Gliding my hand down her forearm, I gently help her to the floor. My jeans are soaked and uncomfortable, my t-shirt clinging to my body like a second skin, but I wouldn't trade this.

Olivia hisses through gritted teeth as I settle her onto my lap. Fuck, what I wouldn't do to swap places with her right now.

Moving her hair over her shoulder, I stroke the ridge of her collar bone, my mouth watering to kiss her, to whisper apologies until my voice is nonexistent.

She didn't feel the same way, her chest heaved with sadness as she looked down at my chest.

"I'm sorry for the way I reacted," I whispered. "You wouldn't wake up in the car and seeing you in that hospital bed… fuck, Olivia, it breaks me to see you this way."

I kiss her jaw gently, avoiding a bruise.

She places her hands between our chests, pushing me away. "I needed you to be there for me, Luca. I thought you were disgusted, that you didn't want m—"

No!

I kiss my apology against her lips. Holding her to me, refusing those fucking words from tumbling out of her pretty mouth, and I pray she accepts my apology.

Her minty tongue is timid in its caress, unsure of me, and I despise my temper for all the pain that it has caused.

I've put self-doubt between us, and I'll be damned if I do it again.

Sighing into my mouth, her hands flutter up my biceps, gently resting on the bandage under my shirt.

I pull away, breathing heavy. "I was angry with myself, and I took it out on you — for that, I'm sorry." Softly, I move her back into the spray and with my hand I tilt her chin, letting the water catch her hair.

Dried blood liquefies, dripping down her back and into the drain where it belongs. With deft fingers I rub her scalp, counting the drops of water on her lashes to stop myself from falling into misery.

Forcing my fingers to soften, I tend to her lovingly, enjoying the soft moan that rumbles in the back of her throat.

She leans forward, blinking away the water from her eyes. "Thank you."

I kiss her shoulder. "Don't thank me." Grabbing the small bottle of shampoo behind her, I squeeze some into my hand and massage it into her hair. "Is that okay? Am I hurting you?"

Her eyes blink up at me. "You're not hurting me."

I'm not so sure about that.

My hands are still in her hair when she leans up and kisses me. I pause with surprise, holding her. "I want to go home, Luca. I don't want to spend another night in this hospital."

Home?

Sighing, she lifts her strapped broken fingers to my face. Her comfort confuses me. "I want to go back to Italy; you'll be more comfortable in your own surroundings, and you can protect us there."

Relief sparks and fire blooms. "You said home. You want to go *home* with me."

Our noses are touching, and I sit, wound tight with anticipation. Her answer floors me. "Yes, I want to go home with you, please. I don't want to spend another night in that bed."

The precious moment is ruined by my own worries.

"The doctor wants to keep you for a few more days," my voice is gruff, as I continue to wash her hair. She should stay here where the professionals can give her around the clock care. But from the way she tilts her chin up I know she's going to push.

"It's just a precaution. It's just bruises, and my fingers will heal in a couple of weeks."

I stop her with a chaste kiss. "You can barely breathe without tears flooding your eyes. If the doctor says a few more days, we stay a few more days. I'm not risking it, Olivia, not when you're in this much pain."

She glares at my chest. "They'll just give me pain meds and I can take them in Sicily, with you."

I love her attitude, fuck it turns me on, but right now I want nothing more than to shake some sense into her. A few more days with professionals looking after her isn't going to hurt.

I rinse her hair and grab for the soap. Fuck, how am I going to wash her without wanting her? I've only just managed to stop my eyes straying to her breasts. Caring for her, in this way, is the most sensual act a man can do for the woman he loves, but mine is injured and the last thing she needs is me fawning all over her.

I swallow down my urges and focus, ignoring my erection that's painfully tight against my wet jeans.

Shaking away my lust, I squirt the soap into my hands. "Let's speak to the doctor first." I rub the orange scented soap across the tops of her breasts "In the meantime, you're safe here, okay? There's security around the whole hospital and my contacts are close to identifying the men from the SUV."

She grabs at my hands, stilling me. "This wouldn't have happened if I didn't push you, would it?"

What?

"It was my choice to stand our security down," I tell her, my hands working the lather across her lower stomach.

She shakes her head, spraying me with droplets of fragranced water. "To appease me. I'm sorry, Luca, I should have listened when you warned me. I shouldn't have pushed." Dropping her head, she sank into my wet shirt "This whole time I thought you were trying to steal me away... I'm sorry," her sob catches me off guard.

Stroking her hair, I try my best to soothe her without applying pressure to her body. But I want to squeeze her, to hold her so tightly that our bodies blend and become one. The fact that I can't frustrates me to no end.

As soon as I'm done showering her, I'll speak to the doctors about giving her more pain meds. Her emotions are probably all over the place from the crash.

"You have nothing to apologize for." I kiss the top of her head, already missing her usual scent that's been replaced by cheap hospital shampoo. "As soon as you're cleared by the doctor, I'll take you home, I promise."

CHAPTER TWENTY-TWO

Olivia Heart

Having Luca watch as an IV was being reinserted into my hand was difficult. He teetered on the edge of pain and violence even as I tried to pin him with my eyes, to silently tell him that it was okay. I wanted to get up and comfort him, but I was stuck in this bed with a front-row seat to his suffering.

The doctor, Dr. Francis Ellins, did well to ignore him while listing off my injuries, until it was time to discuss discharging me. Dr. Ellins confirmed I could leave tomorrow morning and would be able fly. Luca, however, did not agree and began arguing with the medical expert.

"No, she's not ready! She's still in a lot of pain—"

"It's manageable," I hit back, but I was ignored.

Dr. Ellins sent Luca a practiced smile. "I understand your frustrations, Mr. Caruso, but Miss Heart has been cleared for a concussion and her injuries can continue to be treated with pain medication at home. We find patients tend to heal quicker in their own environments."

I looked to Luca whose face said it all. He didn't agree and he was about to say something stupid.

"Thank you, Dr. Ellins," I smiled his way. "I'd like to proceed with the discharge tomorrow."

The doctor sent me a relieved smile, grateful that I had ended the uncomfortable conversation. He advised Luca that he will check in on me in a few hours before leaving to check on the rest of his VIP patients.

Luca steps to me as soon as the doctor leaves, holding out his hands "Olivia, please see reason."

"Olivia and reason? I must have the wrong room."

My head snaps to Dante, who leans against the door of my room. Dressed in dark jeans, a white t-shirt, and leather jacket, he grins over at me—his boyish charm instantly bringing light back into the space.

"Don't be rude," I hit back, playfully glaring at him.

"Rude is my middle name, Miss Heart," he saunters in, nods at Luca, before carefully kissing me on the cheek. "You look like death warmed over."

"Dante," Luca growls, snapping his teeth at his cousin. "Watch your tongue."

The IV pumping drugs into my blood allows me to laugh without much pain "And you look like you stepped off the set of Greece."

He pulls back, his hand clutching his chest. "Now you know where to hit a man where it hurts. But seriously, I'm glad that you're both okay and your injuries aren't life threatening."

In my peripheral, Luca shakes his head and takes a seat by the window. He ignores us both and broods, sipping his espresso from our interrupted breakfast.

"Unlike Black," I mutter, hoping for a reaction from them both.

Dante raises an eyebrow at Luca, who in turn, nods with resignation. They can't keep me out any longer, not now that the threat is very much real.

"There was a rat in Black's security team. They had been providing information to a private source over the past couple of days while he was being moved."

I lean forward, wanting to know more. "Did this person tell you who he was working for?"

Running a hand through his hair, Dante looks at me and sighs. "All communication was done on an encrypted email to a non-fixed IP address. This is where the email to kill Black came from."

A single email had been the reason for a person's life to end. One email was all Black was worth to his conspirator. If I wasn't injured and dealing with Luca's unravelling, then I may have felt sorry for Black.

"We'll find them, Olivia," Luca warns me, breaking me away from my dark thoughts. "You don't need to worry about this."

"We will," Dante agreed.

But I do worry, and I will. It's not just for my own safety, not anymore. It's for the man that bulldozed his way into my life with no apologies and forced me out of my safe cocoon.

Distracting myself from the torrent of emotions running wild, I turn back to Dante. "Are you still questioning the man that double-crossed you?"

He shifts, suddenly uncomfortable, and his eyes slide to Luca. "Ah, not exactly, Olivia."

"What do you mean, not exactly?"

Luca quickly stands up, his shoulders tense, and his eye s pinned to me with lethal calm. "He means, it's been taken care of."

I look between them both, trying to decipher if taking care of it meant what I thought it meant… and I knew it did. I didn't need to feel the energy around them or look at their faces to know that something like this wouldn't be tolerated.

"The men that we employ, Olivia, all follow the same code. These ex-military guys have their own rules for traitors in their units. That's what makes them so employable — they deal with the bullshit for us."

I bite down on my lip, trying to stop myself from caring about the person that had died. Hell, that was two people in the same day, and I could have joined them.

That thought alone sobered my thoughts of remorse. Would Black and this traitor have cared if I had died in the accident, or did they see me simply as a transaction to their greed?

"It keeps our hands clean," Luca mumbled, before returning to his seat. "Black should have died the moment he stepped out on his unit, but well, you know the rest."

Yes. I'd kept him alive.

My fingers twirl the tube of my IV. "Surely, my setting him free wouldn't have mattered to Chen and his team. Black still broke their code."

Dante looked to Luca with a smug smirk, one that said, "Here we go."

Luca glared down at his cousin, warning him to shut up. "Chen made an exception for us, Olivia."

But all I heard was, 'Chen made an exception for you, Olivia.'

I looked away, not wanting to see Chen as anything but an overbearing, calculating asshole. The man that stood silently by

Luca's side had always made me feel uncomfortable with his blank, reserved stares and intense security protocols, not to mention his silent judgment when I broke them.

But he had broken one of his own rules to appease Luca and I—even though it put him and his team in the firing line. There was no denying that it would have been a difficult decision.

Now, I understood why he was so strict with me.

"Fuck," I hissed under my breath, while rubbing my sore eyes.

"He doesn't seem so bad now does he?" Dante mumbled, as he pulled my hands away from my eyes. "They've spent years by your side, so it would be strange if they didn't care for you in the way we do."

A shaky sigh slipped between my lips at the overwhelming over-spew of emotions that flooded my chest.

Dante's smile made it worse. Oh god, why did he have to open the floodgates when I was so emotionally fragile? It almost felt cruel.

I looked to Luca whose face mirrored Dante's. Suddenly, feeling so underserving of those around me. Of Chen and his team who had been there for me just as much as Luca had all these years. Of Dante who stood by Luca's side, protected him, and didn't judge his irrationality.

I want to voice my apologies, make them understand that I had acted out of fear and lack of information, but a drug induced exhaustion begins to tug at my eye lids.

"I should leave you to rest," Dante pats my hand, careful not to touch my freshly splinted fingers. "I'll be back to see you this evening."

Luca stands up with him and nods towards the door, signaling another conversation I won't be privy to, but I don't mind. There's only so much my mind can absorb right now.

Floating on fluffy clouds, I sink slowly onto the pillows while Luca and Dante leave, leaving me alone with only the sound of my heartbeat on the monitor next to me.

****

It had to have been hours later because there was no sun peeking through the bottom of the blinds or nurses rushing through the hallways to complete their rounds.

My eyes flickered only briefly when the mattress dipped behind me. I didn't need to open them to realize Luca had shifted next to me on the bed, pausing, unsure whether to take his position next to me.

"You won't break me," I mumble, moving over to make space for him.

His hand strokes along my bruised ribs, feather soft. "I don't want to keep hurting you," the ache in his voice hurts. He truly believes that this is his fault.

"You won't. Lie down with me." I slip my hand to his. I squeeze. "Please."

Neediness wanted to snuggle into him, to caress and whisper all of the admissions I was yet to make. But I was still so weak, and my eyes had yet to fully open.

Luca sighs while leaning down onto the pillows, careful not to press his body against mine. Yearning for his body warmth, I reach around and grab his hand, pulling him over to my side.

He stiffens against me.

"The drugs have made me numb," I mumble.

"I couldn't stay over there." He presses his lips against my shoulder. "I know I should leave you to rest, but I'm a selfish man that needs to be close to you right now."

"I like your selfish tendencies," I mutter, snuggling into his arm that smells of him, of his clean citrus scent, and the orange shampoo he washed my hair with. "Especially, if it means they'll keep me warm tonight."

His arm draped across my waist tenses and his sharp inhale delights my ears. I love having this effect on him, it fills me up and spills over with a dose of pure happiness.

His husky voice kisses my ear. "I'll keep you warm every night."

"I know."

He chuckles. "The drugs they have given you are working in my favor, you're very affectionate this evening, Miss Heart," his lips brush my neck. "Amenable even."

Luca is right. The moment the very nice, but strict nurse switched my pain meds so that I could sleep, I had felt weightless—completely free of all cares and worries. My mind had switched off and the inane chatter had ceased.

"Olivia," he whispers.

"Mhm?"

He sighs. "I don't want you to worry about this, but I know you will. Just know that the people responsible for this will not come within an inch of you again. I'll cut the hands off anyone who dares to touch you."

The certainty in his deep voice catches me by surprise, but I'm too tired to focus on the sudden change in his emotions.

My lips part with a small sigh. "I know you will."

He kisses my hair. "Good, now sleep. Tomorrow we are going home."

CHAPTER TWENTY-THREE

Luca Caruso

W e left the hospital after breakfast, much to my disapproval, but I had made a promise to Olivia, and I intended to keep it—even if she could barely stand without her eyes filling with tears or her cheeks flushing with pain.

I'd helped Olivia into the car that was waiting for us in the basement of the hospital. Dante was up front with Chen, and the rest of our security would surround us in unmarked vehicles when we moved out.

The palpable relief I felt from Olivia instantly stole my attention away, at least one of us was pleased she was being discharged. Katrina had been the perfect friend and organized for a sweater, jeans, and flats, for Olivia to travel home in and to also disguise the injuries that littered her perfect skin.

But I still knew they were there.

The thin navy sweater couldn't stop me from remembering the bruises that were slowly turning a deeper shade of green. Her body could be coated in steel, and I'd still know where every single one was.

I kept watch over Olivia when she slept under a comforter, reclined next to me on the plane. We hadn't spoken much this

225

morning; I'd been busy being briefed by Chen and Dante. We know the men who had tried to take Olivia were ghosts, their records didn't exist, their fingertips had been burnt off. They were pawns who had been used for one specific purpose, kidnap Olivia or die.

Someone had gone to great lengths in case they botched the kidnapping to ensure their untraceability.

Dante was certain it was the Russians; we had recently cut their shipments down to two a month when local police in Spain became suspicious. It would have hurt their bottom line tremendously.

I wouldn't put it past them to use ghosts to throw us off, but something still didn't fit. It wasn't their style. They were slick in their revenge, unlike the men that had caused a huge scene in the middle of Paris.

"Veen's close to cracking Black's laptop." Dante took the seat across from me, his eyes gently skimming over Olivia's sleeping face, making sure she's still asleep.

"Anything on Black's family?"

"Nothing and there's no unusual transfers to their accounts or communication. They probably don't know he's dead," he sneers, his disgust for Black evident on his face.

"There has to be something we're missing. How can a fuckwit like him have teamed up with someone right under our nose?" I lean forward and hiss.

Dante joins me, dropping his voice. "What about when you and Olivia were at her cousin's wedding? Chen and his guys were busy ensuring she didn't run—he could have slipped undetected," he narrows his eyes at me. "We underestimated him. Remember he managed to get a note to her right under our noses."

Looking over, I peer down at her face which is half buried into her cover. Olivia looks so innocent and vulnerable, and I itch to scoop her up and wrap her in my arms.

"If he wasn't dead already, I'd kill him myself."

Dante sniggered. "That I do not doubt. Aside from your blood thirst, have you spoken to Aida? She wants to know how Olivia is, and apparently, you're still dodging her calls."

Even with all the shit I'm buried under, I still have space left in me to be furious with my sister and her meddling.

"I assumed you would fill her in on everything." Leaning back into my seat I surveyed the frustration on my cousin's face and dismissed it. There wasn't any more space to care about his feelings right now.

"I wouldn't have to if you—"

I dismiss him with a wave of my hand "Does her offer to return Olivia to her life still stand?"

He groans, rubbing under his sleep deprived eyes. "Yes, of course."

"Until it doesn't, there will be no further communication from me. Aida knows she's overstepped."

At my side, Olivia moves, and I freeze. My eyes track every small movement of hers as she brings her hand to her chest while she cuddles down. Peering down at my watch, she has another hour before she has to take her next round of pain medication, otherwise, she'll be back to wincing with every breath.

"She doesn't want to take her away from you, Luca, but you gave her no choice. All she wants is to protect you from..."

My eyes snap back to Dante and I bite out. "Hurting her? If Olivia had taken up Aida's offer to return to her life, she'd have been kidnapped the moment she got off that plane. Now imagine what they would have done to her, Dante, and then tell me Aida is right."

His face contorts into uncomfortable rage before slamming back into his chair to stare at the roof of the plane. Silence fills the void around us and my eyes slip back to the sleeping beauty at my side.

****

"Take them, now."

She rolls her eyes at me, scoops up the pills from my palm, and pops them into her mouth. Smirking, I hand her a bottle of water and watch her swallow them down feeling a little victorious.

We're back in the custom-built SUV's that are completely bullet proof, a forethought after Olivia's arrival in my life when Black was still roaming free. My shoulders relax slightly now that we're in the one place I can control.

"How's your arm?" she asks me.

My arm is fine, nothing I or a pressure bandage cannot handle, but her worry touches a sensitive nerve. She shouldn't worry about me, not when she had come out of the situation far worse.

"You don't need to worry about me, Olivia. My arm's fine."

"But I do," she bites down on her bottom lip, leaving small indentations "We were both in that crash, but only one of us was conscious for it."

Looking away, forcing the memories to recede, I focus on the familiar passing countryside of my beautiful home.

I jolt when her hand touches me and I look down to find her fingers slipping between mine, adding comfort to her hold.

This new, beguiling side to her was not something I could easily accept even though I wanted to. Even now as her fingers squeezed mine, I was waiting for her to pull away in disgust.

Always waiting for rejection.

"Stop it," she whispered, leaning up. "Stop whatever it is you're thinking about." Her kiss to my jaw sent waves of pleasure across my skin. "*Please.*"

Turning my face to meet hers, I captured her face with my hand. "There's only one way to make it stop."

Her laugh is small, to protect her ribs, but its effect on me is huge. The tight feeling in the pit of my stomach unfurls and the weight around my heart disappears—just like that.

Her lips crush against mine, her taste filling me. She's sweet in her kiss, but her hands are not, they grab at my shirt, pulling me down to her, reminding me of our unfinished business before the crash.

There's nothing I want more in this life than to give her everything that she needs, but the caring, rational part of me douses my lust in ice. It would be impossible to be gentle. To take her to the heights of submission I need her strength and trust, and neither of those things are between us right now.

I pull away, touching her lips with my fingers. "We can't go there."

She narrows her eyes, pulling away from me. "Why not?"

I swallow my groan. A week ago, I wanted nothing more than her acceptance, her lust, her desires for the burning connection between us, but now I had it I couldn't think of anything worse.

The monster would come out and relinquish his merciless desires on her beautiful, but damaged body whether she was hurt or not. I'd seen what she wanted from me in the streets of Paris, saw the suffering it had caused, and our quick fuck in the bathroom barely scratched her newly awakened sexual urges.

What I had planned, to satisfy the building inferno building within her, would have to wait. I just hoped she could find patience.

I'd managed it for eight years, so a few weeks should be nothing for her.

"Are you going to answer me?"

I shake my head. "I have some work to do when we get back and there will be a therapist waiting for you, to start taking care of the bruises."

"What kind of therapist?" her fingers squeeze within mine.

"A physical therapist," I mutter, thinking about the specialist who I had flown in from Switzerland. According to Katrina, he was the best in his profession. "He's going to start you on hot and cold therapies to help with the pain — that's if you want it?"

She touches the purple bruise that wraps around her jaw right down to the side of her neck. "I don't see why not."

"Just like that?"

Her lips twitch at my confusion. "The quicker these fade, the sooner you stop looking at me like I'll shatter into a million pieces."

You nearly did.

My jaw hardens at the memories that storm in, causing chaos with my pulse. I look out the window, needing something else to focus on other than my new obsession to punish myself.

Sighing, Olivia drops her head onto my shoulder, but doesn't say another word. And I'm grateful because the seething anger that splinters into my blood stream shouldn't be allowed to escape.

Not again.

CHAPTER TWENTY-FOUR

Olivia Heart

A rnik Olomando was not what I expected, nor was the reaction he threw my way when I stepped into Luca's gym. This tall man, with white as paper skin and copper hair didn't bother to hide his surprise at the injuries across my face.

He was upon me before I could take a step back. Sticking out his large, boney fingers to shake my hand.

"Hello, I'm Arnik," his voice was gruffer than I expected. "Mr. Caruso and his head of security have updated me on your injuries. Please take a seat." I look at the chair sitting by a treadmill and sigh with relief. Another minute on my feet and I'd suffer for it later.

"Nice to meet you, Arnik," I smiled up at him.

He grinned back, showing me his very white and very large teeth. "Your boyfriend made it impossible for me to say no," he laughed, while moving to a large blue storage box with clipped lids. "But I can see why he was so eager for my services. Just from the look of your face and jaw, I can see you've had a rough few days."

Boyfriend? There was that assuming word again that didn't fit Luca and I's situation.

I grimace. "It's not as bad as it looks. The bruises look a lot worse than they are."

Unclipping the box, he fixes me with a comforting smile. "They always do. What we'll do today is assess your injuries and put a plan together on how we can speed up the process of your body breaking down the bruises and reabsorbing the blood."

I perch on the edge of my chair. "How long will this take?"

My mind is still very much thinking about the man who's locked away in his office with Dante, Chen, and the rest of my guards.

"Usually, about two weeks."

Two weeks!? What? No... that won't do. If I have to wait any longer for what Luca had promised, a few bruises will be the last of my problems.

Arnik laughs heartily down at me. "But if you follow the regime, we might be able to cut a few days off," he claps his hands together. "Right, if you don't mind could you take off your sweater?"

"Um..."

"I've seen it all before, don't worry."

I shake my head trying to dispel the thoughts running amok in my mind. Surprisingly, Luca would know that this man would need to see my injuries, to see my half naked body and yet he wasn't here to protect me.

His trust was showing.

I begin the torturous task of removing my sweater, only wincing when it was time to pull it over my head. The bra that I was wearing, even loose, had deepened the bruises across my ribcage.

"Ah, I see my work is cut out for me," he offers me a tight comforting smile and a hand. I take it gratefully and he moves me over to the sports table that stands in front of the wall-length mirrors.

Not only will this hurt, but I've got to watch myself endure the pain.

Once on the table, he pulls out a clipboard and begins noting down all my injuries — all without judgement. While he deliberates on his treatment plan, I look around the gym and admire all the state-of-the-art equipment that glistens under the white light.

No wonder Luca is in such good shape.

"If you're up for it, we'll start with cold therapy first. This will reduce any further blood flow to the area on your torso. Once we have this under control, we'll move to the hot therapies."

"When you say cold therapy... do you mean, ice baths?"

If he meant ice baths I was already out. There was no way on this green earth that I'd put my body in that fresh hell.

He shakes his head. "That's too extreme for you. We have to tread carefully, so to start I'll place ice packs on the severe bruises for fifteen minutes and add to this over the next few days."

Ice packs for fifteen minutes. I could do that. Once the bruises disappear, Luca might be able to look me in the eye once again so fifteen minutes of ice on my skin would be easy.

"Okay, let's do it."

****

No. I wasn't as brave as I first thought. Hell, I cried like a little bitch at the start and even tried to get off the table, but Arnik was a gentleman, and coached me through the pain.

He distracted me with such ease, with questions about my family and Luca, all while massaging the less severe areas on my body. My family was an easy subject, we talked about my cousin's wedding, and he told me that he recently married his husband in a small ceremony on a private beach in Greece.

I even managed to laugh when I realized the real reason Luca wasn't fazed by Arnik and his sexual orientation.

Grateful for the session to be over, I slipped on my sweater with a little more ease than before and listened to his list of instructions before agreeing to meet him here again tomorrow.

Chen and Bones were standing outside the room waiting to escort Arnik out and me back to my room — not Luca's. I sensed something had changed in the time I had been away from him, but didn't bother to ask Bones whose arm I gripped. It would be useless.

Marie was waiting for me in my room with a motherly smile and a plate full of alfredo pasta that made my mouth water. Pretending to clean the already immaculate room, she waited until I had finished my lunch to hand me over my pain medication.

"Do you need anything else?" she asked, while taking away my empty glass.

My eyes looked at the plump pillows on the bed and the soft duvet that called to me.

"I'm okay thanks, Marie. I think I'm going to rest for a little bit."

She moved to the bed and pulled back the duvet and removed a few of the dress pillows "Mr. Caruso asked that your mattress be changed for something softer. It should help keep the tension off your injuries while you rest."

My heart spasmed, stealing away my breath for what felt like the hundredth time today, but this time it was from his tenderness.

Marie left me to rest, and I was grateful for her female intuition. My emotions were starting to get the better of me and she would certainly think I was losing it over a mattress if she stayed any longer.

But it wasn't just a mattress or the physical therapist he had flown in to help me—it was the thought behind it that struck me. My comfortability and care were still his top priority even when faced with one of his biggest fears.

My guilt from being selfish swallowed me whole once I pulled the covers over my head, and even sleep didn't have the power to save me this time. Instead, I returned to The Butterfly House where he would leave me over and over again.

Soft, tender lips pressing down on my cheek pulled me away from my sleep and to Luca who sat next to me on the bed. Dressed in a fresh suit, smelling of his recent shower, he looked divine as he smiled down at me.

Blinking away the pulls of sleep, I watched him silently as he lifted his hand to move a strand of hair that had fallen in front of my eyes.

"Hey." I sat up, ignoring the dull ache presenting in my diaphragm.

His eyes track my every movement, waiting for me to prove I'm still very much fragile, but I hide myself well. The last thing I wanted was for him to dwell on this, especially knowing he would use this to hold out on me.

"You talk in your sleep," his smile twitched within the corners of his lips and just like that, he transforms into the most beautiful creature I have ever seen.

"I do not."

Did I?

He shakes his head with amusement twinkling in his eyes. "How would you know? You were asleep."

I narrow my eyes at him. "How long were you watching me sleep?"

Shrugging his shoulders, he smirks. "Two hours, give or take." His smirk widens, enjoying my horror. "Two hours of your sleepy confessions have been the perfect distraction. I must say, I've learned some very interesting things about you in that time."

Great, just bloody great. Even when I'm asleep, I'm an open book for him to peruse at his leisure.

I pull the covers tight around me, flushing bright red. "What did I say?"

He tuts, shaking his head. "I wouldn't want to embarrass you anymore."

His eyes told me that he was very much enjoying himself and that I'd have to work harder to pry away my sleepy secrets. This new, free and teasing side of him was worth more than a few idiotic mumbles, and I didn't want it to end.

I smile. "You wouldn't because you have nothing, you're bluffing."

His eyes widen with surprise. "Oh, you think so?"

I tilt my chin in defiance. "I do."

He leans forward, catching me by surprise when his fingers capture my face. His clean scent mixed with the faint smell of whiskey tips me from sleepy to lustful in seconds.

"Interesting," he whispers, "do you think I'm still bluffing when I tell you that you uttered words about torn dresses and spankings?"

"Um…"

He chuckles into the arch of my neck before burning me further with a chaste kiss to the hollow of my throat. I shiver into him. "Even when you're asleep, you have the power to surprise me, Miss Heart."

I swallow thickly. I don't feel very powerful right now. In fact, I feel the opposite. Under his overwhelming presence, his teeth tease the bottom of my ear.

"I can't be held responsible for what I say when I'm asleep and under the influence of drugs."

He lets go and laughs, catching me by surprise. "No? Well, I'm going to hold you accountable for everything you said because that's the type of man I am." His fingertips sweep back into my hair as he lifts his nearly black eyes to mine.

I open my mouth to respond, but I'm cut short by his lips capturing mine. His tongue, that's sweet as heaven, licks into my mouth sending me into a tailspin of confusing need.

I forget myself and our conversation and focus on him. Replacing my embarrassment is a desire so harsh, that it leaves me panting and desperate. The tingling in my blood turns sharp under my skin. My chest aches and pounds with every kiss he delivers.

Pain and lust mix and there's nothing I can do to stop it.

More, more, more.

I rip at his jacket, my nails tearing at the material that's in my way.

Luca hisses, trying to grab my hands. "Olivia," my name is a breathless warning, but I ignore him. Slipping his jacket off, I throw it onto the bed, all while keeping my lips on his.

"Steady."

I can't. Not now.

I bite down on his bottom lip. His hand shoots to the nape of my neck, kissing and licking me back while the pain in my chest intensifies. It doesn't matter because the fire in his kiss gives me the strength I need to rip open his shirt and sink my fingertips into him.

He hovers above me, breathless. "Fuck, Olivia, if you keep pushing, I won't be able to stop."

"I don't want you to stop," I hiss, claiming his mouth for the third time.

The little restraint he had left snaps as he squeezes my breasts, massaging, and luring my body into him. It's not enough for him, I'm too far away and he fixes that by yanking me onto his lap.

Pain pummels quick and fast underneath my diaphragm, shredding through the veil of lust until it's nothing but ribbons between us. I cry out, dropping my hands from his chest to clutch myself.

Luca freezes against me, his body turning to stone. "Shit-shit!" he snarls, but doesn't move an inch. I feel his heart pound through his chest. "I shouldn't have done that — for fuck sakes!"

I can't speak nor lift my head to meet his eyes, too afraid to see the destruction my little slip has caused. But a small, tiny part of me wonders if playing it off would get him right where I needed him.

"Look at me," his demand burns my ears.

Nope, not a chance in hell he'll want to carry on now.

"Luca…" I lift my head and face the fury that waits for me. It's bad. I don't think I've ever seen him this furious.

"How bad is the pain right now?" he barked.

His hands are back in my hair, forcing me to look at him when I don't answer.

"Your pain, how bad is it? Tell me how bad it is."

Shaking my head, I try to dislodge his grip. "I was caught by surprise for a few seconds, but I'm fine now."

"Don't fucking lie to me, Olivia." He slowly moves me off his lap and I land back onto the soft bed. Not missing a beat, he stands up and scrambles to fasten his shirt. "Shit! I knew I shouldn't have—but fuck, how am I supposed to deny you when..." he turned to look at me and groaned. "Can you stop looking at me like that?"

My lips twitch to deny his request. I want to look at him, to take a mental picture of the way he looks right now and to remember how good he felt under me. I wouldn't let a little pain get in the way of that.

Cocking my chin, I fixed him under my stare, refusing him.

He threw his head back, pinching the bridge of his nose. "Olivia, I want nothing more than to... finish what we started, but you can't expect me to fuck you in your..."

"Condition?" I murmur, hating the boundaries falling in around us already.

"Yes," he sneered. "Your *condition*."

I tried to stand up, but the pain returned with a vengeance, taking Luca's side.

"See?" He angrily fastens his shirt that's missing several buttons. "We need boundaries until everything's healed."

I balk. "What kind of boundaries?"

I'll accept sleeping in a separate room, but if he cuts me off completely, I won't be able to focus on anything but him. He must know that whatever is happening to me is coming in hard and fast. Hell, I'd have accepted all the screaming pain in my body if it meant we could finish what he started.

I need resolution.

I need to feel like *me* again.

"This," he waves his hands between us, "cannot happen until you've been signed off by a doctor."

"What!? No!" I stand up this time, ignoring my zinging pain receptors. "You took me by surprise. Look at me, I'm fine!" I take a step closer to him.

Luca bristles, taking steps back. "It's a few weeks."

He may as well have said years.

My brain had become a muddled mess the very moment he opened himself up to me in the back of that car. He'd filled my mind with ownership and desires and now all he had left for me was denial.

Unfairness wells in my eyes.

Suddenly, he's in my space, snatching up my hand and inspecting the splint around my broken fingers. It had torn away during our moment and from the look on Luca's face it's the final straw.

"Sit on the bed. Don't move and do not say another word," he hisses, dropping my hand and heading to the bathroom.

I do as I'm told knowing I've lost the battle.

When he returns, with his hands full of bandages and tape, he takes the seat next to me and waits for me to give him my hand.

I sigh and give him what he wants. Gently, he begins removing the old bandage, revealing the black skin underneath. My knuckles are swollen and the damaged bones ache beneath the skin, but it's nothing compared to the silent treatment I find myself in.

I'd pushed when I shouldn't have.

But he did kiss me first…

I peer at him from under my lashes. With brows furrowed and eyes narrowed he exudes aggression, but I know it's not aimed at me — well I assume it isn't.

"Sorry," I mumble. "I shouldn't have pushed... again."

He shakes his head, wrapping the new bandage around my fingers, and pulling it tight. Once it's tight enough, he tapes them together and pulls back, getting off the bed.

"You should rest. I suggest you take a warm bath for your muscles, and I'll have Marie bring in your medication."

"You're leaving?"

"Yes, I have work to do."

Black thoughts smother me, drowning me with insecurities. I'm transported back to that hospital room where he couldn't stand to look at me.

I feel worthless and weak. Damaged and not worthy of his time.

That's not true. You're overthinking it. The drugs are playing havoc with your emotions.

It doesn't matter. I should let him deal with the more pressing matters of who put me in this position in the first place. That's more important to him right now.

"Olivia..."

Pulling the covers over my body I sink back down onto the pillows, sucking in a breath as I lay down.

"You're right. I need to rest," I smile, knowing it's what he needs to be able to leave.

"I'll come check on you later this evening..." he hovers in the middle of the room.

"Okay."

I knew he wouldn't return to my room that night. It had been written all over his face the moment my cry had broken our kiss. Luca saw me as nothing but fragile glass.

And he was just waiting for me to shatter.

CHAPTER TWENTY-FIVE

Luca Caruso

W e had been stripped of our phones, wallets, and checked for weapons the moment we stepped onto the small plane. We were forced to leave them with Chen who would have to wait on the runway for us.

Yury Belov, the head of the Russian Mafia was a paranoid man, so paranoid that our meeting was scheduled on a runway with all of his men under one roof—incase things went south.

In case I put a bullet between his eyes.

I couldn't help the smirk on my face as I took my seat across from him because the runway we sat on was mine.

Mistake one.

My eyes glare him down. The last time I saw him, he was dealing with throat cancer. Today, he looked healthier and had gained back the muscle mass he'd lost all those years ago. But he was still an ugly fuck with disastrous ink covering eighty percent of his face.

A shot of vodka was pushed across the table. I grabbed the glass and downed the liquid hello without hesitation.

"Belov," I greeted, slamming the shot glass back onto the table.

"Caruso." He pours us another drink.

Dante takes his seat to the side of us, eyeing up the heavy that's keeping a keen eye on my hands.

Behind them sits eighteen other men who never leave Belov's side. They were a mix of family and security. Their beady eyes where to watch Dante and I to ensure no harm came to the man who sat across from me.

"What's this about?" Belov, the man of little words asks, in his usual drawl. "I have places to be."

Those 'places' involve a string of prostitutes in a remote hotel, in a foreign country, away from his psychotic wife.

I slip my hand into my jacket and the heavy across from Dante lurches forward.

"Relax. He's pulling out a picture. You took our guns remember?" Dante hisses.

Belov nods at his guy to relax. I pull out the picture and place it down onto the table.

"Do you know who this is?"

He leans forward, skimming the photograph with utmost boredom.

"Yes, I know him."

I thought as much.

The men that had ran Olivia and I off the road where all suspected to be English, but after an extensive search we had found a Russian passport—with ties to Belov.

"He's dead, Belov."

Belov leaned forward and picked up his glass, tipping it back and downing the contents in one messy gulp. Wiping at his crusty mouth, he waved for me to continue.

"He was a part of a crew that tried to kidnap someone I care about, but you knew all about that didn't you?"

Belov leans back into his chair, eyeing me before opening his mouth and revealing all gold teeth. Retribution itches at my fingertips to smash them down his throat, but right now being smart is more important.

"I heard about the accident, but I know nothing of this," he points to Yurik Lebedev's mug shot, the tracker who had been specifically hired to find Olivia.

Belov wants to play games, and right now, I don't have the patience. I lean forward, taking the bottle of vodka from his side of the table and pouring two drinks.

"Here's what I know: you were paid a large sum of money to help with the kidnapping of..."

"Olivia Heart?" he offered smugly, coating her name in his dirt.

Mistake two.

I grit my teeth, fighting back the urge to crush my glass into his right eye. It would feel so fucking good to watch his eye pop underneath the glass while his blood ran down my fingers—too fucking good.

I tip my glass to my lips and swallow.

"That's her."

I pour another under his watch, denying him his own alcohol and enjoying the disrespected scowl he sends my way.

"Money talks, Caruso, and I had to get it from somewhere. You can't expect my respect to continue when you cut my shipments in half without as much as a phone call. You broke our deal."

Of course. It always falls to money with these people.

"It should have been obvious, Belov. The product you where supplying was below standard, and demand was falling. If anyone broke our deal, it was you."

Belov snapped forward and swiped his glass across the table. I watched as it rolled onto the floor, landing by Dante's perfectly polished shoe.

"You dare to insult me?"

"I do. Now listen carefully, as I'll only say this once. Tell me who you're working with, and I'll call this quits. I'll move your product as per our original agreement without issue, but I need a name. Give me the damn name, Belov."

"Luca!" Dante hissed.

I held up my hand for him to be silent.

Belov glowered. "You would let this go even after the woman that you love got hurt?"

Flashes of Olivia hanging helplessly snatched away my calm. Memories of her naked body covered in black bruises turned me from businessman to monster.

"I will."

For the first time since we met, all those years ago, his eyes widen in surprise. "Everything was done through email and whoever it was wasn't exactly the talkative type."

"I need a name," I bite out.

We've spent too much time on this already.

He drags his tongue across his front gold teeth, contemplating whether or not to answer me. The fucking nerve of this guy.

"Everything was signed off by a Kenwood."

It matched the emails Jack, my IT specialist, was slowly uncovering. Soon we would have an IP and the matching bank account.

"When did they reach out?"

Belov grinned, crinkling up the spider's web that sat on the corner of his mouth. "A couple of weeks ago. I thought it strange that they were more interested in the girl instead of you.

Well, that was until I did a bit of my own digging and found out who she was to you."

Dante moved at my side which caught the eye of the heavy across from him.

"Calm down," Dante spat with a sneer, holding up his hands.

Ignoring them, I focused on the man across from me. "Then you will know that anyone who tries to take what's mine will only meet one end."

He leaned back, smug. "But you're out."

"Not for her. I'll step right back in if anyone dares touch a hair on her head."

"That's where you fucked up, Caruso, letting a stupid notion such as love get involved. There's no room for that in our line of work. Look at where you could be if you hadn't changed everything your father had built," he leans forward, washing me with his acidic breath. "You could be a king, but you choose to be a mere man, all for a bit of timid pussy."

Mistake three.

I stare at the man across from me, looking into his dead eyes, and see nothing but weakness. He speaks of royalty and power, yet he holds neither. Belov is too stupid to realize that there is no such thing as a king without his queen.

And right now, mine was asleep, broken and bruised, because men like him cannot control their greed.

"Your men were going to take her for the final pay off, weren't they?"

He nods without fear. "Five million was hard to pass up."

I stand, picking off lint that had fallen onto my jacket. "I won't take up anymore of your time. I have what I need."

Dante follows, keeping his eye on the men that tense around us.

Belov nods. "Always a pleasure seeing you, Caruso. Be sure to explain to your woman that it's no hard feelings — just simply trying to recover my costs." He grins viciously, taunting me.

I pictured carving his face open. Stretching the spider's web across his face until he's nothing more than mauled flesh.

I motion for Dante to go ahead. My eyes take one last look at the men who snigger over at me, their twisted faces taunting me from their seats until they land on the head of the snake.

If there wasn't a part of my heart on the table, I could have walked away. I'd have bided my time and cut Belov off slowly, until I crushed his whole supply chain and then I'd have bought the loyalty of his people when he could no longer afford to support them.

But I didn't have time to play the long game and I'm an impatient bastard.

I bid Belov goodbye with one nod and followed Dante to the front of the plane.

A young blonde airhostess stood waiting, her eyes wide and smile tight from the men on the runway pointing their guns up at her. My head tells me to leave her, she had made her bed the moment she got involved with men like these, but then what would Olivia think?

Would Olivia still see her as innocent?

Shit.

"Move with me," I whispered, grabbing her by the elbow and yanking her out of the plane.

Shouts explode behind me, but they're silenced quickly by Chen slamming the door shut. Rum and Red move forward, their hands making quick work of drilling Belov's only exit shut.

Dante grabs the air hostess by the elbow and pulls her down the stairs, ignoring her bubbling panic as she looked out to the runway that was covered with my men.

They stood, camouflaged in all black in a tight formation around the plane, waiting in complete silence.

While Belov had sat on his matchstick throne, my twenty men were surrounding the plane, aiming their weapons at the tiny windows, and preparing.

I take the final steps and cross the runway to my car where Bones waits. With a face lit up with vicious desire, he hands me his lighter and steps to the side.

I lean against the car and look up at the plane that's full of men trying to escape. Each window is blocked by clawing hands, trying desperately to free themselves under our silent watch.

Dante and Chen take my side.

"All secured," Chen nods my way.

"Tell your men to begin."

Chen grins at me, easily falling into step with what he does best, and that's serving revenge. His hand comes up to his ear and our work begins.

Tiny red dots cover each window of the plane. Two men, dressed in all black begin drilling holes into the plane's fuel tank, letting the fuel pool onto the runway.

Gunshots ring out, but I don't flinch. They're coming from inside Belov's plane. Hopefully they'll continue to rain their bullets on the inside of the impenetrable plane, so I can return to Olivia in time for dinner.

"That didn't take them long," Dante sniggers, shoving his hands into his pockets while looking up at the night's sky.

"Sir, you have a call," Red grins as he passes me my phone.

I take the buzzing device, accepting the call and hearing the guttural curses before I'd even placed it to my ear.

"Ah, Belov, miss me already?"

"You fucking cunt. Open the fucking door, open the door right now or I'll—,"

I sigh. "You'll what?"

I'm deafened by more screams and a string of Russian curses.

My mind wanders to the woman that brings me to this moment. It's been a whole twenty-four hours since I last saw her beautiful face or heard her softly spoken voice. Twenty-four hours since her desire burned brightly against my lips. But as I stand on this runway, covered by nightfall it feels as though a century has stretched between us.

I need to see her.

I snap back to the now, desperate not to waste any more time.

"Belov. Be quiet."

He senses that I won't be wasting anymore time. The line falls silent, "Tell your men to take their seats." The silence stretches on until I hear his final command. Light from the windows is restored as his men move back to their final positions.

"Caruso. Open this door." I hear the panic vibrate in his voice as panic steals away his power. He drops his voice to a shaky whisper, "Open the door, now. Let's talk."

"Unfortunately, that's no longer an option. The moment you decided to break our deal, you forced my hand, Belov. You tried to take what's mine and that's unforgiveable."

"Let's talk about this like men," he snarls down the line, touching my last fraying nerve. His voice was grating against me, urging the monster to finish this quickly so we can return to her.

"You have nothing left that I want. I'm going to dismantle your whole empire, Belov, and give your product away for free; but don't worry I'll let that wife of yours live. Something tells me she'll be happier without you," I laugh into the phone, enjoying the taste of revenge.

He screams more rapid Russian curses into the phone, but I'm able to pick out a part of his anger, especially the part where he calls the woman I love a two-bit whore. In his desperation, he promises to hurt her if I don't open the door, to make her bleed until she's nothing but a broken shell.

It's been a long time coming. My muscles coil and spring into action and I push off the car. Images of bruises and broken bones smear their way into my conscious. Olivia's cry against my lips as I moved her on my lap scalds me. The repulsion returns and I explode.

"Have a little dignity, Belov. Don't embarrass yourself like this." I click back the top of Bones' lighter.

Chen whistles, motioning for the men under the belly of the plane to move, and they quickly disperse to their waiting vehicles. Once the space around the plane is empty, I click down and the flame flickers alive.

His growl echoes into my ear. "Open the door. Don't do this… please just open the door."

Ah there it is. The sweet music of his begging that weaves itself under the tight ropes in my chest and begins tugging them away. For the first time in days, I feel the satisfaction of oxygen filling my lungs.

I'm so close to making this right.

"The moment you took that money, you signed your death over to me, but don't worry, it won't be in vain. Now, everyone will know if they even as much as utter her name I'll destroy them. So, for that, thank you."

The lighter drops to the ground and I take a step back to watch the fire spread, eating at the surface covered in fuel until it surrounds the plane.

"No," Belov whimpers. "Not like this, not like this Caruso… please, let me out. This isn't the way to let another man die."

Screams echo down the phone and chaos ensues, but I don't feel an ounce of pity.

I end the call and return to Dante whose eyes are alight from the bursting flames in front of him. The yells for help and bangs against the window don't defer my cousin from his worry.

"You good?" he asks cautiously.

"Yes." I shove my hands in my pockets and watch the scales even out. In under a minute, the fire will lick its way to the body of the plane where it will begin to eat away at all the evil that fills it.

"Will you tell her?" he asks me, as we watch Chen round up Olivia's team to move out.

The rest of my men will stay behind to make sure the mess is cleaned up and my runway is restored. Like nothing ever happened.

"No."

He turns to face me, not bothering to hide his annoyance. "Your secrets are what hinder you from getting what you want."

I snarl, ripping open the car door. "My secrets will make sure she heals with as little stress as possible. I'll tell her when the time is right."

CHAPTER TWENTY-SIX

Olivia Heart

For the first time in three days, I feel more human, more like myself before the accident. Even though my bruises had gone from black to green, I was able to move a little more freely with only a little pain. My fingers, although still splinted, didn't throb anymore and the bruise on my face had easily been covered by make up this morning.

I could hide most of my injuries in a loose dress-shirt.

I was on the mend.

I'd eaten breakfast alone, had my second ice therapy session with Arnik before given an impromptu Italian lesson by Marie and Laurel, who I'm pretty certain were distracting me from the disappearance of Luca and my guards.

The security around the house had been replaced by a hundred faceless men who were armed and scarily silent. Laurel had been the one to tell me that these where men that guarded several of Luca's businesses across the country, but I didn't need to ask why they were here.

I'd picked up the basics in Italian quickly and Laurel seemed impressed as we walked through the gardens and settled by the pool. But it was Marie who surprised me at lunch by delivering a beginner's book on the beautiful language.

"I'm sure it would make Mr. Caruso so happy if you could speak his language—you may even surprise him," she smiled, her motherly face blushing as she placed the book down on the table.

I suppose I could learn more than the basics, even if it's just so I don't feel like an outsider when he talks to his staff or when he rants to himself. Maybe this is what I need to unlock the final parts of him by showing him that I'm trying to understand him.

"Grazie," I replied, while picking up the book.

"You're very welcome. Do you want me to bring your medication to your room after lunch, Miss Heart?"

Had four hours already slipped by? I sighed, resigned to the fact that the pain was still very much making moving difficult, and I'd have to take the tablets that made me want to sleep whether I wanted to or not.

"Yes, please, Marie," my eyes trailed the pool that I so desperately wanted to slip into. I'd be weightless in the water, free to use my body without having to worry about losing my breath to the pain. But if Luca found out... ah, it wasn't worth it.

After my lunch, I'd angrily taken my tablets and settled back into my room with my new book. I'd spent hours fighting medication induced exhaustion and devoured as much of the Italian language as I could. I was rusty and the phrases I repeated were not natural sounding, but it was something to do.

Frustration and loneliness had begun to creep in when I realized there was no sign of Luca joining me for dinner. Marie had come to check on me, passing me my phone on Luca's approval, and told me to return the calls of my aunt who was going out of her mind.

I sank into my pillows and took the brunt of her questions for the first fifteen minutes. How was I after Luca's recent exposé in the paper? Were we talking? How was work? When was I going to return my grandfather's emails... it was too much, but I took it all.

"I'm fine Aunty Sarah. I've just got a lot on my plate at the moment"

Her tut down the phone told me she didn't buy my excuses. "You're pulling away, Olivia, and I'm worried about you. I speak to you less now than I did when you were in New York."

Ignoring my pain, I sat up straighter, suddenly burning up from the suspicion coating her tone. "I know. I'm sorry, but things have just been —"

"Busy? Yes, you've said… multiple times."

I bite my tongue, sensing that she has a lot more to get off her chest.

"Look, Olivia, I'm happy that you've found someone, but I worry about you. Your whole life seems to be wrapped around this man and I know from personal experience how intense a first love can be..."

A first love... what?

"Aunty Sarah..."

"You've got all your eggs in one basket with Luca. Your job is tied to him, you're living with him now and you're so far away from your family. I worry that he's rushing you."

My grip on the phone tightens and my heart's trying to beat its way out of my chest.

"He loves me, Aunt Sarah," I breathe, expelling a tiny morsel of anxiety. "He would never take me away from you. If anything, he's the one who reminds me to keep in touch. You know how bad I am with these things..." I try to laugh away my awkwardness, but it sounds so painfully strained.

The sound of my Aunt Sarah's dog barking in the background cuts through the tension. I hear her terse voice as she tells him off, sending him back to his bed. At least it's not just me facing her wrath today.

When her voice returns to my ears she's calmer. "I know he loves you, that much is obvious by the way he looks at you. I just worry about you. Ever since your parents' death, you haven't exactly been welcoming to the idea of a relationship or letting anyone new in. So, you can imagine my surprise when you invite Luca to your cousin's wedding, out of the blue..."

The line falls silent. Her perception of me is the same as it is with everyone: fragile, cold, and void of needing companionship. And for a while, it had suited me, but now... now it's not a life I want to return to.

"Luca's different. I'll admit, he's a little intense and his way of doing things may seem different, but his appearance in my life isn't out of the blue." I pause, questioning whether or not a bit of the truth will help the situation. "He's been there for me for a long time."

Behind the scenes, stalking my life, and putting incredibly protective measures around me all without me knowing. But it's true, he's been there for me when nobody else was.

"Oh," she inhales deeply. "Why didn't you say?"

Why didn't I say? Well, I didn't know myself for nearly all of it, but I can't tell her that. God, if she only knew a fraction of the truth, she would be on the first plane here, demanding I return home where she can lock me up in a padded cell.

"I was a little overwhelmed."

"You know if things get too much you can always come home, you know that don't you? I'll be here with an open ear and a warm cup of tea."

Of course, I do. I know that her door is always open to me, but right now I'd bring danger right to her doorstep and I wasn't willing to do that.

"I do."

But I can't.

"Good. I'm sorry, Livie, I shouldn't have lost it like that with you. I forget that you and Alice aren't teenagers anymore," her girlish laugh returns, and all tension dissipates from my muscles.

We're not. Alice is beginning her married life and I'm in the middle of a crisis where a looming kidnap awaits me — but hey, at least we're far away from the troublesome teenagers we once were.

****

Later, in the evening when the house had fallen silent, I'd ventured into the kitchen and found myself transfixed by the beautiful room. Well, the parts I could see from the warm lights illuminating underneath the cabinets. The glossy kitchen is twice the size of my apartment in New York, with its high ceilings and large windows that look out to the vineyard.

I pad through, in the dark like a ghost. My fingers trace across the granite work tops that are littered with the latest appliances that look as though they've never been used.

Back in New York, I hadn't had the time to cook, I was too focused on my cases and looming deadlines. The one time I tried, I had managed to blow up a blender and burn rice until it resembled plastic.

I laugh to myself, remembering having to stand on the sidewalk in the freezing cold as the maintenance company shut off the fire alarm system while my neighbors glared my way. What would Luca have thought of me if I'd have burned down his building...

Maybe he would have been so furious, he would have no choice but to have spoken to me.

Shaking my head, ridding him from my thoughts, I pause by the island to look around the darkened room. Marie is an excellent cook, who would know this kitchen like the back of her hand, and it would have been easier for me to call for her, but it was late, and I'd feel bad disturbing her for nightly ice cream cravings.

I'm more than capable of finding a freezer.

I see a doorway at the end of the room and move. It leads into a pantry, and at the back of that is a walk-in freezer.

Perfect. More ice therapy.

I pull open the door with my hand that's not broken and take a moment to adjust against the light. Each shelf is stocked with enough food to feed a small army, possibly for the small army that watches over me outside.

Ignoring the returning cold, I look around until I find what I'm looking for. Snatching up the black cherry ice cream I smugly return to the warm kitchen to hunt for a spoon.

I'd been craving this ice cream since our visit to the little gelato shop in the city. It had tasted sweeter when I'd licked it off his lips, catching him by surprise—back when things seemed a little easier.

"Ugh, Olivia, just stop."

Dwelling wasn't going to help me find a spoon. Ignoring my pity party for one, I search a few drawers until I find what I need and settle on the worktop across from the window.

There's something about the silence and eating ice cream in the dark that helps clear my mind. For the first time in days, I'm able to enjoy my own company without falling into a pool of worries.

Of course, I fretted over whoever wanted to steal me away. And I worried about the distance Luca was putting between us, but right now there was nothing I could do about it, and there wasn't any point worrying myself to death.

That was tomorrow's problem.

The second scoop of ice cream melts into my mouth and I sigh, content.

I'd all but scooped my third spoonful when a click behind me stole my attention. A spattering of lights above begins to light up the kitchen, illuminating only small sections of the space.

I turn, spoon in mouth, to find Luca standing in the doorway, perplexed by me, the half-naked woman sitting in his kitchen.

He looks exhausted under the lights. His usually pristine hair is ruffled and in need of a cut, his shirt is crumpled with the sleeves rolled up, his jacket long forgotten. I've never seen him look so... normal.

"Hi," I breathe, my eyes greedily drinking him in as he stalks his way over to me.

"You should be asleep, Olivia," he leans against the counter across from me, rolling his tense shoulders. I catch his scent and the usual scent of cologne and spice has been replaced with the smell of fuel and smoke.

"I can't sleep."

Even though he looks as though he'll drop at any minute, he still has enough energy to look at me sitting on his kitchen worktop. His eyes hungrily make their way from my legs to the silk shorts I'm wearing.

The intense look of desire spreading across his face makes it near impossible for me to focus on anything but wild thoughts of removing them for him. Desperately trying to ignore the look of lust that taunts me to do just that, I scoop a spoonful of ice cream into my mouth.

"How's the pain?"

Is he asking because he wants to give up on his rule of having a doctor sign me off or is he just being nice? Either one is fine with me.

"At a four. Arnik is starting heat therapy tomorrow so hopefully that will help."

He nods thoughtfully to himself, pushing off the counter until he's in front of me. My gaze falls upon his hands that reach out for me. I trace the lines in his hands, the callouses from his time in the gym, and wonder what they would feel like gliding up my inner thigh.

"Come with me," his gentle request grips me by the throat. Something's different... he's distant, his full attention elsewhere.

"Where?"

"To my room."

I can't. We can't. I'm not ready for another dose of rejection when he realizes I'm not fit enough for his needs. And Arnik will kill me if I undo all his hard work.

I lick my lips, ridding the stickiness of the sweet ice cream, and I place the tub on the counter, "I'll go back to my room."

"You won't," he shakes his head. "Take my hand and I'll help you down."

Taking his hand was easy. Ignoring the electricity that snapped across my palm was not.

Once on solid ground, he checks me over once more before pulling me out of the kitchen and towards the stairs. We go at a comfortable speed, for my sake, but I sense the urgency rolling off Luca and his desire to get me alone in his room.

Panic swirls. Something's wrong. The usual desire that swarms us feels dull and distant. Even as he helps me up the stairs, he doesn't look at me, he's too focused on getting me alone.

"What's wrong?" I ask him once we reach the open landing. "Why do you suddenly want me in your room?"

He bristled, but doesn't stop. Opening the door, he pulls us both in, turns around and snaps the lock into place.

"I always want you here, Olivia," he mumbles, ripping at his shirt. "Sit on the bed."

My eyes sprint to the door, to the lock that's in place, and back to him. The urgency I felt from him was turning to rage, rushing in waves with every moment that passed between us.

He shifts a little too quickly towards me. Fear spikes ruthlessly down my spine in warning.

I'm in trouble.

I take a step away from him, my toes sinking into the plush carpet.

He snaps at me, stealing away the heat from my skin. "Sit on the bed, Olivia, or so help me I'll tie you to it."

Every instinct in my body told me to run, that a threat was imminent, but he kept me pinned under his cold stare, warning me not to move.

Luca's penetrating gaze never left mine as he stalked forward. "Don't push me tonight, Olivia. Do as I've asked, or I'll tie you down."

My lips part in surprise—he's serious about tying me up. The monster was back, waiting for me to push so that I'd give him a reason to exert his power over me.

"I'll sit," I snap back.

"Good." But something told me he would prefer it if I was tied up, submissive and at his mercy.

I pad over towards his bed and gingerly perch on the end, ready to get up if I need to make a run for it.

Luca rips off his shirt, forgoing the buttons and ignoring them as they land on the carpet between us. The bandage that was once around his arm is gone and I see the neat stitches across his bicep are healing well.

"Where have you been?" I ask, trying to distract him.

"You don't need to know," he hisses, gripping at his belt and yanking it free.

He kicks off his shoes and pulls down his trousers, ridding himself of the smoke-covered clothes. I look away, choosing to focus on the locked door instead of his mouth-watering body.

"If I don't need to know about your evening, then why am I here? You seem upset about something and—"

"You're here because I want you here and I get what I want." He turns, stalks to the bathroom, and disappears out of sight.

Okay...

I hear the shower turn on. I stand up, ready to leave when the shower door slides open.

I'll return to the safety of my room and wait until he's calmed down. Luca doesn't need me in his space right now. I'm probably making whatever it is that's bothering him worse.

He catches me halfway across the room, teetering nervously with embarrassment.

"Where are you going?"

"Luca, let me go back to my room and we'll talk tomorrow when you've slept a-and..."

He draws closer to me, using his full height to keep me from running.

"We'll talk now." Grabbing my hand, he laces his fingers with mine and pulls us into the bathroom that's filling with steam. "That's what you want, isn't it? To know everything, to *talk*."

Humidity clings to my skin, coating me in suffocating heat. Standing awkwardly, I watch him stalk to the door and slam it shut. Placing another lock between me and my room.

"Sit," he points towards the chair by the vanity. I take my seat, ignoring the way he watches me, and focus on controlling my breathing.

My ribs ache under the suffocating heat coming from the shower, but I hold myself together until Luca decides to either tell me what's bothering him or lets me go back to my room.

By the shower door, he drops his boxers. His cock hangs hard and heavy between his legs, taunting me. Without another glance my way, he steps into the glass box and allows the water to rain down on his head.

He lifts his head to face the spray and scrubs at his face. His torso stretches, his muscles tightening with every movement. I shift in my chair, uncomfortable with the heat pooling at the back of my neck and between my thighs.

"Tell me what's wrong," my voice, full of husk that echoes across the bathroom.

I need a different distraction, one that doesn't include taking off my clothes and joining him.

Not that he would want to stare at my body in its current... position.

He scrubs at his face once more. "I thought I would have more time," he turns to face me; his midnight eyes haunt me through the fogged glass.

I need to see him properly. Need to be able to read his face.

I stand and slide the glass open, clinging to the door as I watch him wash his hair.

"Time for what?"

He tilts his head back. "More time before you realize just how fucked up I truly am."

My heart drops. "Something's happened. What is it?"

His snarky laugh tells me that he expected my question. "I had a meeting with the Russian Mafia. It was their men that were hired to track and take you."

A small, minuscule part of me had prepared me for this news and it made it easier hiding my emotions, locking them away to deal with later. Luca was already on the edge of decimating his control, and I wouldn't be the one to set him off with my fear.

Not when he needed me.

I step into the shower, ignoring the heat to stand in front of him.

"What did you do?"

Void of light, he answers me with a smirk across his face. "I killed them, wiped out their entire blood line. That's what I did with my evening, Olivia."

Wiped away their blood line... scrubbed them all from history. Turned his back on his eight years' worth of good to destroy those that had put me in the hospital.

His words echo in my skull, trying to reach the part of my humanity that seems to have gotten smaller in my short time of knowing Luca. I don't feel pain, fear or anxious... I don't feel anything but relief now that there are less people reaching in, trying to steal me away.

Luca interrupts my inner turmoil and steps away from the shower until he's dripping above me.

"Did you hear me, Olivia? I killed them. I locked them up in their fucking plane and set fire to the runway." His hands grip into my hair—forcing me to listen to his confession.

Fire.

Fear prickles across my skin.

"They didn't deserve to keep breathing for what they did. Betraying me; hurting you. Shit, you'll never realize how much I enjoyed their screams as they slowly burned to death. Fuck, it makes me hard just thinking about them begging for our mercy."

The smoke on his clothes... the pungent smell of fuel was from a massacre, a wiping out of evil. He hadn't pulled me into his room to punish me, he'd pulled me in here to watch him wash away his sins.

"Luca..."

His grip hardens while he presses against me, setting me on fire. "They thought they could take you away from me and live to see another sunrise." His fingers move from my tangled hair to trace my lips, leaving droplets of water in their wake. "I couldn't let that message get out there, couldn't let my enemies know that I was weak."

Weak? *Weak?* The freedom he has in his darkness makes him a king of sin. One that's willing to shred his soul and bathe in death to keep me safe. There's nothing weak about him.

But yet, even as I stand with him my fear for the real man before me doesn't disappear. Instead, it multiplies until I'm a breathless mess beneath his touch.

I want to kiss him. To slap his hands away. To scream at him for ruining my life and forcing me to live in this pit of darkness with him. But my reckless heart wants to kiss him, to whisper my appreciation across his skin until all he can think about is me and not the men that he burned to ashes.

I'm consumed and confused by my own devilish thoughts.

Completely ruined.

"Are you happier now that you know what kind of man you've let in?" He pulls me into the spray, dousing me in tiny hot bullets of water.

I gasp, trying to pull away but he holds me to him.

He lifts my chin, so I have no choice but to stare up at him. "Does it make you happy to know that you let me into your bed, Olivia? That these very hands that have killed have also made you come?"

He twists his knife into my memories like the savage he is. Luca has no idea what his hands have done to me, no clue at all about how they had freed me from a cage that only offered isolation.

"And I'll do it again. I'll gladly use these hands to rip out the throats of those that dare to speak your name."

"Stop it. Don't do this," I whisper, trying to create space between us with my hands.

He shakes his head, raining me with droplets. "You need to know more about the man that stole you away." He uses his hips to pin me against the glass.

I resist the urge to squirm and focus on finding a way to reach him. "Not like this, Luca. Don't open yourself up to me out of spite."

He barely registers my words. "You need to know that I lied to you about letting you go because I won't. And if you try to leave, I'll just keep dragging you back until you break, until you give in to me." He twists a wet strand of my hair between his fingers and tugs. "Because that's *who* I am."

"I know." I ignore the tremble in my voice.

A small voice in the back of my head reminds me of Aida's promise and that she would be strong enough to keep Luca away if I chose to leave. It's a tiny blade of hope that I refuse to let go of.

He leans down and licks a drop of water from my cheekbone. "You don't know how badly I want you to break," he nips the apple of my cheeks "Fuck. I want it so bad; it makes my bones ache," his hands snap to my throat, catching me by surprise. "I want you."

His desperation made my ribs ache. "You can't have me like this, Luca," I breathe, panic squeezing at my lungs. I was careful to place my fingers around his wrists, squeezing my warning into his skin.

I'll fight him if I have to. I'll tear at his eyes and rip out his heart if he hurts me.

His nostrils flare, enjoying my fight. "The moment I first saw you, I knew that I could never leave you alone. You're just lucky I didn't take you back then," he chuckles darkly, tracing a finger across the bruise sitting on the top of my right breast, "because I'd have devoured your innocence without a second thought. I'd have taken everything I wanted from you."

His vicious confession stripped my body of all heat and plunged me into the depths of the unknown. The depraved confession clung onto me, digging itself deeper and deeper until it embedded itself into my heart.

"Tell me, Olivia, can you accept me now that you know the real me?" he commands, pressing his forehead to mine. "Do you still want to fuck me?"

I freeze.

He breathes hard and fast, teetering between screaming lust and exhaustion.

Barely hanging on, his tortured mask fades and I see into the pit of his pain, his anguish and uncontrollable thirst for my acceptance. I see the real him and he's just as broken as I am.

I'd spent most of our time seeing a monster, but now all I see is a man that fights every part of himself to not let monster win who 'would have taken everything from me back then'. Luca had waited, watched, and protected me from others and himself.

I tilt my chin up to him and our noses brush. Kissing him softly under the water, stroking along his jaw I try to show him the words that I cannot say.

He snaps at my touch and yanks me forward by my sodden top without removing his lips from mine. His kiss seers me with impatience and we drown together.

CHAPTER TWENTY-SEVEN

Luca Caruso

I devour her mouth hoping for words.

I demand her touch hoping for release.

But I'm repaid with cautious touches and reservations.

Those shapely lips of hers won't open and deliver me from these chains I'd locked myself in years ago. They won't whisper the words I need to return to the world of sanity. She's sealed them shut and condemns me to another night in my cell.

And Olivia Heart has every right to keep me prisoner.

I'm every sin that should be kept in the dark and locked away. I'm hell and she's heaven. Two entities that should never meet.

When I open my eyes, I push her out of the shower spray and against the glass where she'll be safe. Where I won't be able to reach out and strip her of her clothes that have turned completely see through.

Her small breasts tempt me to touch them, to roll her pebbled nipples under my thumbs until she's breathless. And when I'm done with them, I'll lick the mottled bruises that have turned her into the finest water painting I've ever seen.

270

My mouth waters to taste her.

My hands twitch to pull her back to me.

My cock twitches to take her.

She steps towards me, fueling my dirty thoughts and right into the devil's den.

"Stay there. Don't move," I drag in a shaky breath, ignoring my tingling mouth that tastes of her and cherry ice cream. "I need a minute without you touching me."

And looking at you—fuck!

She teeters back to her spot—hurt I think, pressing her palms flat against the glass, watching me as I rinse off the smell of smoke from my skin.

"What happens now?" she asks, distracting me once again.

"Chen's tracking down who facilitated the wire transfer to the Russians." I squirt shampoo into my hands and lather up my hair, scrubbing harshly at my scalp hoping to wash away my unclean thoughts. "Once we have that, we'll know exactly who were dealing with."

"So, the Russians wouldn't say?"

"They didn't care to know who they were dealing with. They took the money with no questions asked."

She grimaces. "Why would they do that?"

Because they were scum with no manners.

I tip my head back and wash out the death that clings to me. "Because they weren't happy, I'd cut their cocaine shipments in half. Whoever wants to take you, knew the Russians could easily be bought."

I watch her carefully, seeing just how much more of the truth she could take. And by the look of steel glinting in her springtime eyes I know the woman that stands across from me can handle it.

"Someone's going to a lot of trouble to get to me…" she pushes off the glass, steps out of the shower, giving me a perfect view of her ass in those see-through shorts. "Do you have the files from Black's laptop yet?"

I take the towel that she holds out for me, "We have most of them, why?"

"Can I have a look at them?"

Not a chance in hell.

"No," I step out and stand in front of her, taking great pleasure in denying her. It's only fair after how much I'm being denied, "You don't need to worry about this or what's on that laptop. I'm taking care of it,"

She crosses her arms over her chest, "But what if there's something on there that I recognize? I can help. You're forgetting that it was my job to scour evidence."

I bristle, "This isn't your job, Olivia. This isn't a regular case of yours, this is a man's laptop who was obsessed with extorting you and me. There's stuff on there that I don't want you to see."

She throws her towel down, glaring at me, before storming into my room. I follow, feeling the pulls of exhaustion and watch her slip into my wardrobe.

"It's a few files, Luca. I'm pretty certain I've seen worse," she calls before returning to me wearing nothing but a black t shirt. I'm transfixed by her long slender legs and how fucking good they look making their way over to me.

I love her in my clothes.

I love her with no underwear on.

The primal part of me likes the stamp of ownership.

"The answer is still no."

"Fine. Be stubborn," she pushes by me and makes her way to my side of the bed. I watch as she yanks at the covers Marie had expertly tucked in. Her time with Arnik is clearly paying off because there's no quiet hisses of pain or teary eyes.

Just fading bruises and bones trying their best to fuse back together.

"What are you doing?" I bark, too tired for this shit.

"I'm going to bed. What does it look like?"

Pinching the bridge of my nose, I try to remember how we had got here. One minute, I'm losing my sanity the next, I'm standing in the middle of my room, perplexed by the most complicated woman on this earth.

I've just admitted to murder and what a small part of the illegal activities in my business estate are, and they haven't frightened her away.

Only words of affection and need do.

"You have your own room with your own bed."

"I do," she tells me, while she slips under my covers.

"So, why are you in mine?"

She smirks, catching me off guard. "Because you'll be in it in a few minutes. My bed, in *my* room doesn't have you in it."

Just when I think I've reached the end of the road, she reaches in and pulls me back. How does she do it? Turn my life upside down and then right it again with just a few meagre words.

"I'd love to stare at you all night, Luca, but don't you have sleep to get to?"

I do. I haven't slept properly in days. Every time my eyes close, I relive the crash—see her half-naked body on the hospital bed, helpless and damaged.

"Ah, touché, Miss Heart."

I drop my towel and make my way around the bed, under her heated gaze, until I'm at her side—trying my fucking hardest to keep my thoughts clean.

It's been far too long since we shared a proper bed.

My thoughts of holding her in the tiny hospital cot are interrupted as she leans over me to switch off the light. Her soft scent of vanilla entices my nose, awakening a desire that pools in my lower stomach.

The light snaps off and I feel her sink down onto the pillows. Too tired to tell her I don't think it's a good idea sharing a bed, afraid I'll catch her bruises, I follow suit and lie by her side.

I'm barely on my pillow when she slides over to me, placing her head down on my chest. Instinctively my arms wrap around her and pull her in, just like the night she had snuck into my bed.

We fit so perfectly together.

"Luca," she whispers, "thank you."

My hand that trails her spine freezes. "For what?"

"For protecting me all these years, even when it comes at such a big cost to you. I'm sorry you had to do what you did tonight..." her lips gently touch my chest, enticing a fierce reaction from my heated skin.

"I'll always protect you." I kiss her hair, committing her scent to memory. "There will never not be a day that I won't. So don't be sorry. I made that choice, not you."

"I know," she brandishes me with one more kiss, before settling her head back down onto my chest. "And to answer your question, it doesn't make me happy to know what you did, but it does make me feel safe."

She pulls in a shaky breath, one that tells me her admission was a difficult one.

My heart leaps appreciatively into first gear, ready to pull her up the bed and for me to cover her mouth with mine.

Did she mean that? Or was she saying it to please me?

Shit. I'd dragged her to my bedroom like some feral beast to soothe my guilt and she had done just that. In one, accepting — maybe too accepting — sentence, she had soothed the burn against my heart and spilled calm into my nervous system.

Doubt began to trickle in until she shifted, sliding her hand up my sternum, and lifted her head to look at me. Even in the darkness, I could see the soft glint in her eyes and just make out those soft lips that I loved so much.

Wordlessly, she pressed her lips to mine. The kiss was all too quick and too innocent for what I wanted, but it was exactly what I needed.

"Good night," she whispered.

****

Olivia looked so serene with her hair fanned around her face and her lips slightly parted while she slept in my bed. I'd spent the last thirty minutes trying to wake her, but she was as stubborn asleep as she was awake.

"Olivia," I traced my finger across her collar bone. "It's time to wake up. You have an appointment with Arnik in twenty minutes."

"Mmhh," she mumbles, ducking her head into my shoulder.

"Come on now."

"I don't want to," she moans. "I want to stay in this bed forever."

You're not the only one.

Against her ear, I whisper, "As much as I'd like that, you need to go to your appointment. Don't make me drag you from this bed, Olivia Heart."

"Ugh!" she groans, rolling onto her back. "You talk too much in the morning."

Throwing me a filthy look, she slips out of the bed and stands. I watch the muscles in her shoulders tense and her arms fly to her waist. Before I know it, I'm out of the bed and in front of her, trying to find the area of her pain.

Not that I'd be able to help.

How much longer?

"I'm fine," she wheezes. "Stop looking at me like that. I'm stiff from sleeping and I stood up too quick is all."

She looks up and I see that the apples of her cheeks are red and there's tears in her eyes. She's not fine at all. I make a mental note to discuss her treatment with Arnik after her appointment.

Maybe we should up her meds, too.

I swallowed hard against my urge to chastise her. "I'll get Marie to bring your pain medication. Do you need anything else?"

"Yes. Can you walk me to my room? I want to shower before Arnik puts me through hell."

I move, snaking my arm around her waist and pulling her into my hip. If it gets too much, she'll be able to lean into me.

"Uh, Luca…"

"What?" I look down at her feet that don't seem to want to move.

"You might want to put some clothes on."

I enjoy the way her eyes brighten with humor, even if it's at my expense.

"Here's me thinking you enjoyed my nakedness." Gently, I remove my touch and quickly dress in my walk-in wardrobe. When I return to my room, she's at the door talking to Bones in just my T shirt that barely covers her ass.

"Sir," he nods over her shoulder at me. "We need to talk."

"Where's Chen?"

"In his office with Dante."

Dante's here? Shit.

"Can you help Olivia back to her room?"

"Of course, sir."

With a gentle smile, he holds out his arm for her to take. Gingerly, she takes his arm and returns his smile. I'd give anything to be the one to take her back to her room, but I feel the pull of my bigger responsibilities.

I watch them leave, making sure Bones keeps his eyes in his head before heading down the stairs and into Chen's office where grim faces greet me.

Dante is the first to ruin my morning while thrusting a black coffee into my hand. "We've traced the bank account."

I sip, devouring the bitterness. "And?"

Chen twists around his computer screen. "It traces back to the Canary Islands, and as far as I can tell, it's been set up under the name Kenwood Corp. We've checked and there's no such company."

Is this it? Is this all they have? A fucking shell company…

I step forward, exasperated. "Please tell me we have more than this."

"You might want to take a seat." Dante places a hand on my shoulder, his power offering me little to no comfort from what's probably going to tip me over the edge.

I shake off his hand. "Spit it out already."

"Sir, there's only three outgoing transactions from the account. One is to an offshore account in Black's name. The second is to the Russians, and the last…"

With urgency spilling into my blood, I click my fingers, "And the last?"

"The last is to Emilia Vicolay."

"Fuck!"

"Exactly, sir," Chen mumbles.

Emilia, my ex-fiancé, the woman whose heart I had tortured until it broke, was involved with the person who wanted to hurt Olivia.

It couldn't be… she wouldn't. It didn't make sense. We had ended badly, yes. Fuck I'd pretty much destroyed her life, but I'd taken care of her after our split.

I'd made sure she would never need for anything again.

Promised her a life of luxury.

Resisting the urge to crush Chen's screen with my fingers, hoping to erase the truth, I turn to Dante.

"Are we certain the account is hers? Could they just be using her name to throw us off?"

Without meeting my glare, he takes the seat in front of the desk and nods for Chen to continue. Dante struggling to open his mouth only means one thing, that what they're saying is in fact true. No matter how much I want it to be a fictitious tactic to throw me off.

Chen, sensing my towering rage, passed me over a file and takes my cup. "It matches the account details we have on her. They sent her two million euros, four days after we took Olivia from her apartment in New York…"

My hands clenched the file until my knuckles popped. Hot air hissed from my tight lips as I fought my urge to find Emilia, to make her fucking pay for being so reckless.

Wasn't stringing her along for four years enough? Wasn't turning up late to dinner dates and then leaving her sitting alone as I enquired about Olivia in New York enough? Or my constant push back when she spoke about marriage… or the final night that I'd whispered the wrong name into her ear.

I slam the folder back onto Chen's desk and begin to pace. Red and Rum step out of my way, pushing their backs against the wall. Bones entered the space with a nod to Chen before joining his colleagues.

"I need to speak to her."

Dante answered. "No, you're too close to this. I'll speak to her."

I turn on him, itching for a fight, to feel my fist connect with something solid. "Too close? She's betrayed me, Dante, you can't get any fucking closer than that. It's me she needs to answer to. I need to know why the hell she would do this."

"We don't know the severity of her betrayal and if you go in hot headed, she will deny you the information we need to get this cunt once and for all."

I growl, "I don't give a shit about Emilia's hot headedness. If there's information to be had, I'll be the one to get it from her."

Chen eyes us both with an envious calm, waiting for one of us to give him the orders he needs.

Dante stands up, glowering my way. "She might not want to see you."

Of course she won't, and a small part of me doesn't blame her. I was nothing but a rotten bastard who used her as a distraction, and a way of making it look like my life wasn't falling apart.

But she's working with someone who wants to take Olivia, to hurt her, beat her, or worse—all to destroy me for something I've probably done.

I wouldn't be able to forgive Emilia for this.

Pinching the bridge of my nose, I sucked in a breath and forced self-restraint to snap back into place where things made sense again.

"I'll speak to her and find out what she knows." I look around the room, glaring at anyone who dares to argue. "And, under no circumstances does this get back to Olivia—not until I know what's happening."

The last thing I needed right now was explaining the situation between Emilia and me.

Olivia wouldn't understand, she couldn't. She's not exactly had much experience in the world of relationships, and indulging her in this mess would only bring up more issues, more stress.

"And what happens to *this* Emilia once you get the information you need?" It's Bones' voice that cuts through Dante and I's staring contest.

I don't know… I don't fucking know.

I've just slaughtered a plane full of people for crossing me, but this is different. This is completely different.

Dante steps in. "We'll take care of it," he fixes his attention on me. "We'll get the truth and then we will fix it. None of you will be implicated in the mess Emilia has gotten herself into."

Bones takes a step forward, his gnarly scar crinkling as he opens his mouth. "If she hurts Olivia in any way, shape, or form, we will step in. Woman or not. If she gets in our way, we will take her out with or without your approval, sir."

Red joined his side. "Olivia's been through enough shit," he nodded at Chen.

"So have we," Rum added.

I look to Chen, who didn't need to open his mouth to tell me that he agreed. Olivia's team had been put in place for one reason and that was to protect her at all costs.

Now these 'costs' were coming at us from every angle, dredging up my past and trying to ruin her future with it.

Dante cleared his throat. "We're all on the same page here, right, Luca?"

Are we?

Could I let them hurt a woman I had cared about? My skin crawled at the thought of Emilia being hurt anymore, even when she had betrayed me in the worst way.

Fuck.

CHAPTER TWENTY-EIGHT

Olivia Heart

Arnik was a breath of refresh from my night of dark truths and stomach-churning tension. In just under an hour, he had turned me from tense to supple with heat pads, magic hands, and normal conversation.

The bruises across my torso were looking better. The edges that had been black only days ago, were now turning to a faint green. In a few days, eighty percent of my skin would return to normal and the splint around my fingers could be eased.

I was on my way back to full health and thank God. I couldn't stand the fussing, the worried stares, and Bones telling me to take it easy every five seconds.

I'd forgone my pain medication, choosing to spend the rest of my day present, instead of in and out of consciousness, much to Marie's fussing. I needed one clear day to sort through the mess of the past few days.

With my phone and a strange smoothie concoction from Laurel, I'd sat by the pool and found the perfect distraction by catching up on the photos Alice had sent me.

"How are you feeling?" Dante asked, before dropping into the seat by my side.

Dressed in a white t shirt and bleach faded jeans, he looked completely different to the usual all black suit or leather.

I leaned back into the chair, looking up at him from under my sun hat. "Much better, thank you."

He followed me and leaned back, tilted his chin up to the sun and closed his eyes. "That's good. You had us scared for a while. I still don't understand how you both made it out of that car in relatively one piece."

"Luca made sure I made it out, well that's what I know from my short conversation with Bones this morning."

He doesn't open his eyes, choosing to bask in the sun. "He should never have dismissed your security."

I shifted uncomfortably. "That was my fault. I'd pushed him that morning."

His eyes snap open. "No it wasn't. It wasn't your fault that you wanted some normality back in your life, Olivia. Nobody blames you for that..." he sighs, sitting up and turns to face me. "Anyway, that's not what I want to talk to you about. Aida has invited you both to her birthday dinner tomorrow night and —"

"Luca is refusing to go?"

Dante rubs at his face, revealing his frustration of being caught in-between the stubborn siblings. "Yes. He's still pissed at her for coming to find you and the whole going behind his back, revealing the deal they have. You know the usual sibling drama."

I feel my lips twitch at the memory. Aida had forced her way into my life, just like her brother but she had outsmarted him, using his own tactics against him.

I could see why Dante would find them frustrating. Being stuck between two equally stubborn, but powerful people, would not be easy. I didn't envy his position as peacemaker one bit.

Looking out, focusing on the glistening pool that was calling to me, I watched the water softly lap over the edge. "I'm not leaving him... not with everything that is going on, so everyone can relax. He shouldn't miss his sister's birthday because of me and our issues."

"I was hoping you would say that," he laughed nervously. "He'll need persuading and you're the only person he'll listen to at this point."

I caught his eye, trying to ignore the flush threatening to take over my cheeks. "I'll give it my best shot, Dante, but I cannot make any promises he'll listen. Ever since the crash, he's kept me at a distance, treating me like glass that's ready to shatter at any moment. This might just tip him over the edge."

I wanted to slap my hand over my mouth. Words had tumbled from my tongue, revealing feelings that I was still trying to understand.

Dante shifted to face me, his eyes turning near see-through from the sun. "You're the only person in his life that he's ever had to worry about, Olivia. He was fixated on you the moment you handed him that damn ticket," he laughs without humor, "and trust me, there's been plenty of days I had wished you hadn't. I'd spend some nights talking him down from some crazy request or accompanying him to New York."

"Wait!" I sit up, my ears prickling. "How many times did he visit?"

"We had planned on just one visit. I'd hoped just seeing you in person again would calm him down and help him refocus. It was the only way of keeping you in New York and him somewhat sane."

My throat felt thick with all the questions I wanted to ask. My whole body tightened with expectation, but Dante was right there to fill in more of the gaps and preventing me from fumbling over my questions.

"We were in your boss' office once. You had just arrived like a whirlwind of energy with your eyes buried in casework. Luca forgot that we existed, and his focus was on you. I don't believe in God, Olivia, but you best believe I prayed silently that you would walk in and interrupt us. I wanted nothing more than you and Luca to meet again, so it would all be over."

I tried to picture myself meeting them both in that situation. Would I have recognized Luca then? Would he have told me who he was?

I opened my mouth, waiting for the right words to form, but Dante beat me to it.

"You left before he could do anything," his smile was tinged with sadness. "And then, if fate wasn't cruel enough, a few years later while we were checking in on your security team you walked into the same restaurant we dined in."

"How the hell did I not notice you?!"

Dante shrugged, his eyes slipping behind my shoulder towards the house. "We can be quite inconspicuous when we need to be."

Anger spit fired, ricocheting down my spine. "Why didn't you come over? Why didn't he *speak* to me?"

"Because dismantling our family business became his gatekeeper, preventing him from making the mistake of taking you when it wasn't the right time to do so. He had people wanting to slit his throat the moment he decided to change the business, to stop working in the black markets. It wasn't safe for either of you, so we walked out."

I heard Dante, loud and clear, but all I took away from this was the missed opportunities for Luca and me to have met on better terms.

But does that matter now? I know him now. I'm starting to understand him more every day.

"Why isn't he the one telling me this?"

Dante, for the first time since we met rolls his eyes and scoffs. "Because like you said he treats you like glass. He forgets that you dealt with people like us in your job every day. It's quite frustrating having to drill it into his thick skull every day. But anyway, I'm telling you this because you have the right to know and you're the only one who can prove to him that you are far from fragile."

"I guess we'll find out if you're right about that."

He grabs my hand, being careful not to pull at my splint. "When I saw you in the hospital with him, I knew something had changed — you had changed. You've softened to him haven't you, Olivia? You've found it in your heart to care for him, to forgive him."

Looking away, I ignored the heat spreading across the apples of my cheeks and focused on the truth instead.

I'm done with hiding the truth, hoping that If I buried it deep enough it would disappear once and for all. But it didn't, instead, my emotions were spreading into a galaxy-worth of space just waiting to explode.

"Yes, I care for him," my eyes slide to Dante's. "I don't understand why I feel the way I do about him, but yes, I have feelings for him. Have I forgiven him for upending my life? That I wish I knew…"

The exhale that falls from his lips mirrors the emotions celebrating inside my head. Relief tastes sweet on my tongue and my heart feels lighter in my chest already.

"Does he know how you feel?"

I try to pull my hand from his. "I'm pretty certain he knows."

He would have known the moment I jumped him in the busy streets of Paris or last night when I slept in his arms.

Dante grins wildly, prematurely celebrating what he conceives as a win. "I doubt that very much, Olivia. You're not exactly an open book when it comes to your feelings — maybe it's because you're British," he chuckles at my scowl, "or it's because you and Luca have never had a frank discussion. Either way, I think you should tell him how you feel so we can stop this nonsense."

I pull my hand away and cross my arms defensively over my chest, protecting myself. "I tried that once before and it didn't end very well."

Luca had retreated into defense mode when he sensed I wanted to talk. I'd seen it in his eyes the moment I'd stepped into his room in Paris and dropped my dress.

"Try again," standing up, he peers down at me. "Something tells me you won't get the same result as last time."

I blink up at him, the Lothario giving me relationship advice.

Well, at least he has some experience in the world of dating.

"Dante, you know how bizarre this is don't you? Taking relationship advice from a man that changes his women as often as he swaps his suit?"

He fake scowls, enjoying my teasing. "I'll have you know, Miss Heart, I haven't had time for a relationship. I've been too busy making sure Luca kept his shit together to even entertain the idea."

"Oh."

Dante winks. "Don't feel bad for me. I've had plenty of fun along the way."

Shaking my head, trying to hide my smirk I reply, "Oh, I don't doubt you have for one second."

CHAPTER TWENTY-NINE

Luca Caruso

We have dinner plans tomorrow night."

Snapping my head up from my monitor, I see Olivia standing in the doorway of my office, with her determined glare. Barefooted and dressed in a white wrap dress, she looks an angel that's been sent to rid me of my sins.

"We do?" Leaning back into my chair I watch her carefully, devouring the way she bravely steps into my space.

She glances around the room that's decorated to my darker tastes. Her eyes travel around the walls, drinking in the black and grey artwork hanging on the walls before settling back on me.

"Yes, we've been invited to your sister's birthday dinner, but you already knew about it, didn't you?"

Dante. Of course, my big-mouthed cousin jumped at the first chance to speak to Olivia without me being there. This would no doubt be a part of Dante and Aida's scheming to either check up on my sanity or to pull Olivia further away.

"I do, and we aren't going."

She scowls, stepping in front of my desk. "Yes, we are."

I frowned, not liking where this was going. She takes a seat across from me and crosses her slender legs. The near see-through dress inches higher, testing me.

Fuck, she has the sexiest legs I have ever seen.

They would look even better wrapped around my waist.

"You're still pissed at her, aren't you?" she asks gently.

Yes. Of course, I'm still pissed at her. She's gone behind my back and stuck her nose and ultimatums where they didn't belong. Just like she had been doing the moment she found out about Olivia.

"She went behind my back, Olivia. You must know by now that I don't forgive that sort of indiscretion."

"I went behind your back and you've forgiven me," she traces a finger across the edge of my desk, following the deep oak line.

I don't move. I watch her, trying to understand her sudden honesty and appearance in my office.

"You're different," I bite out, hating how cold I sound. I had forgiven her, but it still caused me discomfort to remember the moment she chose Black over me. It always will.

She sighs. "Because you love me, right?" Her eyes snap back to mine before I can prepare. Before I can control my reaction.

My spine snaps and locks into place under her expectant stare. Every muscle in my body tightens and prepares for the worst. Dread washes over me and clings to me like a second skin.

How can she sit across from me and speak the words that she was so afraid to hear? Why now?

"Olivia..."

"It's not a trick question, before you let your mind run away with you," she smirks, pulling her hands back from the table and placing them on her lap.

I grit my teeth. "What does my feelings for you have to do with my sister?"

"Well, you're worried that if we attend tomorrow, I'll take her up on her offer, but we both know that can't happen now, not with everything going on," she stands up. "So, there's no reason to sulk anymore." She slinks around my desk until she's by my side. "Or any reason to avoid Aida."

She's too close for my liking. I can smell her sweet perfume and the sun on her skin. It taunts my senses until I feel the familiar pull of intoxication tugging at my heart.

Sensing my sudden inability to form a proper sentence, she squeezes in front of me, pressing her ass against my desk— waiting for me to agree.

"Okay?"

The switch of power had happened so subtlety this time that I hadn't realized it until her hands reached to touch my chest. It was a simple gesture, sweet and soft, but it set me on fucking fire with lightning speed.

I was up, placing her on the desk and in between her legs, capturing her face between my hands in seconds. Her delighted gasp is music to my ears as I press myself against her.

I try to be gentle, try to stem the urgency pounding underneath my skin while tilting her head back to kiss her neck. I lick from the bottom of her throat, tasting her skin before meeting her lips—Fuck she tastes so good.

"Okay, Olivia," I press my hard cock harder against her flimsy panties. "You win, we'll go tomorrow night."

She squirms, her hands grabbing at the paperwork of my desk as I lick the shell of her ear.

"Don't tease me, Luca, if you're just going to pull away," she whispers, melting into me. "You're driving me insane."

Her breathless confession was all I needed.

"Good." I push my hips forward, just a fraction more. Olivia lifts her head to look at me, her lips slightly parted and her cheeks flushed with desire.

"Stop it," she whispers, but her eyes tell me she wants the complete opposite. Olivia Heart's body wants to finish what we started in Paris, to find meaning in the emotions that are running amok in that beautiful brain of hers. And I'm the only fucking man who can give her what she needs.

I trace my thumb across her lips, relishing in the softness.

"You're the one who walked into my office."

"To talk," she tries to dislodge herself from under my hips, but I have her pinned. I slide my hand across her smooth thigh and lean over her, waiting for the blush I love so much.

I smirk. "Well, we've done that. I've agreed to your demand so now, tell me, Miss Heart, what's your pain level at today?"

I pull back, enjoying her, loving her heated gaze that follows my step back. My attention is on her dress that's bunched high across her waist, revealing the white panties that stand between me and my next want.

"That's another thing I came to talk to you about. I'm fine, my pain is nonexistent and... well, I want you to stop treating me like glass and give me what you promised."

Pain and pleasure coursed together.

I wanted to trust that she wasn't lying, that the bruises covering her beautiful skin don't hurt anymore, but I've pushed her too far before.

She's all I have in this world.

And I can't afford to keep pushing her away.

Maybe I should call Arnik and get his opinion. He's spent the most time tending to her injuries and would have no reason to lie to me.

"I need you to trust me when I tell you I'm fine," she pulls me back to her, wrapping her slender legs around my waist. "I have no reason to lie about this."

She doesn't.

Her light shone through one my darkest of thoughts, destroying it before it could take hold. Olivia was far from weak, hell she was one of the strongest people I had ever met. Life had thrown her plenty of curve balls wrapped in misery, but she always got up, protecting herself and kept going.

Just like me.

I close my eyes, distilling the urgent desire to kiss her, and focus on accepting what she's telling me.

"I'm okay. We're okay." Her lips touch mine, her hands resuming their spot on my shirt.

We're okay. She's okay.

I'm reminded of the moment she asked me to take her home, here, with me. In my urgency to protect her and bring her home, I'd been blinded to the fact that she had wanted to be by my side instead of returning to her old life.

Wasn't that the acceptance I've been craving this whole time?

I open my eyes to the thief of my sanity.

"You have to say it, Olivia."

She bites her lip, teetering between lust and nervousness. "Say what?"

I capture her face in my hands. "Say you want me. Say that I'm enough and that you can forgive me for everything that I've done, and I'll give you everything."

Her legs tighten around me. "I want you. You're more than enough for me and I'm working on the forgiveness part." Her blush is my undoing.

It's more than I deserve right now and more than I can ever ask for.

I steal her mouth for mine, kissing her gently, licking and caressing her tongue with mine. She moans when I swap her lips for her neck, trailing kisses against her bruises.

My fingers make quick work of her dress, pushing down the straps until the material only covers her stomach. Her breasts, although still covered in fading bruises, capture my attention and the needs of my hands.

Olivia arches her back into my touch as I roll her nipples under my thumbs.

For the first time in weeks, I feel free.

I need more space to love her.

Leaning behind her, I swipe my arm across my desk, clearing the contents in one quick motion. Everything that was neat and organized clangs to the floor, smashing and banging with papers flying up into the air.

Olivia freezes, her eyes widen with shock, much to my amusement.

"What the hell did you do that for!?" she asks me, peering down at the computer that sits on the carpet at an odd angle.

I smirk. "I need more room to start making good on my promise." She tries to resist as I gently push her back onto my desk, but I follow her, kissing her lips until she softens against the cool surface. "Don't move."

I pull back, removing her legs from around my waist.

She tries to follow. "Wait, where are you going?"

"To lock the door. Lie back down, Olivia."

I enjoy the flush that creeps across her face and the way she covers herself. Like that's going to stop me from devouring her.

Once the door is locked, I return to her, to find she hasn't obeyed my order. She's sitting on the edge of my desk covering herself, hiding herself from me.

This just won't do.

"You agreed to obey me in Paris, Olivia, or have you forgotten?"

By the way she shivers into me, I know she hasn't. The worry that she finds so hard to let go of glares out at me, trying to steal this moment.

I press my lips to her forehead. "I won't take this a step further unless you're with me the whole way. I need to take you to edge of no control and for that I need all of your trust."

"And you plan on doing that in here?" she smiles shyly, looking around my office.

"Oh, I plan on starting it here. What I have planned could take all night in many different rooms."

If she feels shy being half-naked around me then I'll just have to remedy the situation. Pulling at my shirt, I ignore the buttons and tear at the material until it's thrown on my chair.

"I love when you do that," she licks her lips, breathless and back with me.

"I know." With my lips, I push her back to where she belongs, watching her eyes flicker from fear to relief. I stand over her, trying to regain my control and to steady my heart that feels as though she's filled the once useless organ up with her butterflies.

The naivety shining in her eyes has an expected effect on me. I'm coming alive with blind lust, knowing that I'm her first for many sexual exploits she's yet to experience.

"You have the most beautiful body, Olivia. I want to worship every part of it."

She looks down at the space between us, hiding behind her beautiful hair.

This won't do.

I prevent her from overthinking this, overthinking us, by smothering my mouth over hers. I ruthlessly grab at the top of her panties and rip them away, shoving them into my back pocket where they belong.

Her gasp is sweet just like her.

Ruthlessly, I slide a finger into her, stretching her, enjoying the sweet sound of her cry against my swollen lips.

"That's right, baby. Moan for me."

Her hands grab lightening quick for my trousers. I shift out of her reach, pulling back enough that I can deny her.

"Not yet, Olivia, you impatient thing."

She arches her back, meeting my fingers with flushed cheeks. "But I want you. Now... *please*."

"You have me."

Always.

I drop to my knees to begin the worshipping of my queen.

Appreciating her shivered response, my teeth scrape the sensitive skin on the inside of her thigh before sinking into her sensitive flesh, catching her by complete surprise.

"W-what are you doing?"

What I've wanted to since the first moment I met you.

I answer with my hands. Olivia lifts her hips to meet the rhythm of my fingers, desperate for more. She's so wet and just knowing I can turn her on this much, sends blood pumping straight to my cock.

Fuck, if I don't move this a long, I'm going to embarrass myself.

"What I'm going to do is take my time with you, Olivia. First I'm going to fuck you with my mouth."

"Oh."

I press my greedy mouth to her, plunging my tongue with little to no mercy. Her thighs close around my head. Her hands grip my hair, enjoying the ride of my tongue as I devour her.

She's sweet and mine. Breathless and arching on my desk, trying to get away from the orgasm that's already building within her.

With each tremble I swirl my tongue, working her with my fingers. Loving her muffled cries as she breathlessly begs for more.

She tenses around me. I push her to the brink with a second finger and pick up my speed, fucking her while drinking every glorious drop. My face is covered in her, coating my skin like a badge of honor and I still want more. I could do this forever.

"Luca... please I can't take anymore"

I bite, lick and suck in quick succession as punishment for her wanting to speed up my fun.

She's such an impatient little thing. So greedy.

I blow on her sensitive flesh.

"Ah! My god-I..."

The grip in my hair becomes near painful, turning my lust up to a burning notch.

I repay her in kind with my hand that slides up her stomach until it tugs at her nipple. She cries, pushing her pussy into my face just in time to meet the final plunge of my tongue.

"No!" she cries.

Oh, yes.

Every part of her tightens around me, throbbing until she combusts around my fingers. With my hands still enjoying the fading embers of her orgasm, I stand and pull her back to me.

She's dazed, flushed, and completely fucking gorgeous.

"Sei moi," You're mine.

I remove my hands, taking great care in licking my fingers, savoring every drop of her first submission.

She nods quickly, gasping for air. "Lo so adesso." *I know that now.*

I stumble back, tripping over a keyboard, hearing the keys crunch under my shoes. Did she just—

She pins me with her stare, waiting for me to say something.

Have I lost my mind? Did she pull out all of my sense when she pulled on my hair?

I scrub my face, trying to clear the lust filled fog in my brain. "What did you just say?"

"Ho detto, lo so adesso," *I said, I know that now.*

If it wasn't for the pretty little smirk forming across her lips, I'd have thought I was simply dreaming, but no, she just spoke Italian to me; perfect fucking Italian with all the confidence as if she spoke it every day.

Pushing me away, she pulled up the straps of her dress and pulled down the hem.

I stood, covered in her orgasm without a single sentence in my head while watching her begin picking up the contents of my desk.

"When did you... how long have you... what!?"

She turns to me and giggles, her eyes alight with happiness.

My brain registers that I've made her come and laugh in the space of an hour, but right now it doesn't have time to unpack all of that.

"A few days," she places a stack of files back on my desk. "Marie and Laurel have been teaching me bits in their spare time and the rest I taught myself."

My voice croaks, giving me away. "But why?"

She stops with her hands around my keyboard that's now missing a few keys. "I wanted to be able to understand you and well, surprise you." Her smile is heavenly. "And from the look on your face I think I achieved that one goal."

I scrub at my face, suddenly embarrassed at being caught off guard, but also fucking elated that she would do this for me. What a combination.

God, I need a drink.

I need to be inside her.

"For the first time in my life, I don't know what to say."

She shakes her head while dropping the broken keyboard on my desk, the desk I'll always be fond of now, and she returns to my side.

"Luca Caruso, speechless. Now what a turn of events," she teases, stroking her finger across the band of my trousers.

I grab her hand, careful not to press her splint that's miraculously still in place "I was the only one who was supposed to be handing out gifts tonight, Miss Heart, but you've upstaged me. I must say you've been rather rude."

She unleashes her new power with a fuck-me smirk. "Bene, cosa hai intenzione di fare con la mia maleducazione?" *Well, what are you going to do about my rudeness?*

Jesus-fucking-Christ.

Her speaking Italian is an aphrodisiac that pulls at the simmering lust in my veins until it's burning under my skin.

I don't know whether to fire Marie and Laurel or give them a raise.

Before she steals any more of my power I lean down and pick her up, ignoring her squeal, and place her over my shoulder.

"Hey! What are you doing?"

"I'm going to deal with your rudeness, Miss Heart. First, we're going to go to the kitchen and get a bottle of your favorite wine and then I'm going to fuck you into next week. Now, be a good woman and be quiet."

She laughs, trying to wiggle out of my iron grip. "O cosa?" *or what?*

I answer with a full palmed slap to her pert ass.

"Oh," she breathes against my back.

"Oh, exactly."

CHAPTER THIRTY

Olivia Heart

L uca placed me on the kitchen floor, leaving me to prowl the kitchen for wine. He looked so lost in the space, so handsome without his shirt on. Sensing my admiring gaze, he sent me a breathtaking smile while snatching up a bottle of my favorite wine from the cooler. While he looked around the gigantic kitchen for the glasses, I took the opportunity to study him more.

Every step was calculated, precise and confident. He moved gracefully, owning every inch of space he entered, his presence calling to me to go stand by his side.

With his brow furrowed, he grew frustrated with every cupboard that didn't have what he needed.

It was the most normal I had ever seen him. Luca's common frustration made it incredibly hard not to laugh. God, it was times like these that made it incredibly difficult not to see the light in him.

"Screw it, we'll have to drink it as it is," he mumbled, grabbing my hand and pulling me out of the kitchen with him.

I bit my lip, stopping myself from laughing at his lack of patience.

"Where are we going?" I ask.

We're leaving the front of the house, coming up to the pool that's lit up from all the underwater lights. All is quiet, but I know on the other side of the walls are guards lining the perimeter of the house.

"We're going to the vineyard," he looks down at my naked feet and scowls. "Come here." Before I can protest, I'm back over his shoulders, barely keeping my dress over my bare ass. With one arm he holds me to his naked chest and the second holds up the wine we are to share.

"Luca! I can walk you know! Or better yet, let me go put some shoes on." While swaying over his shoulder, I catch sight of my underwear hanging out of his back pocket. I balk and lean down, trying to grab them, but he swats my ass.

"Ah ah, no touching, Olivia. They're mine now."

His perverted words imprinted against my body in the form of goosebumps.

"You're a pervert."

"Oh, you have no idea of my perversions for you. We're just scratching the surface tonight."

I'm not sure if the blood rushing to my head is from being over his shoulder or his filthy mouth. Either way, I'm desperate to return to solid ground. Thankfully, he senses I've had enough and places me down onto soft dewy grass.

Shoving my hair away from my eyes, I look out to the space before me. It's more beautiful at night with the twinkling stars above and the crisp breeze capturing the leaves of the trees that surround us.

Small circular lights buried in the surface of the ground light up the alleyways of grape-bearing vines. Each row bursting with grapes has been expertly manicured, ready for the harvest in the next coming weeks. The smell is exquisite, and the silence is perfect.

My sigh is stolen by the breeze. "It's so peaceful out here."

There are no guards, none that I can see, and the only noise is the sound of the leaves rustling in the wind.

"It's one of the reasons I bought this piece of land," he takes my hand, pulling me over to a spot of grass. Carefully, he drops to the ground and brings me with him where I take my seat on his lap.

"Dante said you built this house a few years ago." I feel his hands snaking around my waist as he pulls me into him, cocooning me into his body.

There's something about feeling his heartbeat against my back that melts away all my residual armor, allowing me to be present in the moment with him.

"I did. I wanted to live out of the way of all the noise and prying eyes. This was the perfect place to do just that," his lips kiss my bare shoulder.

"It's such a big house. Weren't you lonely?"

I want to slap a hand over my mouth and curse myself for asking such a stupidly obvious question. Of course he had been lonely out here, all on his own, worrying about me a million miles away.

Around him, I find it incredibly hard to think first.

Well, he did just fuck you senseless with his mouth.

"I kept myself busy," he shifts under me. "Because if I didn't, I'd make irrational decisions like flying to New York just to shout at you," he chuckles darkly into my neck.

Something begins to niggle at me from the back of my mind, an unanswered question from weeks ago during our tender negotiations. I'd shoved it to the back of my mind, paying no attention to it, but now it was crawling its way forth.

Had he really been as lonely as I thought?

But didn't he mention a fiancé?

I move quickly in his arms until I'm straddling him. Swallowing hard, I tried to focus on the way his skin felt on mine rather than how he may perceive my next question.

"Do you remember when you told me about your tattoo?"

He stiffens against me, and the hand tracing circles at the bottom of my spine pauses. "Of course, at Alice's wedding—why?"

My fingers nervously tap his chest. "You said you had the tattoo to stop yourself making a mistake with someone else. Who..." My bravery faults and I suddenly wish I'd kept my mouth shut. I don't want to have this conversation any more than he does.

A bubble of what feels like anguish is sitting heavy in my chest at the mere thought of Luca having a past. I have no right to feel the way I do, no right to pry into his history, but the small voice in the back of my mind wants to know everything about him.

The good, the bad, and more of the ugly.

His jaw hardens at my prolonged silence. "Who was it?" he finishes with a pained sigh.

"Sorry, you don't have to answer that." The smile that lifts my lips feels heavy. "It's none of my business."

I hope the kiss I place on his lips will help drop the subject, and for a second, I think it's worked. Until his hands cup my face, keeping me from looking away.

"You have every right to know about my history, Olivia. After all, I've had an open book into yours," he presses a kiss on my nose. "So, if you want to know about her, I'll tell you."

Do I want to know about her?

Right now, she's a blank face with no personality and nothing for me to compare myself to. I don't have to worry about the reasons for their split or take any responsibility. For the first time since Luca and I met, I feel safer in the dark.

How ironic.

"It was four years of my life. I'm not proud of those four years, Olivia, not one bit. My businesses were suffering, my family was worried, and my relationship with Emilia..."

I hear her name and the rest of his sentence fades away into a pool of oxygen starving confusion. What feels like anguish, seizes the blood in my heart clogging up my arteries. Just when I thought it couldn't get any worse, her name rings in my ears, loud and clear, taunting me.

Emilia.

It sounds like Olivia.

His hands cup my face, trying to reach me but I'm lost, trying to press the reset button in my brain. Trying to scrub her name away.

But it's no use, I fall and fall into a pit of gloom and picture him with a faceless woman, his adoration washing over her while he kisses her. My mind pushes me further down the well of torturous visions: he's angry at her, jealous for her, loving her, worshiping her, and I don't exist.

Oxygen is scarce as the waves of... jealousy, yes, it's the only emotion that describes the waves of pain that overwhelm me. I'd felt this pain only once before, when I was younger, when I thought Alice was flirting with Will at the school dance.

He shakes me gently. "It was you. It was always you."

I can't see him. All I see is black fog.

"It must have been hard for her." I squeeze the words from my throat.

He sees right through me and tilts my chin. "It was, but that was my fault. I was wrong for using her as a distraction, for hoping to push you out. I hoped for years that she would be strong enough to push you out of my head, but she wasn't. Nobody would have been."

My vision starts to clear. "Did you love her?"

I need to know.

No, I don't.

Please say you didn't.

My fingers itch to cover his mouth before he can answer but I'm too slow.

"No. I didn't love her."

An exhale of relief explodes from me, and my brain begins to work again.

He pulls my face so that I'm only an inch away.

I stiffen at the way he narrows his eyes in on me. "I couldn't love her, and trust me when I tell you that I tried. I had stupidly hoped that one day I would wake up and she'd be the one to own me body and soul," he kisses me once, commanding me to relax. "But how could she steal my heart when you had stolen it from me all those years ago?"

He stops, sucking in a deep breath. "I'm not proud of myself for the way I treated her, Olivia. Using her to forget you will always be one of my biggest regrets—she didn't deserve to be treated like that. Nobody does and I should have left her well alone."

"What happened—in the end?"

He tips his head back, his closed eyes pinched in the corners, finding courage in the stars. "What was always going to happen. I hurt her for the final time, and she left me."

Emilia was either an incredibly strong woman, strong enough to hope that she could change his mind, or she was just as damaged as Luca and not able to see he was far too gone to give her the relationship she wanted. Either option helped clear some of the jealousy that wreaked havoc in my head to replace it with a little compassion.

"I-I don't know what to say."

Truthfully, I didn't.

His soft smile does nothing to soothe the tension still simmering between us. I'd ruined our peaceful moment by dragging out his painful history. This is what I did when things became too real between us and yet he had enough patience to deal with it.

"I feel awful." I scramble to find the right words. "I hate the thought of you going through all of that because of me."

Fingers touched my face. "My past isn't your burden to carry, Olivia."

But it is. I'd been the one, like he said, the rogue to have stolen his heart and left. And what had I done since realizing it? I'd been the one to prolong his torture by denying I even had it in my possession.

He was right.

I owned him, but hadn't allowed him the same courtesy.

My heart stopped.

My mind slowed, finally giving in to the truth that was coming in fast.

"I'm sorry for stealing your heart," I whispered, shifting on his lap. "I'm so sorry for not realizing what I had done sooner."

I kiss him quickly, catching him off guard for only a second. The man that has infinite power over my senses pushes his hard body into mine, deleting the remaining space between us and taking back control.

Where we both feel safe.

My moan against his searing mouth, tasting myself on his devilish tongue becomes his undoing.

Luca moves quickly, turning me until my back is against dew-covered grass and he's between my thighs.

We pause. Words flourish silently between us.

Luca stalks me with his eyes, greedy and hungry for more of what we started in his office. I feel his right hand grip the top of my thigh, digging into my flesh with an intensity so bright I feel it vibrating through my flesh.

"I need to see you," he begins to remove the straps on my shoulders with his teeth, tugging the fine cotton down my chest. "It's been too long."

CHAPTER THIRTY-ONE

Luca Caruso

Olivia Heart, the only woman who has the power to ruin me, holds out her understanding with grace and strength just when I need it the most. My mind orbits around her, worshipping her, savoring her smile and forgiveness until I'm love-drunk.

I move to pull her dress over her hips, but she stops me, grabbing at my hands shyly.

"Luca, there's guards and..."

"They can't see us," I kiss her collarbone, inhaling her perfume while freeing my hands of hers. "Only the moon and my eyes will watch you tonight, Olivia."

The relief on her face is beautiful, lightening her eyes and lifting her cheeks as she smiles up at me.

Fuck, she's breathtaking when she smiles.

And just like that heaven returns to me.

My heart jumps into overdrive while I watch her shimmy the dress over her hips and down her legs. The moon glints off her naked body, turning her bruises from black to silver, transforming her injuries to a work of art that requires the right kind of worshipping.

I'm lured in by her sweet sigh, lost as I touch her.

Her nipples peak at my touch and I tug, relishing in the sound of her innocent gasp. Everything about her is perfect, her soft skin, the tiny freckle on her right breast, her long legs that should be around my waist.

I pause before I lose complete control "I need you, right now, Olivia. Tell me no if you don't want this."

Challenging me with a fierce stare, she wiggles underneath me, her fingers resting on the waist band of my trousers, giving me the approval, I need.

What she needs.

"I want you," she tugs at my fly.

Three simple words that hold enough power, echo inside my chest until they imprint on my heart.

"La mia sirena." *My siren.*

Impatience rules Olivia when her greedy hands tug at my trousers with surprising quickness. My hard cock springs between us and the innocent alarm returns to her eyes.

What an ego boost, Miss Heart.

Even with every cell in my body demanding I sink myself into her, there's a much stronger urge that requires my attention. I palm her pussy, my lips on hers, reeling from her reaction as she presses herself into me.

Fuck me sideways, she's wetter than the ocean.

I want more. Moving down her body I'm reckless with my kisses and licks until I land on the sweet spot of her lower stomach. I listen carefully, enjoying the hitch in her breathing as she realizes my intention.

"Wait—again?"

I look up, finding her peering down at me with worry. I'd forgotten myself for a second, forgotten that she was sexually inexperienced to realize that she could come more than once.

"One taste was never going to be enough for tonight."

Olivia gasps with delight, her eyes rolling back into her head when my lips meet her inner thig. I feel completely untouchable. I feel like royalty between her legs.

"You have the most reactive body, Olivia. I want to worship you until every part of it recognizes me." I slide a finger into her, enjoying the sweet sound of her cry as I ready her.

Olivia lifts her hips to meet the rhythm of my hand, desperate for more.

The devil inside me has plans of one lick, one claim, and one command.

Breathless and arching her back, she tries to wiggle away, trying to get away from the heat that's already building within her.

Not today, not now, I'm ready to take what she owes me.

I grip her hips, pulling her back down to my mouth.

I lick her pussy once in a slow sweep, savoring every drop of her while pulling away.

Moving quickly, I free myself. I lift her to me, enjoying the insatiable look in her eye and her soft breasts against my chest.

"Mine."

She stifles my growl by smashing her lips against mine as I enter her, the woman that I love beyond measure.

Olivia is tight and slick with need as our bodies join. I'm overtaken with the urge to take this slow, to savor every moan, every gasp, but she takes control.

The bite to my lip tells me everything I need to know.

"Take me," I demand, my hands slipping to her hips. "Take what you need from me."

Her curious gaze warms me as she pauses, unsure and worried. Sweat beads across my brow as every cell in my body screams at me to take back control.

"Like you did at the butterfly sanctuary." I take her nipple in my mouth, swirling and nipping with urgency.

I need to give her this or I'll take from her until she cannot breathe.

I'm rewarded with her sweet moan and the roll of her hips.

Pulling her head back by her hair, I slide my tongue up her throat and meet her again with a hard thrust.

Grabbing her ass, I tighten my hold, trying to grip on to my sanity as she slides back down onto me with her head back in ecstasy.

The next slow, deliberate roll of her hips is torturous and perfect.

Just like her.

"Oh, god," she cries, falling forward against my lips. "Oh.fucking.god."

"That's it, baby."

With every downward take, I lift my hips to meet hers, to force her to feel every part of me. Even as her cries become incoherent, and I'm blinded by her hair in my face, I feel her nails dig into my biceps, alerting me.

My body reacts to hers, my cock suffering from short spasms of delayed relief until she bites down on my shoulder.

I hiss through my teeth while enjoying the pain she dishes out. If this is what it feels like when she's in control she can forever have it.

"No, no, no, no," she pants.

Yes, yes, fucking yes!

With my hands, I slam her back down onto my cock, groaning at the intensity of her heat as she grips me.

"Luca- I..." she shakes her head before pressing her forehead to mine. Even in the darkness I see her as clear as day. See her battling against the relief, afraid of letting go.

"It's okay, baby, let go for me." My hands slide the way up her spine, holding her, forcing her deeper. "Ti ho qui e per sempre." I've got you, here and forever.

She moans incoherently while watching our bodies join over and over again.

Fuck, why is this so hot?

I'm going to come.

Sudden hands grab my face before I can pick up our speed, and she stills mid glide, keeping me on the edge of my orgasm. Bright emerald jewels glitter with clear clarity, stealing my attention.

"What's wrong?" I growl, trying not to thrust into her.

"Luca, I..." she drops her claiming hips, pulling me deeper. "I love you."

"Shit!"

Her words trigger an explosion of fireworks before I can stop it. My orgasm comes in high and bright reacting to hers. I'm just on the first wave as she bites down on my shoulder, setting me on a spiral of harsh ecstasy.

The hiss from my clenched teeth releases her and she cries out for me. I reach for her throat, holding her down to me until I'm meeting her orgasm with my own. My eyes slip into complete darkness as she clenches around my cock, stealing every drop of my sanity.

My body halts its bliss too quickly, winding me until I'm breathless.

Her words are ringing loud and clear in my ears.

But what if this isn't real, what if I'm not really here and I've fallen asleep at my desk?

What if this is a cruel joke?

I growl against the confusion that slips between us and I kiss her, wanting to silence the sudden rush of insecurities that are pouring in quickly for me to control.

I pull away, testing my throat. "Olivia," my voice is barely there, but she hears me. Her gaze settles onto me, wide eyes full of surprise and fear beam back at me.

"What did you just say?" My hands trace her lips, willing her to say those precious three words again.

I stiffen when she fails to open her mouth.

"Say it again," I demand, kissing the corner of her lips.

Say it or so help me, I won't come back from this. Not now I've heard it once.

She sucks in a shaky breath and I'm suddenly aware I'm still inside of her.

"I couldn't stop myself," she whispers. "I had no control—the words came out before I could stop them," she tries to grab her dress by our side, but I turn us, pushing her down onto the grass where she can't hide.

Urgency poisons my blood. "You said you love me. Did you mean it?"

The color drains from her cheeks.

Fuck, this is bad. She regrets it.

I need to get away. I can't do this. I'm not fucking strong enough for this.

Her voice keeps me grounded. "I thought all this time I was losing my mind, that it was just lust, and it would stop." Her hands shake before touching my chest. I distill her tracing of my tattoo and force her to look at me.

"Did you mean it?"

It's barely audible, but I hear it. "Yes."

Yes.

YES?

Fuck. What the hell just happened? She's knocked the air from my lungs and ripped away at any sense left in my head. But she's also cut the barb wire that clings to the muscle of my heart and freed me from years of doubt.

With three words.

I need to focus on that. On her. But there's too much doubt overshadowing what should be the happiest moment of my fucking life.

"Will you say something?"

I blindly grab for her dress and pass it to her.

I feel her watching me as I dress. "Give me a minute."

We're both a mess. There's grass in the back of her hair, my knees are covered in mud, rubbing against my trousers and our clothes are completely ruined.

She's yours. She's given you what you need. Say something.

I take her hand, tugging her to me. My mouth twitches to say something, anything to solidify the moment that means the world to me, but I freeze.

For the second time in my life, I don't know what to say.

"I've caught you off guard, haven't it?" she tells me, worry etched on her face.

My heart rate spikes in agreement.

"Caught me off guard is the understatement of the year, Olivia," I bite a little too harshly, but I'm fucking dying here. I don't know what to think.

She smirks, the woman in front of me *smirks* and I think I'm on my way to my first coronary.

"Well, while you deal with that, do you think we should head back? I'd really like to wash the grass out of my hair," she tried for humor, but it doesn't reach me.

I take her hand and we walk in complete silence back to the house.

CHAPTER THIRTY-TWO

Olivia Heart

No matter what I did, I couldn't stop the shakes rattling through my body. I'd gone from completely consumed to freedom with three little words and barely enough time to register what they meant. I'd hit the maximum high and came down far too quickly to be humanly possible, but I survived.

I, Olivia Heart, had survived opening up and letting love in.

Lights, stars, and the moon had exploded into my vision on the release of my confession. I was up there with them, untouchable, reeling in my feelings for the man under me.

I was finally free.

My compulsions, urges, and desires had combined their magical powers until my heart shed its last lock. I was no longer the woman that was scared to open up and let love in.

I was as brave as the man that loved me enough to see through my damage and still want to be the one to fix it.

Even when Luca had taken me back to my room, kissed me once, and left without a single word I knew he would be back.

And I was right, once I stepped out of my shower he was sitting on the bottom of my bed, freshly showered in just a pair of shorts holding out one of his black T shirts that I'm so fond of sleeping in.

Over on the bedside table, is a glass of water and my pain medication that he turns for once I'm in front of him. The light hits his smooth shoulders and I'm drawn to the teeth marks on his shoulder. I move so quickly to him, that I almost trip out of the towel covering my body. He looks from me to his shoulder, confused until he realizes why.

Grabbing my hand, he removes me from the wound I've inflicted and looks down — impressed.

"I'm so sorry. I don't know what I was thinking."

"Do *not* apologize for what you felt in the moment, Olivia," he growls, "because if you do, I'll get it tattooed on my body. Now, put this on," he pushes the t-shirt between us.

My eyes only leave the indents on his broad shoulder when I pull the soft t-shirt that smells of him over my head.

"I'm still sorry, and you wouldn't do that."

You sure about that? Your initial is already tattooed on him — what's a few teeth marks?

"No? Oh, but I would," he smirks, before passing me the glass and the tiny three tablets. "With a little note underneath that marks it as the day, Olivia Heart told me she loves — "

"Okay I get it," I huff with a roll of my eyes, fighting the burn of my cheeks.

He kisses my cheek after I've taken my meds "I hope you do because the tattooist is coming tomorrow."

I almost choke. Luca throws his head back and laughs, his hand to his chest as he enjoys himself at my expense.

I can't help it, but I smile at the beautiful sound of his laugh.

Hand on my hip and an eyebrow raised I snap, "You better be joking!"

He pulls back my covers, still laughing. "Wouldn't that be romantic, having your lover's teeth etched into your skin as a permanent reminder of how good you made her feel?"

He's enjoying this far too much.

I turn the light off at my bedside and try to use the covers to protect me from his merciless teasing, but he pulls me into him, wrapping his warm arms around me.

"Go to sleep, Luca."

He chuckles into my hair. "I won't get the tattoo if you give me something I want."

"Haven't I given you enough tonight?"

His fingers find me in the dark and tip my chin up to him. "You certainly have, but I'm a greedy man, Olivia, you should know this about me by now," his lips touch, gently caressing mine. "Say the words again and I'll leave the permanent markings for another day."

My hands find their way into his hair, and I whisper, "Are you blackmailing me?"

"I am."

Well two can play this game.

I press my lips to his once and delight in the feeling of his arms tightening around me. "Ti amo." *I love you.*

But before he can relish in his win, I cut him off, "Now go to sleep."

CHAPTER THIRTY-THREE

Luca Caruso

Emilia hasn't been to her apartment in three weeks," Dante tells me, eyeing up the mess of my office with his usual curious stare. I watch as his eyes land on my empty desk and bounce back up to me, an eyebrow raised.

I shrug, smug and proud of the mess I'd made with Olivia last night.

"I tried to speak to her sister, but she told me to 'fuck off' and leave Emilia alone."

Of course, she had. Everette hated the very air that I breathed so there was no way she would speak to us.

Ignoring the paperwork scattered everywhere, I took my seat. "She's either gone into hiding or she's left the country."

Dante shook his head, grimacing. "I've checked. Her passport hasn't been swiped either."

None of this made a lick of sense. Emilia and I had been over for a year now, and when I'd seen her a month ago, we had an amicable conversation. Now she was out to destroy me...

"What if we're looking at this the wrong way? What if she's being blackmailed to supply information and the transfer is just to throw us off?"

"Or she's out for revenge?"

Revenge for wasting four years of her life. That's what Dante wanted to say.

He brushes a hand over his face, exhausted. "Look, whoever this Kenwood is they clearly have an insider knowledge on how best to get to you. Emilia had been by your side long enough to provide them with plenty of information. Luca, she's lost her innocence the moment she put Olivia in the hospital."

My anger rolls hard and fast. Images of Olivia covered in my blood pollute my mind.

"Have Jack track her phone and all those close to her."

We're interrupted by a timid knock at my door. Arnik stands awkwardly in the doorway, unsure whether to take another step into the mess that's my office.

"Sorry to interrupt, Mr. Caruso, but do you have a minute?"

No, not really. My past and future are colliding, the woman I love is in danger, and I'm barely holding on to what's left of my sanity.

"Take a seat." I nod for him to take the chair next to Dante, but he doesn't move a muscle. Arnik looks to Dante and I'm suddenly aware of the problem.

"Dante is fine," I wave him off. "Please, take a seat."

Arnik slinks into the room, narrowly missing the top of the doorframe, and takes up the space by Dante. Just by his right foot is a file I'd been working on before Olivia interrupted me last night. The temptress had been in my office all of two minutes and I'd destroyed everything to get to her.

Worth it.

"It's just a quick update on Olivia's progress, Mr. Caruso. After this morning's visit, I think it's best if we extend Olivia's treatment for another week."

My body stills. "Why? I thought she was improving."

She looked like she had improved last night when she was under me.

Dante looks incredibly irritated, wanting to continue our previous conversation, but right now he has to wait—this is far more important.

Arnik shifts in his seat, looking everywhere but me. "Well, everything was on track until this morning's session. I've had to restart the ice treatment because of the number of new bruises that have formed across her torso."

"Sorry?" I bark.

Arnik sighs. "She's incredibly prone to secondary injuries so any amount of pressure right now can set us back days, sometimes even weeks."

Dante turns in his seat. "How has she sustained new injuries?"

Last night.

Last night when she told me she wasn't made of glass, that she wasn't in anymore pain... when she told me she loved me as we fucked in the vineyard.

"She wouldn't say."

Arnik pins me with a 'don't make me say it stare' while Dante looks around my office, until he lands on my desk, a smug smirk tugging at the corner of his lips.

I clear my throat. "I wasn't aware of any new injuries."

Truthfully, I wasn't. This morning when I'd left her to sleep, she'd been covered by my T Shirt, wrapped up in her duvet cover. I'd kissed her cheek and relished in the return of a soft sigh that made it almost impossible for me to leave her side.

Dante cuts in. "Well, it's a good thing you're here Arnik. What would you suggest Olivia does to prevent this from happening again?"

Dante, the smug bastard turns to Olivia's therapist with his fake concern, and I suddenly wished I'd have hit him harder this morning during our sparring match.

One black eye wasn't enough.

Arnik has the good sense to ignore my death glare towards my cousin. "I've already had a discussion with her about what she should and shouldn't be doing so…"

"So, no desk sex then?"

That's it. I'm going to shoot this motherfucker right between his eyes.

Arnik has the good sense to pretend he didn't hear Dante, but the tips of his ears turning red gives him away.

I stand. "I'm sorry, Arnik, seems my cousin here has forgotten his manners. I'll speak to Olivia and make sure she follows your list of do's and don'ts and if you're able to extend your services that would be great."

Dante sniggers, but his attitude is quickly remedied when he catches my eye.

"Great. I'll send over next week's schedule when I'm back at my hotel," he stands, relieved to be leaving. "See you tomorrow."

I nod my goodbye and wait until he leaves the room, shutting the door behind him.

"Not another word. Not another fucking word from you, Dante, or so help me I'll put a bullet through each of your knees."

****

Olivia's perfume wafts underneath my nose as soon I enter her room. My eyes find her slipping on heels, her fingers working the dainty clasp around the ankle. The figure hugging, dusky rose dress that she wears covers her all in the right places.

Hiding the evidence.

She catches me as she stands, "Hi…"

In four strides, my hands are in her hair and her lips are on mine. I kiss her once before letting her go.

"You're mad," she purses her lips. "Arnik came to see you, didn't he?" She moves over to the vanity in front of the window and picks up the butterfly earrings I gave her in Paris.

"I'm not mad at you," I push her hair over her shoulder while she places in her earrings. "I'm mad at myself. I should have been more careful with you last night. I didn't realize… are you in any pain? Do we need to cancel tonight?"

"No, I'm fine, Luca. Honestly, I can barely feel them," she steps into my arms, sliding her hands into my suit jacket.

Her body on mine is the balm I need to soothe away all the tension. Today had been a day of dead ends. Emilia was still unaccounted for, our search for anything Kenwood related was a bust, and Chen's suggestion to start questioning Olivia had pissed me off.

What information could she provide? It was clear whoever wanted to take her wanted to do so because I'd wronged them.

Kissing her hair, I mumble, "Come on, let's get this dinner over and done with."

Chen and his team where waiting for Olivia and me by armored vehicles. The rest of our security would be following in front and behind. Until everything was dealt with, I would place an army of men around Olivia with no expense spared.

I refuse to feel that helpless again.

Our drive to Aida's house, my childhood home, was short and uneventful but the air in the car was super charged with apprehension. Olivia did her best to ignore it, but by the time we were pulling up to the large black gates she was wound just as tight as I was.

Our security in front and behind joined Aida's and dispersed to their posts leaving us to travel the long-pebbled drive. At the top of the drive, there are eight vehicles parked haphazardly around the water fountain that stands proudly in the middle of the drive.

Some small dinner this is going to be.

"I don't know what I was expecting but... wow," Olivia smiles, shaking her head.

"It's our childhood home," I tell her. "Aida took it over when our Ma died. A lot of it has been changed over the years to suit her modern tastes, but there's some parts that are original."

Unfortunately.

The cellar that has been untouched remains deadbolted and out of bounds. There are still rooms that were locked years ago that are kept that way. Parts of the garden that are not to be visited.

To me, this is a place of horror — a shrine to the monster that raised us, but to Aida it's her childhood.

"I can imagine this place was quite fun for you and your friends to get lost in."

I squeeze her hand. "We weren't able to have friends over... my family required complete privacy at all times given our unusual business."

She bites her lip before turning to peer out of her window now that we've stopped.

I want to tell her that my history is now hers. If she wants to know about all the dark corners of my life, I'm willing to share them. After all, she needs to know what type of man she's fallen for.

"But you had Aida and Dante, right?"

"I did." I'm the first to open the door, willing for the cool breeze to catch my face. "And the rest of our cousins on my mother's side. Thankfully, I come from quite a big family—speaking of which, Aida has left out a few details about tonight. From the looks of the vehicles here, this is more than an intimate dinner so be prepared."

"Does that make you nervous?"

She steps out of the car and smiles at Bones and Rum who are waiting to escort us to the door.

I laugh without humor. "More annoyed. My family... they can be a little... full on. If it gets too much, at any time we can—"

She shakes her head. "It will be fine, Luca: you don't have to worry about me. I won't say anything I shouldn't."

"No," I flare. "It's not *that*. It's more what they'll say."

"Oh, I hope they'll say a lot and show me lots of pictures. I imagine you were quite the cutie growing up."

I wouldn't put it past Aida to pull out the photo albums just to embarrass me. As I help Olivia up the stairs to the top of the house, I make a mental note to find them before she does.

Once Bones and Rum depart from our sides, I know they'll join Chen at the security desk, keeping an eye on the entrance at all times. It should distill the urgency running havoc in my blood, but it doesn't. There's far too much up in the air for me to relax.

"I was far from cute," I grumble.

She beams, her playful smile catching me off guard. "I imagine you were stealing hearts left, right, and center."

We stop at the top of the steps before the open doors. A faint thrum of music and laughter catches my ear. My heart constricts—Aida's birthday dinner has gone from intimate to a party.

I pull Olivia to me, using her touch to center myself. "No stealing of hearts, Olivia. I was saving myself to steal yours."

Dainty fingers slide up my shirt and tug on my collar, straightening it out. I don't think I'll ever get used to her care. Every time it floors me. "It's not stealing if I give it."

"What are you two doing in the doorway? C'mon everyone's out on the lawn."

Olivia's blush is beautiful under the warm sun light. I watch her as she peers over at Dante who stands in the foyer, hands in his pockets, waiting for us to make a move.

"So much for a small dinner," I mumble.

Dante comes over and holds out his hand for Olivia. "Come on, there's people that want to meet you."

Taking his hand, she steps into the house where I had spent most of my young life trapped. Unlike back then, the house had been brought into the twenty-first century with its white marbled floors, white staircase, and rich purple art pieces that hang on the clean white walls.

Aida could change every single part of this house, but it would still bring back bad memories. Still reek of violence.

We move through the center, underneath the stairs, until we enter the kitchen. Staff rush around, taking care of drinks and preparing the dinner, but part as we head through.

As soon as Olivia steps through the veranda doors, the whole party stops and turns to face her. There are thirty of my closest family members in clusters across the patio, armed with drinks and judgmental stares.

"Olivia!" Aida is the first to steal her attention, leaning in and air kissing her cheeks. Dressed in a rich plumb dress that floats to the floor, my sister doesn't look a day over thirty. "So glad you could persuade him to come. How are you feeling? I'd have visited you in the hospital, but my brother here thought it would best if I didn't."

The glare she throws me tells me that tonight isn't going to be comfortable.

"Hello, Aida," I drawl, my jaw flexing to say more.

I shove my hands in my pockets to stop myself from taking Olivia and getting the fuck out of here.

"I'm much better now, thank you." Olivia takes a step back to me and links her arm with mine. "Happy birthday, by the way."

Aida's eyes follow Olivia's touch, carefully gauging the situation. If Dante hasn't filled her in on recent events, I'm pretty sure it wouldn't be long until she's pulling the information from Olivia herself.

"Thank you. Come on, there's some people you should meet."

Ah, here we go. Time to parade Olivia to the family.

I need a drink.

CHAPTER THIRTY-FOUR

Olivia Heart

A glass of red had been thrust into my hand and I'd been thrown in headfirst into the introductions with Aida at my side. Everyone was so careful to greet me, trying not to touch me or press too hard when they kissed my cheek.

I sense the bruises down the side of my neck are on show.

I keep my smile loose and polite but after every introduction I itch for Luca to return. It's only with his hand in mine do I feel less like a car crash victim and more of a woman wearing a nice dress and incredibly sexy heels.

"This is my best friend, Laura," Aida introduces me to her best friend, a beautiful red-head with pale skin and a dusting of freckles across her dainty nose.

Laura pulls me into a firm hug, and I instantly like her. "So, you're the elusive woman that everyone has been whispering about since I got here."

I sip my wine, trying not to blush.

"Laura," Aida chastises her. "Real subtle."

Laura grins. "Being subtle is overrated," she sips her mojito with gusto. "Olivia deserves to know that she's upstaged your event by being the talk of the night."

Coming to my rescue, Aida rolls her eyes and squeezes my arm. "She can upstage my event all she wants if it stops people asking how old I am," she gives me a warm smile. "Anyway, how are you feeling, Olivia? Do you need to take a seat?"

"I'm fine don't worry," I spot Luca making his way out of the house with Dante, both of them in a hushed conversation. "It's just a few bruises and broken fingers."

"Just?" Laura steals my attention once again. "You were in a wreck, Olivia. I'm surprised you're even here."

"Me too," Aida agrees. "Are they any closer to finding out who it was that tried to take you?"

I look from Laura to Aida; both wait for me to respond, and I assume that Laura has been made aware of Luca and I's situation.

Brushing a hand through my hair I answer, "I don't think so. The Russians didn't know anything, and Luca isn't exactly forthcoming with information right now. He wants to protect me from whatever's happening..."

Aida swears under her breath and rolls her eyes. "That brother of mine can be an idiot at times."

Laura raises her glass. "I agree with Aida but don't worry, Olivia, I've known Luca as long as I've known Aida and there isn't a chance there will be a second time."

My eyes look for him without realizing it. Standing by Dante and an elderly gentleman he smiles, his perfect sharp cheekbones lifting, stealing my breath away.

"I hope you're right."

There was no doubt in my mind that Luca would find those responsible for hurting me, and when he did it would be over for them. I'd seen it in his eyes the moment we both assessed my injuries in that hospital bathroom. He wasn't going to stop until my bubble of safety returned.

"A man who's as in love as Luca is, will do anything to protect the woman he loves."

I turn to the voice that's captured everyone's attention. Standing before me is the mirror image of Luca's mother with a soft smile, dressed in a cream pant suit with pearls decorating her tan neck. She regards me with regal hospitality, extending herself to me in an instant.

"Olivia Heart, what a beautiful young woman you are."

On instinct, I take her hand and she pulls me in, enveloping me in the scent of roses on a warm summer's day. I'm careful not to spill my drink down her expensive attire as I hug her back.

"Olivia, this is my aunt and Dante's mother, Fia."

Fia reminds me so much of my Aunt Sarah with her blonde hair and crisp blue eyes.

"It's very nice to meet you, Fia."

"And you my dear. Now let me get a good look at you." Her hands slide underneath my hair, pushing it over my shoulder before I realize, and she tuts at what she finds. I open my mouth, to tell her that I'm okay but she clocks my fingers and frowns. "Luca will find the people responsible for this my dear, and when he does you must let him deal with them as he sees fit."

Our eyes connect and an understanding forms between us. "I will."

Aida's eyes widen with surprise. "I see that you two are on better terms."

Fia smiles at her niece, patting her hand. "Of course, they are. It was obvious the moment they walked in together. Her eyes never left his."

I resist the urge to down my glass of wine. I don't like being an open book, especially not to people who know more about me than I know about them. I'm constantly on the backfoot here.

"Nothing like a near death experience to bring people together," Laura raises her glass in the air before downing the thimble of alcohol left in her glass.

I wish to follow her actions, but I'm caught off guard by a young boy running across the grass with his arms outstretched. Luca catches him in one swoop, chucking him up in the air and returning him back to the grass with a bright laugh.

Mateo, grins up at his uncle, enjoying whatever it is Luca has to say while having his raven hair ruffled.

"He loves Luca," Aida tells me. "It has a lot to do with the stupidly expensive race cars he keeps buying him."

"Race cars?" I ask, with a raised brow.

"Well, mini versions for Mateo. Luca used to race as a child, and he's passed the addiction for fast cars and lack of safety on to my child."

Fia sighs, patting my arm. "It's a Caruso thing. They have no fear for danger." She looks to Dante, who's filling Mateo's hands up with cash from his pocket.

"Now all the fast cars make sense," I mumble.

Just as I finish, Luca looks up and catches me staring. He tenses for a brief second but relaxes when he sees that I'm okay, that I'm withstanding the company of his incredibly nice family.

I don't understand what he was so worried about.

Ensuring I don't dwell on his concerns, he winks my way before picking up Mateo once more.

Aida and Laura were just about to give me a tour of Luca's childhood home when he appeared by my side, stealing my elbow, and pulling me away.

He didn't say a word until we were out of ear shot of the rest of the party, but I could feel every bit of tension building between us. The familiar electric snap was hard to miss when his fingers entwined with mine.

"What's wrong?"

"It's been too long," he kisses me hard and fast, his hands in my hair. "Too long since I've kissed you." He kisses me again and sears me with a bite to my lip.

I'm breathless. "It's been thirty minutes, Luca."

"Thirty minutes feels like a lifetime to me, Olivia," he rubs his nose down mine. "My impatience for you has no bounds. Especially made worse when others take up all of your attention."

"You're being ridiculous," I laugh, trying to disengage our bodies before I lose myself in him entirely.

"I know," he smirks, his hands sliding around to my ass, exerting a dominant squeeze on my tender flesh. "Would you think it ridiculous of me if I suggested we ditch Aida's party so I can take you home to my bed?"

A flurry of heat pools in my stomach, tingling bright with neediness.

"We can't," I whisper weakly, so close to taking his hand and leaving. "You know that Arnik's banned any extra activities until everything has completely healed."

He fixes me with a challenging smirk. "I don't have to touch you to make you come, Olivia."

Oh hell. What kind of fresh torture is this?

"Stop it!" I'm breathless, pulling away. "You're not using your dirty mouth to get out of having dinner with your family!"

He laughs deeply and I feel it echo into my chest. God, I love that sound and what it does to me.

"You didn't mind my dirty mouth last night."

I want to desperately to push the heels of my palms into my eyes, trying to rid the memory of him between my legs, but I'm wearing mascara. Fuck.

"Please, Luca, play fair," I take a step back, trying to ignore the familiar pull in my stomach.

He stalks me, pushing me further and further towards the trees.

"Come on, Olivia, let's go and I'll show you how fair I can be," he reaches for me, but I dart out of the way.

"Fair is being here to celebrate your sister's birthday and getting to know your family."

Even though all I can think about is exploring the idea of him turning my world upside down without even touching me. Now that would be something else...

"I can tell you all you need to know about them," he studies me, his eyes dark, willing me to agree to leave. "After I've made you come."

"I know you're uncomfortable right now with me being here. It's two parts of your world colliding but don't worry. Everything is fine. Your family is sweet and they're just worried."

"We don't need their worry," he stops, eyes narrowing over my head at the party behind me.

I've touched a button I shouldn't have but it's the only choice left when you're being stalked by an insatiable man with a mouth full of filthy promises. Ever since I agreed to this dinner he's been on edge, looking for an out but not because he doesn't care for his family. Because he's worried I still want to leave.

I need to do something.

Telling him I loved him clearly wasn't enough.

I snap, ignoring my inner voice that tells me not to be so hasty and close the gap between us. My hands touch his face, my fingers grazing his five o'clock shadow.

"If you're being like this because you're worried about Aida's offer just know that I'm never going to take it, okay? If you need me to go tell her that right now I will."

"I told you that I would have dragged you back if you took it," he said soberly.

I shake my head, remembering his dark confession in the confines of his shower. "You did, but you didn't mean it. You knew if I decided to accept Aida's offer you would have had no choice but to let me go. You would have done that for me — not her."

He shuts me out by closing his eyes.

"That doesn't matter now. That's the past. Just trust me on this, okay?" I kiss his perfectly full lips. He tastes of whiskey and me. "I'm not going anywhere."

"Fine, we'll stay," he opens his eyes. "But on one condition."

I grin, completely shocked, but pleased that he trusts me. "What is it?"

"That we don't have to stick around for dessert and the whole singing happy birthday nonsense."

I bite my tongue, trying not to laugh at the indignant look on his face. Luca Caruso really is not the singing happy birthday type.

****

We're seated on a table that has been put together to accommodate thirty people. Glass vases filled with purple dried pampas grass and diamonds part us into groups of ten. Everything down to our cutlery has been expertly personalized by Aida who sits at the top of the table with Mateo.

Luckily for me, I'm sitting next to Laura, who's on my left, with Luca across from me, and Dante on my right. Both Dante and Laura are the perfect people to stop me from taking Luca up on his offer to leave.

After our little talk in the gardens, he had introduced me to Mateo who was very keen to show me his car collection and to get my views on the latest Marvel film that I hadn't seen. He's such a sweet child whose love for his uncle I found incredibly endearing.

When I'd asked Luca about Mateo's dad, we were called to dinner, but he promised to fill me in later on, telling me it was too long of a story and too private to do in front of Aida's guests.

"I heard about your eventful night last night," Dante whispers into my ear. "Although, I think you and Luca may have scarred your therapist for life."

Jesus—did Luca have to share everything with his cousin?

The glass of red which had been kindly topped up is in my hands in seconds. I sip, hoping the subtle burn in the back of my throat overtakes the one to my pride.

"You're so dramatic."

Dante laughs. "Dramatic is swiping the contents of one's desk while—" He doesn't get a chance to finish his sentence. Fia swats him around the head as she takes her seat.

336

"Non a tavola, Dante." *Not at the table.*

Luca raises his glass to his aunt, appreciative of her swift punishment.

"Sorry, Ma," he rubs the back of his head, transforming from man to child.

Servers begin to pour out of the veranda doors with their hands full of antipasto platters and focaccia with a traditional caponata dip. Laura is sweet enough to keep my attention, asking me about my time in New York and if I plan on returning to my career while we sample our appetizers.

Luca's voice captures our attention before I can answer. "If that's what she wants."

Do I? Could I go back to a career where I felt as though I barely made a dent in the corrupt system that protected the wrong people? I'd been miserable and obsessed with working myself to the bone.

And does Luca mean that? Would he be able to let go enough for me to enjoy a fairly normal life by his side?

My head spins.

A conversation like this, in normal circumstances would be ringing alarm bells, but we all spoke as though this was my 'normal'.

"So, you'll stay in Italy?" she asks him. "Or will you return to New York with Olivia?"

Dante at my side freezes midway through a bite of his focaccia.

Luca however is calm enough not to let his annoyance show, but I feel it anyway.

"We're taking it one day at a time."

That's what we're doing?

I drop my eyes to my plate, wishing for someone to change the subject.

Laura doesn't take the hint. "I suppose that's the smartest option for you both right now considering everything you have going on."

The reminder that there's some unknown psychopath out there who wants to hurt me puts me off my food. My stomach knots and the familiar feeling of dread begins to weigh heavy on my shoulders.

"We're fine," he tells her, his tone on the arctic scale.

"Olivia?" Luca calls my name. I look up quickly, needing to be anchored by him "fidati di me come io mi fido di te." *Trust me as I trust you.*

I breath for what feels like the first time, "Io faccio." *I do.*

"Wait- stop! Since when you have been able to speak Italian?" Dante bursts, his face blushing bright red as he looks between Luca and me.

I shrug. "I'm learning the basics," with my shoulder I nudge his. "Don't worry your secret conversations about all the women you're dating are safe."

He scowls over at Luca who seems quite pleased that the tables have turned onto his cousin.

My eyes catch the attention of Mateo who runs behind his uncle, narrowly missing a waitress that tries to top up Luca's glass and he darts back into the house. Swapping places with the energetic little boy is Chen and the rest of my guards. Their eyes narrow in on the party until they land on me.

All three tables fall into silence.

"Ah shit," Dante whispers, when he sees them heading over.

Chen catches my eye, forcing my stomach to tighten with apprehension. He moves with stealth like precession towards his boss who is unaware of what's happening behind him.

Bones and Rum walk the length of the table until they're behind me, their hands touching the back of my chair — ready to pull me away at any moment.

Chen leans into Luca's ear and I feel the twine that holds in the chaos begin to loosen. Luca looks down while Chen whispers in his ear, his body hardening — preparing for a fight.

"How long?" he demands his answer from Chen with his eyes on me. Suddenly my need to touch him is multiplied.

"She's already here, sir."

Who's here?

"What's happening, Luca?" Aida demands, slipping from her chair to join her brother's side.

Dante grabs my hand under the table, squeezing once before letting me go. He kisses his mother's cheek and stands up.

Luca regards his sister with impatience. "You have an uninvited guest, Aida. Olivia and I are leaving."

"I'll get Olivia out of here," Dante tells Luca, as he leans down and plucks me from my seat. "We'll meet you at the front of the house."

"What's happening?" I hiss, trying to dislodge his grip. "Who's here?"

"I am."

It doesn't take a genius to work out who slips out of the house to stand in front of us all. Luca's ex-fiancé, Emilia, pins me to my spot with her hard blistering stare and smug smile — stealing the attention of anyone that dared look at her.

She looks like an old Hollywood actress with her long straight blonde hair, small pouty mouth, and incredibly sharp cheekbones that could cut glass. Everything about her, from her cool blue eyes and curvy frame are the opposite of me.

We're nothing alike. Opposites. Sudden enemies.

"How dare you do this here!?" Aida sneers, storming over to the woman whose eyes refuse to leave mine. "Do you have no shame, Emilia?"

Luca catches his sister's hand and pulls her to his side. "Let's take this inside, Emilia. There's no need to ruin Aida's birthday."

"Olivia, let's go." Bones touches my shoulder, forcing me to drop my attention from the problem in front of me.

"Shame? You're asking me, your best friend, if I have any shame?" Emilia snaps back, dismissing Aida with a wave of her hand.

Bones nudges me gently to move. I walk the length of the table, surrounded by Dante, Red, and Bones under Emilia's heated glare. Urgency spills out with every moment that passes between us.

Luca regards his ex coldly as he steps forward, trying to steal her attention away from me but it doesn't work. She steps around him, slipping through Chen until we're in front of each other.

I feel her cat-like eyes size me up, judging me. "I thought you would be... more..." she looks me up and down, her red lips curling up into a sneer. "But you're nothing more than a meek little mouse."

"Watch it, Emilia," Luca's voice drops, echoing into my chest. "Say one more word and it will be your last."

My throat dries on his promise.

"Your threats don't scare me anymore, Luca," she doesn't turn to face him. "Now be quiet. I have some business with your little plaything to attend to."

I finally find my voice, her insults pushing me to meet her anger. "What do you want?"

"I don't want anything from *you*. I'm just here to give you this," she reaches into her overly large designer tote and pulls out an envelope. "I have something you'll want to see."

My hands grip the envelope before Luca has the chance to take it from me.

"Let's take this somewhere private," Luca hisses through gritted teeth, grabbing Emilia's elbow and marching her into the house.

Aida looks from me to Chen, unsure on how to proceed with her birthday dinner.

"Miss Heart, we should follow," Chen shadows me. I feel his urgency for me to follow his boss, but I'm rooted to the spot, feeling the weight of the envelope in my hands.

"Olivia, are you sure you want to open that without Luca?" I hear Aida ask.

Luca? He's all but forgotten me for his ex-fiancé who seems quite comfortable on insulting me in front of his family. I didn't need him for this.

I rip it open, ignoring the hushed whispers and stares.

Five pictures spill into my hands of a couple sharing an intimate moment in a restaurant with the sea glittering behind them. The first picture is of Luca, his hand extended out to Emilia's face in a loving embrace. I grit my jaw and flip to the next—Fuck. Flipping to the last photograph, silently praying their embrace doesn't go any further, I see her claws gripping at his collar, with her lips pressed to his... his eyes closed.

A thin invisible wall that I thought was long gone reappears in front of me. Old safety mechanisms begin to work, shielding me from what these photographs mean for Luca and I.

They had kissed and she wanted me to see this? Why? These could be from their time together — before me. Before he stole me away. Or they were evidence of a recent betrayal.

My mind snapped. All this time he had professed his love for me, telling me over and over again that it was only ever me. That Emilia was a distraction, nothing more than someone to keep him preoccupied.

Liar.

Fucking, good for nothing liar.

"Olivia, let me look at those." I snatch them out of Dante's reach and make my way into the house — to find the woman that had chosen this moment to destroy my heart just as the glue was drying.

Standing in the living area they're both embroiled in a row, barely registering that I and my guards have entered their space. They converse in their native tongue, swapping insults quicker than I can translate.

"When were these taken?" I snap, demanding their attention. Specifically, Emilia's who seems quite content in giving it to me.

Emilia grins wickedly my way. "The day before your cousin's wedding. Cute, aren't they?"

The day he had disappeared. When he had told me he had been busy with business, but by the looks of it, she was the business he needed to attend to.

And the day after he attended to me.

Luca finally looks at me, his eyes drawn to the pictures shaking in my hands. That's all I'll allow my eyes to see of him. Any more and I won't be able to hold myself together.

"When I imagined you, I thought you would have more class than this Emilia, but these," I hold up the pictures before throwing them down on the coffee table, "are anything but classy."

She sneers my way. "What happened after wasn't either."

Luca chokes back a cough before narrowing his eyes on her. "No! that's a lie. Olivia, these pictures are easily explained."

If I throw up now it'll be the icing on the cake. Emilia will win.

I turn to Dante, who's flanked by my guards and Chen. "I want to go. Can you take me back to the house?"

"Wait—Olivia. Hold on," his touch to my arm makes it near impossible to keep the rage below the surface. "Let me explain."

I snatch my arm away from him, glaring down at his hand. The same hand that had touched *her* with my initial tattooed on the skin. "Don't fucking touch me."

Bones, Rum, and Red step in around me, barricading me in—preventing him from getting to me.

"Trouble in paradise," Emilia laughs, enjoying the show. "This really is quite ironic."

"Sir, please take a step back," Bones holds out his hand in warning.

Chen steps between the two. "Let's take a minute here."

"Fuck off, Bones. Remember who pays you," Luca snarls, trying to reach between them to get to me. "Olivia, just wait a fucking minute. Give me a second to explain."

The look that passes between Chen and his team tells me all I need to know. Their priorities have changed and now it's only me that they'll take orders from. The moment they saw me in that crash, everything had changed.

I ignore Luca. "Dante, I want to go. **Now.**"

Dante doesn't move. He barely looks at me. Instead, his eyes are drawn to the photographs I had thrown down on the coffee table. He too is taken by surprise.

I give up on him. "Bones. Please take me back," I grab the back of his arm. "I don't want to spend another minute here with these two."

Bones grabs my hand from behind his back, squeezing once. "Chen. We're going to take Miss Heart back. We'll take the first car."

"We'll follow when we're done here," Chen nods before looking over at me, pissed I think at the destruction of his team's loyalty to Luca—already blaming me.

"Nobody is going anywhere. Not until I've spoken to Olivia." Luca stares hard, willing me to step out of my shield of muscles.

Pain confronted me under his guilty stare. My eyes welled before I could stop them.

"Sir, Olivia wants to leave and given your current... company I think it's best if we go."

"Let her go, Luca. We need to talk." Emilia moved closer and placed her hand on his shoulder, putting her man-stealing claws where they don't belong. On the man that I thought belonged to me.

Bitch.

My body shook with jealousy. I hated her condescending tone and how much she was enjoying herself. But what I hated the most was her hand that Luca hadn't shaken off in disgust—he let her touch remain.

"Yes," I spat back. I pulled on Bones' hand, urging him to move. "You two should catch up."

I was so grateful for Bones taking control and pulling me away from Luca before I did something stupid. And Red and Rum who flanked close behind as we moved towards the front door, showing me that their loyalty lay with me.

"Olivia," he called my name, following us down the steps and towards the waiting car. "Don't do this. Don't run from me."

"I didn't do this, Luca. You did!" I fought my tears with my rage. "You did this the moment you lied to me after you kissed *her*. This is on you. So, listen to me for once in your fucked up life and leave me the hell alone!"

Yanking open the door with little to no grace, I slid into the back of the car where I felt a strand of safety. He couldn't get to me in here, not when Red and Rum guarded the doors.

"I didn't kiss her! Fuck! She's lying, Olivia. This is what she wants, she wants to stir up trouble. She wants to pull us apart."

"Mission accomplished."

He tried to get to me, but it was no use. I was done. Pulling the door, I slammed it in his face, hiding behind the tinted windows. Shoving Red out of the way, he slammed his hand on the window, frustration boiling over as he screamed his demands for me to get out of the car.

I was done listening to him.

In the darkness of the back seat, I finally allowed myself to cry.

CHAPTER THIRTY-FIVE

Luca Caruso

I watched Olivia's car pull away without me and exploded. My life was in chaos, my heart fucking burned, and she had left me—again. But this time she hadn't just left me physically, she'd retreated into her mind and barricaded herself into the place where I'd struggled to reach her.

It didn't take me long to find the person responsible for all this shit. Emilia, who took great pleasure in watching my life implode stood proudly from the top of the steps.

"What the fuck are you doing?" I hiss, grabbing at her elbow. "Have you lost your damn mind?"

She rolls her eyes dramatically, as if my questions are nothing but an inconvenience. Fuck, what happened to her? When did she become so spiteful, so full of resentment?

"I'm ending this," she sneers, pulling away from me. "What does it look like?"

"You have no fucking clue the mess you've brought upon yourself by hurting Olivia," I bite, seething with rage. "Do you think you'll walk away from this?"

She invades my space with conviction and malice. "I will walk away and there's not a single thing you can do about it."

Dante slips out of the house and joins us, placing himself in reaching distance.

"You think you can step into my life with your hatred and walk away? You think this Kenwood will protect you?" I step forward, hating her. "Yes, I know about the money, Emilia."

Amusement twinkles in her eyes. "I know. I gathered when Dante came looking for me," she winks over at my cousin. Dante shakes his head with disgust. "But don't worry about me Luca. I have a… personalized deal with my new friend."

A snark laugh erupts from my throat. "If he doesn't kill you once he's done with you, I will."

Unfazed by my threat she grins. "You won't. You can't. Not when I'm the only one who knows Kenwood's real identity and the real reason he wants your plaything so badly."

"Who is he?" Dante asks, "Who are you working with?"

"You'll find out soon enough," she looks down to her wrist, to the Rolex I had purchased for her thirtieth birthday. "I would say within the next ten minutes."

CHAPTER THIRTY-SIX

Olivia Heart

"Are you okay?" Bones asks, his voice silences me mid sob. "Here, take this."

"W-what are you doing?" my voice cracks, as he passes me his jacket from the front passenger seat.

His smile is soft, his eyes full of kindness. "You're shivering, Olivia."

Accepting his jacket, I slip it around my shoulders, burrowing myself into the material. We had only been driving for five minutes and in that time, I'd gotten myself into quite the mess.

I felt so raw. So open to pain that I didn't even bother to wait to cry in private.

"Sorry you had to go through that," Red mumbles from the driver's side. "That was the last thing you needed right now."

Rum at my side grabs my hand and squeezes with kindness I'd never felt from him before.

I was overwhelmed with emotion and gratitude towards them all. They were all I had in this world, and right now they wanted me to know that they were there for me.

"Thank you. All of you. I appreciate you getting me out of there." I wiped my mascara away with the sleeve of Bones' jacket.

Red caught my eye in the mirror. "We told Caruso. We warned him that if she hurt you, we would take control."

"You knew about her?"

"We did," he nodded. "We were told not to tell you about her."

My heart stuttered and slammed to a halt. *Of course*, he didn't want me to know about her. Luca knew it would be easier to subdue me with morsels of information about Emilia rather than admit the truth. And I'd been blindsided.

"We found out about her when her name popped up on the bank transfer between Black and Kenwood."

"Kenwood?"

I lurched forward towards Red, wanting to see his face, hoping that he had misspoken.

"Yes… we think it's a code name for the person that wants to take you. They paid Emilia two million euros and I think her visit tonight was her end of the deal."

My vision blurs and I sway with panic. I no longer see Red's concerned gaze or the leather seat in front of me. "It's not a code name."

It isn't a code name. The person that wanted to take me wasn't hiding behind a company name or gang identity. It was an intimately cruel and personal attack, one that only I would understand.

"What is it, Olivia?" Bones asked.

"It's my mother's maiden name."

Red almost lets go of the steering wheel.

I laugh, snorting into my sleeve. "They don't want to use me to get to Luca. They want to take me from him," my laugh turns into a peel of giggles, nervous, uncontrollable- my-life- is- falling- to- pieces- giggles.

Rum, the poor guy, pulls me into him hoping that his embrace would calm me.

"Do you know who it is, Olivia?" Bones is on his phone, tapping quickly against the screen as he asks me who my next kidnapper would be.

"I think I do," I wipe tears away from my eyes. There's only one person with that much money and knowledge to be able to pull this off. Even if every part of me hopes I'm wrong.

"Shit," Red hisses, slamming his foot onto the break. My seatbelt pulls me back into the seat, bruising me. We coast, our speed dropping down to a slow crawl.

"We have a code red, sir. There's three vehicles up ahead blocking the road on Viale Moro. We need assistance."

The three SUV's that face us are completely blacked out, but I don't need to see inside to know that were outnumbered. I also don't need a magic eight ball to know that they're waiting for me.

"Two minutes is too long. We're outnumbered and outgunned out here. What the fuck do you mean, a team are out? Get Chen on the line."

Red brings us to a stop and the car falls into silence.

"Can we outrun them?" Rum whispers.

Red swipes the sweat from his brow. "No. They've got more horsepower on us. We'll have to go old school."

The passenger door on the lead car opens. Dark brown shoes step out onto the road, followed by a crisp navy suit that is tailored to perfection to suit the powerful body of William Adler.

"Let Olivia go and nobody else has to get hurt," he calls, as he leans against the front of the car, his hands in his pockets. His shrewd and calculating eyes bore into our car, looking for me. "You have thirty seconds."

"Who is this fucker?" Rum hisses, pulling his gun from his pocket and checking the chamber.

"He's…" My old best friend and the man that nearly killed me

"Twenty seconds," Will calls, with an assured smile on his face.

"How many bullets you got?" Bones asks his colleagues.

"If there's three per car we have enough," Red shakes his head.

"No bullets," I squeak. "Let me talk to him. I know Will. I'll be able to sort this out with him if you give me a few moments."

They all turn to me like I've grown several heads.

Will's voice penetrates the car before they can argue. "Ten seconds."

My fingers itch to grab the door handle.

"Two minutes. That's all I need." I look to Bones, imploring him to listen. "Nobody else has to get hurt today."

"Not a chance," he barks and then flinches from the conversation he's having with Chen on the phone.

"Fine," Will calls. It's the last call before several tiny red dots penetrate the car, landing on everyone's chest except for mine.

No. Not them.

"Ah shit," Bones groans, looking down at the tiny dot hovering over his heart. "Looks like there's four per car."

My fingers pull back the door handle and I fling myself out of the vehicle.

"Wait! Don't hurt them, Will!"

We stand meters apart and chaos ensues behind us. My team rushes out to join me, trying to drag me back into the car until Will's men step out, brandishing their weapons and their little red dots of death.

"Liv," he steps towards me, "Are you okay?" His concern doesn't touch me in the way he hoped.

Rage does instead. I teeter forward in my heels. "What the hell are *you* doing? Have you lost your god damn mind!?"

"I'm bringing you home, Liv. You don't have to be scared, okay? He can't hurt you anymore."

Hurt me anymore? You have no idea.

"Oliva, get behind me!" Bones pulls his gun, putting himself between us.

"It was you... you're the one that tried to take me." I race forward, hoping to scratch his eyes out. Bones reacts quickly, dropping his aim to pull me into him.

"It was," he nods in agreement. "But it wasn't my intention for you to get hurt. Things went a little... off plan"

"Get hurt!? Off plan!? I'm covered in bruises! I have broken bones because of you! You nearly killed me, you asshole."

He takes one step towards us and the men behind him join, their boots slapping against the concrete. "And for that I'm sorry — I am. But it was our one shot to get you back and we had to act fast."

"What the hell happened to you, Will? This isn't you." I point towards the men keen on hurting the people protecting me. "Luca's going to tear you limb from limb for all of this. You know that, right?"

"I'm not worried about him," he hisses before spitting at the ground with disgust.

My fear for him mixes into straight, black rage until I'm breathless and hot. I want to scream, to throw myself at him until he's covered in as many marks as I am.

"You should be. You must know what he's done to the idiots that put me in the hospital?"

"He's saved me a job," the savage laugh that infiltrates my ears stops me in my tracks, choking my anger. "Less loose ends for me to clear up."

Black had been a loose end. The English money shoved in his mouth... greedy etched into his skin. Black also had two children, two innocent children who wouldn't ever see their daddy again.

"Who the hell are you?"

This isn't the man I used to know who wanted nothing more than to manage his own paper, who wanted to be on the forefront of a good story. Not this... not this savage...

I didn't know him.

You don't know Luca either.

"I'm your friend, Liv, that's who I am and right now you're in trouble and you need a friend like me."

"Olivia, we need to get back to the car," Bones whispers, edging us back. "Back up will be here soon."

Will clocks us and seethes. "Move her an inch more, and I'll have a bullet put through your chest."

Bones tightens his grip around my forearm. No, this can't happen. Nobody else has to get hurt. He has a little girl to get home to and there was no way I was risking his life for me.

"You wouldn't. Not when she's this close," he barks back.

Forcing my temper to recede, I focus on those willing to risk their lives for me instead. "Will, you need to stop this right now. Tell your men to put their weapons down and we'll talk, okay? Nobody else is getting hurt today."

Will saunters towards us, his hands splayed out in front of him. "Liv, listen to me. All you have to do is walk over here, okay? We'll talk once I have you somewhere safe."

No.

Not a single muscle in my body moves. I'm not going with him.

"You have a minute," he tells me.

"Don't move," Red hisses. "He wants us vulnerable."

So, he can kill them the moment I'm not within reach.

I sense the urgency around me and feel the beginnings of an anxiety attack. It adds weight to my already oxygen starved lungs.

Get it together, Olivia. This isn't just about you now.

My eyes water under the strain. "I know what you did to Black and if you think I'm going to leave, so they," I point to the masked men, donned in all black, just waiting to pull their triggers, "can hurt my guards, you have another thing coming."

He pulls in a deep breath, glaring daggers at me. "Come with me now and I won't need to hurt them. Nobody has to get hurt, Liv, if that's what you want. You have my word."

"Luca won't let you do this."

"Luca is done," his voice steals my attention, and the rhythm of my heart. "If he doesn't let you go after this, I'll use every media outlet to tell the world about the type of man he is and everything that he's done to you."

My ankles wobble in my heels, and I stumble into Bones' back.

"Every shred of proof that I have about him and his family will be made public knowledge. He'll no longer be untouchable by the time I'm finished. Everyone will know about the stalking, the bribery, the kidnapping—hell they'll know about how he set guards up on your family the day he stole you," his laugh steals the air in my lungs. "Did you know about that, Liv? Did you know that if you contacted your Aunt Sarah, and told her the truth, that his men would have put a bullet through her head?"

It's a lie. Luca wouldn't do that to me, he knows that if he ever hurt my family, I would never forgive him—hell I'd kill him if he touched her. I refuse Will's lie from settling in my head and dismiss it as fast as it comes.

"You'll ruin my life if you do this," I tell him. "You'll hurt my family, embarrass them and..."

"They'll understand, Olivia, and so will everyone else. You and Emilia are the victims here. You just need to remember that. Come with me now and I'll tell you everything you want to know."

I'm not a fucking victim. I never have been and never will be. The word alone makes me want to reach over and strangle Will for even daring utter it.

I grip Bones' shirt. "I'm not leaving."

His exhaled harshly. "I can see the pain in your eyes. You know about him and Emilia, don't you? Liv, c'mon you know deep down that any feelings you have for him aren't real. It's just a coping mechanism for all the evil shit he's done to you."

I swallow back the urge to vomit. "You don't know a thing about him or my feelings."

"It's you that doesn't know the real him, the real monster that lurks beneath the surface, because if you did, we wouldn't be having this conversation. You would have run into my arms by now."

I know who he is. Well, I thought I did. Photographs of his lips pressed to *hers* remind me of how I got to be in the middle of this road with guns aimed our way.

Will pulls me away from my spiraling. "You said that he wouldn't let you go, well now he doesn't have a choice. Come to me."

"No," I snap. "Will, stop this now. I don't need you to save me, okay?"

Will takes a step closer to me and ignores the guns aimed at his chest. "I'm sorry, Liv. I'm sorry that I have to do this, but you've left me with no choice." he turns his attention to Bones and glowers.

"Give her to me or the men," Will slowly glares down at each of my guards, "that are watching your families will go in and kill those that you love. Is she worth it? Is she worth losing your loved ones over?"

None of us move.

"What are you talking about?" Bones snaps, pushing me further behind his back.

"You have a little girl, correct? One that attends Aberndale Academy. From what I gather, she has quite the high IQ for a girl who's missed a lot of school due to a heart condition."

"No…" my own voice sounds distant, over the rapid thump of my heart.

Will smirks, taking great pleasure in rattling my team. "It would be such a shame to leave her without any parents."

"Motherfucker!" Bones lurches forward, forgoing his gun. Red and Rum bolt to grab him and yank him back. In the scuffle, I'm shoved forward, tripping and landing on my hands and knees.

My groan of pain is cut off as Will leans down and pulls me to him. His men snap in union and surround us, waiting for Will's command.

I stare at my guards who look at me with horror. They had let me slip away. They couldn't protect me anymore, not when the people they loved were in the firing line.

Will's hand snakes down my arm until his fingers clasp mine. He cuffs me without apologies.

"Let us go without any trouble and you have my word that no harm will come to you or your families."

Pain slices right through me at the horror dawning on Bones' face. He'd let me go in his rage and pushed me into the arms of my new monster. But I couldn't blame him or Red and Rum.

They had done their best. They had been there for me when it mattered, and I would always be grateful for their protection.

"It's okay," I tell them. "I'll be okay. Just go home and protect your families. Forget about me, forget about…" I couldn't say his name. It was too painful to think about him in this moment.

"Listen to her," Will demanded. "Nobody else has to get hurt because of Luca Caruso," he spits his name with venom. "We're going to leave now. Stay here for ten minutes, and no harm will come to you or your families. Try and follow us and their blood will be on your hands."

Will roughly dragged me away from them and towards his car. I didn't drag my heels or try to stop him. I followed quietly, resigned to the fact that this was the only option for me now.

Luca had betrayed me. My guards couldn't protect me. Will wasn't going to stop until I was safe with him, even if that meant hurting innocent people. Once again, I'm left without a choice.

"I'm so sorry," Red yelled, his voice cracking.

"Don't you dare give up, Olivia," Bones yelled. "Fucking fight."

"Every step of the way," Rum finished.

Tears pooled and spilled as I stole a single glance back.

I'd spent so long looking at them as the enemy but this whole time they had been my protectors, my friends who were just trying to do their best.

Will didn't care for their display of friendship. He shoved my head down and into the back of his car with frustrated haste.

Once the door was shut, he captured my jaw with his harsh fingers and pulled my face to his. "Forget them. Forget him, Olivia. All you need is me now."

Imprisoning my mouth with his cool fingers, I felt a smooth pebbled like object press against my lips. Chocolate wafted, reminding me of the chocolate ice cream Luca and I had shared.

Will pressed the chocolate into my mouth, forcing it past my lips. I gagged, trying to pull away, but he pinned me to the seat with his hand. My throat worked hard to swallow as I fought against the drug. I choked as the chocolate melted and bitter gel slid across my tongue to the back of my throat.

There was no kindness in Will's gaze. The boy that walked me home every day after school holding my backpack didn't exist anymore. The teenager that had stolen my first kiss in the rain lived only in history.

The man that shoved his drug-filled chocolates into my mouth promised a future of karma, pain, and domination.

And there wasn't a single thing I could do about it.

Extras

Keep a look out for *Beautifully Broken*, A Before I Break Novel
set to release in 2022. Keep reading for a sneak peak.

CHAPTER ONE

Theodore Belmont

K atrina's hand shot out and captured my knee, stilling me with a quick squeeze. "Relax. They'll be here soon."

"Why do we have to wait so long? I thought the whole point of paying for a private service would mean, we wouldn't have to *wait.*"

She didn't bother to hide the roll of her eyes as she stroked her small bump, choosing to subtly remind me that our unborn child would pick up on any frustration through the womb.

I wonder how mad she would be if her pregnancy books ended up in the bottom of our river.

"I pray that our son has more patience than his father," she mutters under her breath.

My smirk pleases her. My beautiful wife all but knows of my impatience and secretly loves it. It's kept her on her toes all these years and ensured that nobody would ever fuck with us.

Leaning in I run a hand over her stomach, loving her and our little boy that I pray will take after her. "Now, why would you pray for such a thing mon amour?"

Katrina captures my hand and places a kiss across my palm. "Because I can."

Before I can kiss her the door finally opens, and the sonographer announces our pictures are ready. We're handed a light blue envelope with three tiny snapshots of our healthy baby.

I take them and help Katrina to her feet. "Let's go celebrate."

She grins wickedly, knowing exactly what I mean. "Only if we can get ice cream after."

Of course, more ice cream. Katrina, since finding out she was pregnant, has sampled every ice cream flavor in France and has yet to find the one that satisfies her cravings. Even our staff were hunting down new flavors in hopes of pleasing her.

"Of course," I kiss her cheek and grab her hand. We move quickly out of the poky all-white room and into the waiting area where more couples await to find out the sex of their babies.

We're halfway out of the door when my phone buzzes violently against my chest. I try to ignore it, wanting only to focus on my wife and how many ways I can satisfy her before she tires.

Work can wait a few more hours.

It buzzes once more just as I open the car door for Katrina. Once she's safely inside, I pull out the irritating piece of metal and see that I have two missed calls from Chen.

I look into the car at Katrina who waits patiently for me and back to my phone.

Chen never rings. Ever. We've always communicated by email because nothing has ever been urgent enough to warrant a chat. Unless…

I stab roughly at the device, putting it to my ear. On the second ring, he picks up.

I wait to hear his terse voice, but nothing.

"Chen?" my demand echoes back into my ear.

"I've fucked up, Theodore."

On instinct alone, I move around the car and get in. As my phone connects to the speaker, I pass the pictures of our unborn child to Katrina.

"What's happened?"

"She's gone," the man that speaks to me doesn't sound like the man I've known nearly all my life. His hollow voice reeks of fear and a lack of discipline.

"What do you mean, she's gone, Chen?"

Katrina looks at me when she hears what I do, her eyes swimming with worry.

His fast exhale echoes into the car. "Olivia's gone," he clears his throat. "She's been taken and we're all fucking screwed."

Katrina flinches at my side, understanding who exactly Chen was talking about.

"Put Luca on the phone."

"I can't."

Fuck. I don't have time to baby him right now. "Why?"

"He's gone looking for her," Chen's voice drops to a whisper. "If he would have just listened to me, I could have prevented this. Protected them both."

"Who's taken her?"

"William Adler."

Katrina lurches forward to the sound of Chen's voice. "William Adler? Are you sure?"

"Yes."

Katrina looks to me, silently forgiving me for what I was about to do. "I'll be on the next flight out. Find Luca. Look him the fuck up if you have to, but make sure he's there when I arrive."

We hear Chen's sharp intake of breath.

Grabbing Katrina's hand, I bring it over to my lap, holding her to me while I destroy one of my promises—hoping for her understanding.

"I'm bringing my own men and we do this my way, Chen. If you know of anyone on your team who won't deal, now is the time to get rid of the dead weight."

His voice comes in stronger, vibrating through the speakers. "They're all in."

"Good." I end the call.

Katrina is on me, bump and all before I have time to process my next steps. Falling into my lap, her haste lips meet mine with consent and love.

"I've already forgiven you," she whispers. "Just make sure you come home to us, okay? That's all I ask of you, Theodore. Just come home to us in one piece."

About the Author

A. L. Hartwell lives in Nottingham, England with her wonderfully patient husband and sassy dog Lyla. From the age of fifteen, as part of an escape, she spent years writing short stories, accumulating them, and sharing them online. With a vast taste in genres, she found herself drawn to the wonderful twisty world of Dark Romance. When she discovered the freedom in writing within this genre, she delved headfirst into writing her first novel, Bending to Break.

When she's not working or spending her time locked away in her writing cave, she's reading, drinking tea, or obsessing over her niece and nephew.

Also by the Author

Bending to Break

Breaking to Pieces

Beautifully Broken (Coming Soon!)

About the Publisher

Kingston Publishing Company, founded by C. K. Green, is dedicated to providing authors an affordable way to turn their dream into a reality. We publish over 100+ titles annually in multiple formats including print and eBook across all major platforms.

We offer every service you will ever need to take an idea and publish a story. We are here to help authors make it in the industry. We want to provide a positive experience that will keep you coming back to us. Whether you want a traditional publisher who offers all the amenities a publishing company should or an author who prefers to self-publish, but needs additional help – we are here for you.

Now Accepting Manuscripts!
Please send query letter and manuscript to:
submissions@kingstonpublishing.com

Visit our website at www.kingstonpublishing.com

Printed in Great Britain
by Amazon